The Best of Barcelona INK
the city's writing

Volume 1 Issues 1–8

Editor: Ryan Chandler

The Best of Barcelona INK
the city's writing
Volume 1 Issues 1–8
Edited by Ryan Chandler

Published by Catalonia Press
www.cataloniapress.com

Barcelona INK is published in Barcelona, Spain.
C/Vallespir 171, 08014 Barcelona.
www.barcelonaink.com

ISBN Print: 978-1-61150-026-4
EPUB: 978-1-61150-027-1
Kindle/mobi: 978-1-61150-028-8

Contents

Introduction

Ask a visitor for their impressions of Barcelona and you might well be offered the Disneylike spires of Gaudi's Sagrada Família, the coliseum of the Camp Nou stadium, or the city's golden beaches with their plethora of fish restaurants. Or perhaps, less fortunately, memories of a group of drunken Englishmen on a stag night wearing joke breasts and throwing chips at a local transvestite. But as a home to and source of inspiration for writers and poets...in English?

Yet this city has indeed acted as inspiration or home – or both – for many such writers; from Colm Tóibín, who has a hideaway in the nearby mountains, to Steve Toltz, who wrote his novel *A Fraction of the Whole* sitting under a palm tree in a local park. Rupert Thomson has used the city as a bolt-hole for writing his spidery fiction, while other long-term guests have included P.J. Kavanagh, Richard Gwyn, and scores of poets from Alan Jenkins to Philip Levine. These authors, among many others, are featured in this anthology.

The city hosts three international literary festivals including Kosmopolis, BCN Crimeweek and the annual Poetry Week, all of which have attracted writers as diverse as Ian Rankin and Martin Amis. Unsurprising then, to discover that Barcelona also has numerous English writing courses, reading groups and a small but thriving theatre and comedy circuit. At the time of going to print there were four English-language magazines in circulation.

What *Barcelona INK* tries to do is provide a reflection of this literary netherworld where, bizarrely, people write and work in a language alien to their surroundings. At the same time, we publish translations of Catalan writers who we admire – represented here by the cutting satire of Màrius Serra and the melancholy poetry of Joan Margarit. The result, I hope, is a kind of letter to a city that has, I confess, bewitched me like so many others who have fallen beneath its spell. Often, the letter is a declaration of love; but sometimes it might be a request for divorce, or occasionally, even a scrawl of rebellious graffiti sprayed across the façades of this beautiful Barcelona.

The selections in this book have been drawn from the first eight issues of *Barcelona INK*. It is an eclectic and surprising mix: The grizzly post-war city features, as Kavanagh complains beautifully of being offered 'the bed her husband had died in four days previously' by a 'black bombazined widow' and Levine bemoans the Lilliputian size of the locals, 'in a clothing store on

Gran Via a clerk told me they had nothing in the store to fit a man as large as I was – 5'10.' The issues facing contemporary Barcelona are dealt with in Sameer Rawal's story of the Pakistani immigrant drawn into problems with the mafia, and, elsewhere, in David Hall's crime-noir that touches on the the very real problem of real-estate mobbing in the old quarter. Surprises? How about finding punk shockstress Lydia Lunch hiding away in what she describes as 'Grannyville' or Henry Miller travelling to the city, just for a meeting with an old friend...read and enjoy.

—Ryan Chandler

Barcelona
March 2012

The End of Barcelona

Fatally, the city's rulers believed their own propaganda...

Michael Eaude

The city of Barcelona has died, aged about 2030, of multi-factorial systemic collapse amid an excess of self-congratulation. Even as its rulers were hanging banners from every lamp-post proclaiming the city 'the best shop in the world', hundreds of thousands were unable to pay their bills, 10 per cent of the city's housing stock was uninhabited while thousands were being evicted and hundreds slept in the streets. Smog from frequent climate inversion exacerbated by mass car use led to record levels of cancer and breathing complaints, while health services were being closed down. Pushing the city once too often as 'a sustainable city for the 21st century', its rulers committed the fatal sin of believing their own propaganda. They lusted for fame and money whilst ignoring the most basic measures of self-preservation. Thus, in the city's great old age, its rulers committed the same crime of overreaching as they had several centuries earlier, in the city's prime.

Two centuries BC, Rome's rival Carthage was defeated and utterly destroyed, to be covered by the wind-driven sands, harbinger of the destiny of all empires. Tarraco was constructed as the capital of the Roman province of Iberia and then, in the time of Augustus, Barcelona was born on a low hill in the middle of a swamp, known as Mount Taber (with irony, we assume: it rose 17 metres above sea level). Till the city's death, its heart beat in this same place, called then the Roman Forum and most recently the Plaça de Sant Jaume.

In the town's youth, it had the first of its many famous children by different fathers, Eulàlia. In the fourth century, at the age of 13, she was murdered by the Romans for refusing to abjure Christ. Rolled off Mount Taber in a barrel full of broken glass, her breasts were then cut off and she was crucified. Her tender age is why there were thirteen geese in the cathedral cloister. Her apparently uncorrupted, sweet-smelling body was later buried in the cathedral crypt. Barcelona's Christian tradition was founded in this terrible martyrdom, a sobering story of sadistic fantasy at the heart of a system of belief.

As it reached adulthood, the young city, squeezed by the Arabs in the South and the Franks to the North, had to struggle for independence. Finally, sacked by the Arabs in 985, it saw that French protection was of little use and, in alliance with other cities, launched itself on its adventure as capital of an independent Catalonia, a journey lasting the several centuries of its maturity.

The twelfth and thirteenth centuries saw Catalonia's expansion. Frustrated in its venture North after the death of Pere, Count of Barcelona, at the Battle of Muret in 1213, it turned its attention South to Valencia and East into the Mediterranean. By the start of the fourteenth century, the Kingdom of Aragon and Catalonia ruled Naples (all of Southern Italy), Sicily, Valencia and the Balearics. An adopted son, the mercenary Roger de Flor, born in Italy of a German father, led his fearsome, shaggy-haired, half-naked *almogàvers* to Asia Minor. For 70 years, the Catalan flag flew on the Parthenon in conquered Athens.

Plague ravaged Barcelona in the fourteenth century, reducing its population by more than half. The Empire was overstretched, exhausted, as mortally sick as in recent times. Its merchants could not pay for its overseas adventures. Its most erudite section, the Jews, was amputated by pogrom in 1391.

By 1492, when Isabel of Castile and Ferran of Aragon, uniting Iberia by marriage, received Columbus in the Plaça del Rei, Barcelona had recovered from its near-fatal illness, but hostile new powers risen to the West, on the windswept steppes of central Iberia, were hastening its decline. Isabel forbade Barcelona from trading with the Americas in 1518 and the silver and gold from the Indies poured into Seville.

Their imperial hopes dashed, Barcelona's rulers' subsequent dream of the city becoming capital of a small, modern trading nation, perhaps something like Holland, was decisively destroyed in 1714. All its historic rights – laws, language, university, the control of its affairs – were removed by its rival sibling, Madrid. Catalonia was militarily occupied and its sacked capital was subjected between the cannon on the Montjuïc hill and the newly-built citadel (later a park and the Catalan Parliament: History erases the physical signs of military conquest, but not its memory). It looked quite likely that old, tottering Barcelona would soon follow Carthage's fate.

Another remarkable renaissance started in the 1830s. Young intellectuals began to promote public use of the suppressed Catalan language. In 1835 Barcelona's many monasteries and convents were put to flame and replaced by factories. The Industrial Revolution had arrived. Modern Barcelona can only be understood as the intertwining of two great struggles: the national struggle, for Catalonia to be free and independent; and the revolutionary fight for social justice.

The bosses of this industrial revolution were often *indianos*. After the lifting of the ban on trade with the Indies in 1780, many made their money on Cuban sugar plantations run by slave labour and returned to found textile factories. Wages were chronically low, both because of the large reserve army of labour that came off the impoverished land in the rest of Catalonia and Southern Spain and because the bosses – with rare exception – lacked the surplus necessary to buy social peace. Competition with France and Britain was tough.

In 1855 the first General Strike took place, paralysing the city in the fight for a ten-hour day under the banner 'Unions or Death'. When Bakunin's agents reached the city around 1870, they were casting seeds on fertile ground. The struggles for unionization, usually repressed violently by the army, led Engels to write in the 1880s that Barcelona was 'the city whose history records more struggle on the barricades than that of any other city in the world'. It became known as the Rose of fire, *Rosa del foc,* as revolutionary trade unionism led by anarchists dominated the working-class movement between the 1880s and 1937.

In the 1880s, Verdaguer wrote in his *Ode to Barcelona* 'Your splendid present heralds new times'. The movement to regain national rights took many forms, but the dominant current was led by a retired Spanish Army colonel, Francesc Macià, who first attempted to invade Catalonia from France in 1926 and then declared the independent Catalan Republic in 1931 from the balcony of the Palau de la Generalitat on the same Roman Plaça de Sant Jaume (or *de la República*, then). But independence lasted only two days, as Macià bowed to pressure from Madrid.

The 1936-39 Civil War brought defeat for both the revolutionary movement and the movement for Catalan national rights. Bombed by the Italian aviation, battered by hunger, its language banned, its dissidents executed, exiled or jailed and its crumbling Old City pitted with bomb-sites, Barcelona was a crushed city in the 1940s and 1950s.

Yet Franco's grey, ill-smelling city was to live one last great Renaissance. The Socialist Party that governed the city from 1979 to 2011 created a Barcelona brand for the world's tourism bazaars. They opted to promote tourism and business, using the 1992 Olympic Games as an excuse for a huge building programme of new roads, hotels, wealthy flats, conference centres and shopping malls.

The Barcelona brand contained several ideological and artistic strands. Barcelona was the city of Art Nouveau and in particular of the city's adopted son, the architect Antoni Gaudí. Its bourgeoisie, frustrated by lack of political power, had poured their money into financing Art Nouveau buildings between 1875 and 1925, an eccentric style that dominated the city's Eixample or *extension*. It gave tourists two cities in one: the mediaeval monuments of the Gothic Quarter, built in Barcelona's imperial prime, and the modern city of Art, with Picasso and Joan Miró forming an impressive triumvirate alongside Gaudí.

The brand exploited Barcelona's revolutionary image, too: the 1936 revolution celebrated by Orwell. And its down-market image, the degenerate city beloved of French intellectuals and absinthe-drinkers, revelled in by Jean Genet.

Visitors poured in. Young foreigners adored the bars, beaches and alcohol. Business people loved to hold their meetings and trade fairs there. But something was wrong. The old were shoved out to outlying estates. There were no jobs for young people. There was no housing. Large anti-capitalist and anti-war movements from 2001 to 2004 seemed to fizzle out; but as had happened in Cairo before the revolution of 2011, so in Barcelona deep anger built up over the years when the city's inhabitants had to pay for the capitalist crisis with wage reductions and worse social services.

The city had suffered so many apparent deaths and rebirths that its rulers – and many citizens – believed the city was immortal. Its end was sudden. Explosive rebellions wrecked the tourism industry. The rich fled the city. Rosa Luxemburg had prophesied socialism or barbarism. With the rebellious unable to win power, the city sank into barbarism. Already plague has returned and the Mediterranean's gentle waves lap against the shores of Mount Taber and soft sand blows along the deserted streets of the Eixample.

Barcelona, city, born before Christ, died 2015.

Three Rooms

An interview with Colm Tóibín

Colm Tóibín has won many accolades and much acclaim since his debut novel The South *won the Irish Times Literature Prize for a first book.* The Heather Blazing *won The Encore Award and both* The Blackwater Lightship *and* The Master *were shortlisted for the Booker. His non-fiction includes* Homage to Barcelona *and* The Sign of The Cross: Travels in Catholic Europe.

You first came to Barcelona in 75 then again in 89, yes? I'm probably right in guessing you've been back since. What changes have you noticed in terms of atmosphere? How up to date are you in terms of Barcelona/ Spain?

I lived in the city from 1975 to 1978 and all of 1988 and some of 1989 and 1990; after that I have spent a few weeks of each year in the city, but over the past ten years I have been mostly in the Pyrenees where I built a house.

I stay in the city for a few days on my way through to the mountains a few times a year, and usually go to the Liceu four or five times a year. I am not as interested in the city as I used to be, but that is middle age talking. It's not the city's fault. I am setting a long story in the city, in Carrer Sant Pau, among the Pakistani immigrants, so I walk up and down that street a lot, and get shaved every day in one of the barber's shops. I also have another story in the back of my head. I have a *Bicing* (the city's rent-a-bike scheme) card so I like that.

I sit at the bar called Els Tres Tombs and watch the world sometimes in the evening.

Would you say it's a good city for writers? Are there such things as good cities for writers (like Nice is great for painting)?

I think a long cold winter is better for novelists; thus maybe Dublin or Berlin or New York; maybe Barcelona is good for poets.

I read somewhere that you said rooms were more important than cities, what did you mean?

I live in my head and then I live in two or three rooms. They are the important places. This doesn't mean that the great cities of the world –

Barcelona, Seville, San Sebastian, Rio, San Francisco are not filled with excitement and promise. But excitement and promise are no use when you are working on a novel.

Do you find any similarities coming from a Catholic country like Ireland and being somewhere like Spain? Does it have any relevance in terms of your feelings for the two countries?

I haven't been in wider Spain very much and don't really know it, although I have always liked it and enjoyed it. But in Catalonia there is no real Catholicism like in Ireland. You simply don't notice it in the same way.

I suppose having two languages vaguely in conflict interests me in both places. But I like Catalonia for its difference from Ireland, for its work ethic, and its interest in civilised pleasure.

Similarly, have you felt any special affinity for Catalonia and its concept of nationhood coming from Ireland? I say this because many Catalans I meet always seem to express an immediate warmth for the Irish.

I think there is a real connection between Ireland and Catalonia, which began perhaps in 1848, a year in which both places became aware again, with other parts of Europe, of a lost nationhood and began to attempt to restore it. But more and more I find the whole idea of nationhood half mad. I like Catalonia's openness to Europe and I used to enjoy its terrible prejudices, but I am less amused by them now. I still love Catalans' attitude to culture and to infrastructure and to civic space.

You have mentioned that one of the reasons you went to Spain was because you liked *The Sun Also Rises*. Was it what you expected when you arrived? If not, how did it differ from your expectations?

The pleasure in food and light and the night which Hemingway deals with is all there still. Yes, I found it as soon as I arrived. It was even better than I had imagined.

Is it true that despite being set in Barcelona/Catalonia you wrote the *The South* in a Lisbon hotel room? If so, does this mean you prefer to put distance between your experience and the actual process of writing?

I can write anywhere, including at home. But sometimes you need to focus, really concentrate and you can do this in an unfamiliar space. But it doesn't really matter.

> *'I have been here for several weeks. I am grateful that the woman who runs the hotel and her little mouse do not speak English. I remain a mystery to them, they cannot get through to me.'*

How much of this is you? Any? If so what do you mean by 'they cannot get through to me'. Do you miss those little mice and shabby hotels?

Yes, that was an old pension I stayed in at the corner of Carrer del Pi and Portaferrissa. They could not get through to her because they had no language in common. Yes, I miss a Barcelona when there were no tourists, no tourists at all, and the city centre belonged to the people of the city. In the 1970s and 1980s no tourists came to the city, they all went to the coast.

Your prose suggests a strong poetic influence, why haven't you written any poetry? Who are your favourite poets?

I have written poetry, but it doesn't really work. I like Wallace Stevens, Yeats, Elizabeth Bishop, Sir Thomas Wyatt.

When you wrote *Homage to Barcelona* why did you choose non-fiction as a medium when you normally write fiction? What motivated you to write it?

I realized that I could get a contract for the book since city tourism was beginning and people were starting to discover Barcelona and I was always writing out lists of places where people should go, and things they had to see. The idea that someone would pay me to write about the place seemed thrilling.

It has been said that there is a strong mother-figure theme throughout your work. I would be interested to know if you feel any affinity with the film director Almodóvar who seems to pursue a similar vein in his films.

He makes comedies. I make tragedies. We are both gay. I discovered when I interviewed him that he is a really hard worker, a very focussed person. There are some films where there is no mother. I think if you are gay and you write a few times about mothers then people think you must be obsessed by your mother. There are no mothers at all in some of my books.

Plaça Sant Pere

Stephen Burgen

They'd had a row. It's plain in the way they come down the street, side by side, but with a metre of no man's land between them, and how each takes a studious interest in things not worthy of such focused attention, an interest that neither shares with the other. He in a man unloading sacks of cement from the back of a van, she in a wholesaler's window display of catering uniforms; he in a Moroccan wearing a spotless white jalaba, as though he'd never seen such a thing before, and she in a wrought iron balcony of which there are thousands in this city.

They are in their early thirties, stylishly casual and, as they are on holiday in late June before the masses arrive, almost certainly childless. Both, and he in particular, affect the forced nonchalance of people who want to blend and don't want to be taken as tourists, though they could hardly be anything else. His hair is dark, with a fleck of grey, and is cut very short. He wears rectangular glasses with blue frames and a fitted blue shirt that he wears outside his jeans. He has three or four days' growth of beard. She has bobbed, medium-brown hair and is dressed in a white singlet, white shorts and green wedge-heeled sandals. She has milk-white skin. A large pair of wraparound sunglasses cover her eyes. She carries a large leather handbag, the same green as her sandals. He is empty-handed.

V., who has propped himself against the wall of the Espai de Sucre pâtissier school, watches them coming. The guy from the Pakistani mini-market opposite is having a smoke in the doorway. A skinny Chinese pushing a sack truck piled with boxes of clothes is trying to get past the woman who is feeling in her bag for her camera. There is something shambling and broken about the Chinese man, as if he'd been in a car crash and had his bones set by an amateur. The boxes are piled so high he can barely see over them. V. guesses the couple are English, not that it matters. Something about their manner and the way they dress. She puts the camera away and as she draws level with him gives V. a sidelong glance; he can tell she's looking at him, despite the wraparounds. Her cheeks are pink from the heat. He checks her out from behind as she passes. Nothing much to shout about, but the very whiteness of her thighs fascinates him. Their otherness.

She takes out the camera and as she's taking the picture steps into the path of a bicycle. The cyclist swerves and swears, though not directly at her, as she jumps half a step back. Her boyfriend turns to her for the first time since V. has been watching them. Their eyes meet but she looks away; she isn't ready to make peace yet. It's a stupid thing, the argument; it's nothing really, his attitude more than anything else, the way he speaks to her sometimes. He doesn't see it. When she brings it up he just goes cold on her. Sometimes her brittleness drives him crazy.

When they reach the corner of Méndez Núñez he takes a map from the back pocket of his jeans. He has folded it up small and looks at it discreetly, turning over the folds without opening it up, anxious not to give himself away as a tourist. He looks up at the street sign, looks back at the map, then folds it away in his pocket. She meanwhile is studying the goods in the window of a wholesaler that specialises in socks and tights. Two more Chinese pass pushing trucks piled with boxes. He moves to his right towards Plaça Sant Pere and she follows in his wake, half a dozen paces behind.

The cobbled square slopes away from the church. The tall laburnums that line two sides of the square are shedding their flowers and the square is thinly carpeted in yellow. There is an old-style drinking fountain in the middle of the square. She photographs the laburnums and then takes a picture of the fountain. He is studying the menu on a blackboard outside the restaurant, which has half a dozen outside tables. The menu is in Catalan. They are united in their condition as outsiders and their need to understand the menu – she has a pocket Spanish dictionary in her bag but that won't help – but both nevertheless resist this opening for reconciliation. Instead, they exchange consensual shrugs and sit down at the table nearest the fountain. V. sits on the church steps smoking a Winston.

The waiter is young. He is dressed in a black apron over a black T-shirt and shorts. He is wearing black trainers. He wears a look of sullen impatience, as if he wants it understood that working here is beneath his dignity. He takes them through the menu in broken English. She takes off her sunglasses. Her eyes are hazel. She points to the blackboard.

'What's that?' she says. If he'd thought about it, the waiter would have expected her to have a higher voice. *'Trinxat?'*

'*Trinxat*,' the waiter says, scratching his cheek. 'It's potato, chopped with, I don't know how you say this, *col*.'

She hears 'coal' but knows that can't be right. She orders salad with the fish to follow; he orders the *trinxat* – he likes to think he has adventurous tastes, but also to spite her – and the squid with meatballs. He asks for a beer, she for wine. She puts her sunglasses back on and sits with her hands folded over the bag on her lap. He looks around. All the tables are occupied. Aside from a couple with their teenage son, who by their blondness must be

Swedes or Danes, or possibly Dutch, all the others are locals, mainly young and casual, aside from a pair of besuited businessmen who are talking loudly. Two small boys are playing football against the church wall. Three gaunt Moroccans sit on a bench by the fountain sharing a spliff. A busker with a guitar a few tables away is singing *Light My Fire*. Fifty yards away workmen are digging up the cobbles with a jackhammer. V. has moved across the square and is leaning against the portico of the bank. The waiter brings the drinks. The boyfriend raises his glass.

'Cheers,' he says, anxious to break the ice.

'Cheers,' she says, coldly.

'Can't we just let it rest?' he says.

'Pretend nothing's wrong, you mean?'

The waiter brings their starters. The boyfriend pokes at the *trinxat* with his fork.

'Cabbage,' he says with a sigh. '*Col* is cabbage. Oh well, nothing ventured …'

She hangs her bag over the back of her chair and spreads the napkin on her lap.

'Salad good?'

'Divine,' she says, without expression.

She doesn't see anything. All she has is a vague sensation of movement, of the air changing, like the passing of a ghost. Then there is a commotion. One of the businessmen is shouting, knocking the aluminium chair over as he gets to his feet.

'*Lladre! Lladre!*' he shouts. Everyone turns to see what's going on and where he's pointing. V. doesn't turn round; he doesn't break into a run. He lets the bag fall to the ground and keeps on walking at his normal speed. No one's going to run after him; they never do. It doesn't matter, there are plenty more bags.

Only when the businessman picks it up off the ground does she realise that it's her bag. She stands up slowly and the chair grates noisily against the cobbles. The businessman carries the bag by the strap on the end of his finger as though it were a piece of evidence. All eyes are on her. Her boyfriend also stands up; it feels like the right thing to do. The businessman shakes his head – it isn't clear at whom his dismay is directed, her or the thief – and hands her the bag.

'*Gracias*,' she says, flushing bright pink. '*Muchas gracias*.'

She is filled with a mixture of gratitude and embarrassment. She has an impulse to throw her arms around the man and another impulse to cry. She suppresses both. The man returns to his table, the other clients go back to their food and conversation, the boys kick the ball against the church wall. Suddenly the couple feel exposed and awkward and they both sit down.

'I feel so stupid.'

'Don't. It's not your fault.'

'But everyone gets robbed here. You know that. Everyone we know who's come here has been robbed. Everyone warns you.'

'I know, but we weren't robbed, we were almost robbed, we were lucky.'

It feels right saying 'we', although it is her bag with her things in it.

He reaches across the table and puts his hand on hers. The sullen waiter passes, noting their barely touched starters. Her companion is relieved to see she isn't crying; her crying gets on his nerves. She isn't angry with him anymore. That's all history. He sees an opportunity to save the situation, the holiday. He squeezes her hand.

'I love you, Claire,' he says.

She looks at him, then down at the salad, the bag on her lap, then back at him. She smiles.

'Me too,' she says softly.

Around the corner at Arc de Triomf, V. sits on a bench smoking a Winston. Two women with a toddler sit across the way. The toddler keeps running off and the women take it in turns to bring the child back. One of the women wears her handbag strapped diagonally across her chest. Her companion has set hers down on the bench beside her. V. walks in a long loop around the arch and positions himself against a lamppost. The women now have their backs to them. The child is with them, sitting and eating a chocolate biscuit, but V. knows he will run off again soon. It's only a matter of time and V. has time. He's in no hurry.

Pauline Stainer

A Blind Man Passes La Sagrada Família

I
I have no spittle on my lids

I hear the light quadrupeds
squirrel, ferret
on the seven lesser altars

the sough of birds
chloroformed
with outstretched wings

still-born infants
rising on plaster dust
in the Santa Cruz hospital

the triple torchères
tossing their howling manes
for the three holy children.

II
I feel the flexible wire-mesh
of the recording angel
on the Field of the Harp

skeletons
practising deposition
from pulleys and weights

doves of polished iron
in the spandrel
as if heaven were to one side

the billow of incense
through the twelve bell-towers
each blowing a different death.

III
I sense the cranes rust
along their rat-lines, men like trees
walking the spiderdeck

the hare kindle
at the annunciation
in the bloody meadow

Lazarus
densify the ice-house
under the lawn

the desire to crucify
by mirrors, calvary flowing
until it floats

the pestles of mortars.

IV
I see the masons
chip the stone
into blazing accidentals

the spires cast
their Venetian glass like falcons
into the wind

the seraph
at the empty sepulchre
in a suit of lights.

Rebus in Barcelona

Ian Rankin

Ambushed on a recent visit to the city, Ian Rankin, the creator of the renowned Edinburgh detective, answers our 20 Questions...

Barcelona...
Edinburgh with heat

A reason to visit...
it's a great city to walk around

A reason to leave...
fear of pickpockets

A time to write...
late at night…

A place to write...
in a cafe or bar, with a beer or a glass of wine to hand

A good day's work...
can be a single sentence or an entire story, so long as you're pleased with it

A place to read...
trains and planes

The first line of a book...
'Someone – or something – had killed Barcelona. It was his job to find out why.' (I made that up: feel free to steal it.)

A line from a poem...
'Her pleasure whispered through a much-kissed smile' (Douglas Dunn, *Tursac*)

An interesting quote...
When one has been threatened with a great injustice, one accepts a smaller as a favour' (Jane Welsh Carlyle)

Food for thought...
chocolate; chocolate gets me thinking…

A drink to wash it down...
massala tea

The role of a writer...
To create new and interesting worlds

A good author should...
yet rarely does…

A sentence should be...
fitting to the crime

Language makes us...
but also has the power to unmake us

A valuable talent...
invisibility

An essential tool...
a pen, naturally

A memorable expression in Spanish or Catalan...
'A la tercera fue la vencida' (final line of *Los Sueños de un Libertador* by Fermín Goñi)

A final question...
What's the point?

The Bergman Virus

Simon Newman

The room had no windows, buried as it was deep in the bowels of the headquarters of XanaX Systems. Lights twinkled, coffee machines blinked on standby and the wispy-bearded geeks you'd expect to find were dutifully slouched in front of their screens. It was the top anti-virus company in Europe, based at 22@Barcelona, the city's shiny new 'innovation' district. Their corporate strapline said they operated at the cutting edge of technology, conveniently failing to mention that they also worked at the flaky edge of the law.

Computer viruses used to be the domain of hormonally-charged pubescents who, when not otherwise flipping burgers or popping zits, spent their downtime in back bedrooms creating digital mayhem. But the world had moved on, and companies like XanaX simply wouldn't survive if all there was out there to challenge them was some shabby, amateur bit of code that let out a whoopee-cushion every time you pressed Caps Lock.

XanaX reasoned that it was about time that the professionals moved into the virus-creation market. So they set about doing the job properly – themselves. Over the years they covertly enjoyed a string of successes, like the Niagara, the binary equivalent of a cold shower that extinguished firewalls. And then there was Dalí's Paradox, a surreal virus that convinced computers they were an ironing board, making them exasperating to set up and prone to collapse at any moment. Ironically, few noticed the difference.

But Rosalin Connors, founder of XanaX, wanted more. The big one. The one that would totally wipe out the opposition. And now it looked like she had it, thanks to the unstinting work of XanaX's Head of Research, an über-nerd known simply as Weasel, so named on account of the supreme deviousness of his work. Rosalin sensed they were on the edge of a breakthrough. This one would turn them all — PCs, Macs, laptops, desktops, right through to the systems of major corporations — on their heads.

'Explain to me again, Weasel, in language I can understand, just how this virus works? And what are we going to call it by the way?'

Weasel yawned. He'd been up all night, in fact most of the last seven nights, putting in the finishing touches.

He was a pro and at only nineteen Weasel was widely considered to be the industry's King of the Hill. But his world was one that changed fast. There were new, younger kids coming through. Kids that had never heard of Quark-Driller or Kwontum Mekanik, or any of the other greats from Weasel's legendary back catalogue.

And Weasel had decided that he'd had enough. His long nights of continuous subterranean work had started to take their toll.

Quit while you're on top, he told himself. Always leave them wanting more.

He was keeping it from Rosalin, but this one was going to be his swan song. He planned to move back to Dublin and start afresh in something new, even though his stocks in XanaX would give him enough to live comfortably without ever working again.

Weasel yawned once more and turned to Rosalin.

'It's going to be called…the Bergman Virus.'

Rosalin looked at him quizzically. She was used to Weasel's obscurities but this one intrigued her.

'And...it's to be called the Bergman virus…because?'

'Ingmar Bergman, the famous Swedish …'

Rosalin interrupted.

'Yeah, I know. She was an actress. Beautiful, mysterious, the ultimate femme fatale. I get it. She looks like butter wouldn't melt…blah, blah, but just when you're not looking, she slips the salami knife between the shoulder blades. I like it, Weasel. I like it a lot.'

Weasel groaned and rolled his eyes. In business, Rosalin was as sharp as they come, but movie-trivia was his province, his only passion outside of nerding.

'No, Rosalin, that was Ingrid Bergman. She was the actress. This is Ingmar Bergman, the film director. He shot mostly in black and white. Remember? Bleak wasn't in it. Most of his films were about the utter futility of existence. And that was on his up days.'

Rosalin coughed and waved her hand.

'Yeah, right, that Bergman. But hold on, I thought he was a boxer.'

'What? What are you talking about, Rosalin? A boxer? Wait a minute, you're not thinking of Ingmar Johansson, are you? He was a boxer.'

'Was he Swedish?'

'Er, yeah, I think so.'

'So I was kind of half right then?'

'Er, yeah, half right, Rosalin. Look, can we get back to Ingmar Bergman? His films were always about depression. *Through a Glass Darkly* and all that grim, Kierkegaard philosophy shit. No hang on, Kierkegaard was Danish. Never mind. So, Bergman. You're going to love this, Rosalin. The Bergman

Virus is going to cause computers to get the symptoms of real-time, full-on, clinical depression. Remember what happened to Carl in Finance?'

'Of course I remember. Sad case. Good at his job, dependable.'

'Exactly, and then...?'

'He got depressed. Became listless, unfocussed on his work, lost motivation, started making mistakes and missing deadlines. Then it really got bad. He stopped eating, and then went missing for a while. They found him walking the streets. Hardly knew what day it was. Completely lost the will to engage with the world.'

Rosalin paused, and then beamed at Weasel, 'So, Bergman, it'll behave …like…like Carl?'

Weasel nodded. 'You see, in the past, viruses, including mine, have to put my hands up, well, they just got too brutal. Files corrupted, systems frozen, data lost, and so on. But Bergman's going to be different. Subtle. All those symptoms you just reeled off about Carl? They're going to creep out, slowly, insidiously. It'll start with the simple mistakes, but they'll gradually get bigger. Then the virus will cause a deep melancholy to set in. Finally, one day you'll find your PC curled up in the corner, gently rocking in the foetal position, sucking its thumb. That'll be it. Goodnight Vienna. But at XanaX, we'll be ready. Only we hold the antidote. We'll clean up, Rosalin. We'll be the Knight on the White Charger. Masters of the Universe. Think about it.'

Rosalin's eyes were moist.

'Weasel, you are a …genius …a grade 'A' genius. THE top mullah, no question.'

Rosalin kissed Weasel resoundingly on the forehead. Mmmmmw-wahh.

'I love you, Weasel. I love you and I want to have your babies. Well, not literally, obviously, you being a total weed and me being a divine goddess. A virtual baby, maybe. But I tell you something, Weasel, when this gets out, the world's going to be your lobster, I'm telling you, your absolute, total lobster.'

Weasel grinned.

'Yeah, actually I think you mean...oyster, Rosalin...the expression is The World's your Oyst…oh ...right …that was a joke, yeah? Yeah. I knew that'.

XanaX launched the Bergman virus quietly, with no fuss, on a Monday morning, which Weasel thought fitted in neatly with the whole depression thing. No-one likes Mondays. Normally he hated his dad's music, but he'd recently found a vinyl in his collection by some old Irish hippy. The song carried a special resonance for Weasel on that morning. He started singing to himself.

The silicon chip inside her head just switched to overload …something, something …damn, can't remember all the words …

but she can see no reason, 'cos there is no reason

what reason do you need to be show, o, o, o …

Tell me why

I don't like Mondays.

Tell me why...

Weasel shuddered with anticipation, and then hit the Send key. Bergman was on its way.

As ever, there has to be a first one. Whenever a virus hits the web, there has to be a computer somewhere in the world that's directly in the firing line. And it has a special role to play. The self-replicating code that viruses depend upon to spread themselves around, needs that first computer to act as a platform from which it springboards upwards and onwards. It's estimated that a well constructed virus can infect over ninety percent of the world's billion computers in under a week.

The very first Bergman virus entered the ether, just as likely to pop up in a computer in the office block next door to XanaX in Barcelona, or, … the other side of the world.

It was a beautiful day in Alice Springs. Dr Marion Walker was in Rob's bedroom testing the equipment to make sure there were no glitches.

The State had only been running the AVE scheme, Assisted Voluntary Euthanasia, for six months, when they decided to close it down. There had been a fierce backlash from the moral Right. Protest marches, petitions, hunger strikes and sit-ins at Parliament.

Rob's case would be the last to be carried out in Australia for the foreseeable future. Dr Walker had been calling on Rob for the last year and had seen the way in which he had deteriorated. The prognosis in his case wasn't good. MS, Multiple Sclerosis, hits you with a double whammy. First the symptoms themselves, they're bad enough. But worse is the dread of what's to come. Dr Walker knew that most MS patients fall into one of two categories. Those that can keep their head above the parapet, mentally, can both prolong their lives and maintain a decent quality of life for many years. But then there are those, like Rob, who simply can't find it in themselves to generate the supreme effort needed. They collapse into a trough of despair. They just want to pull the plug. And that was the decision which Rob, after much heart searching, endless deep-and-meaningfuls with doctors, friends, family and psychiatrists, had finally taken.

The mechanism was simple really. The software that the doctor had loaded on his PC would take him through a decision tree.

Do you realize that...?

Are you certain that…?

After the next stage you will not be able to turn back.

When you press Return, the software will activate the drip.

The first shot will be a mild sedative.

The second shot will be a muscle relaxant.

The third shot will be an opiate that will send you into a deep, desensitised sleep.

What follows will be the final dose of Betamin 34, the cardiac-arrest drug.

Do you fully understand the implications of …?

Rob had been on the Net just an hour earlier. He'd cleaned out his message box and sent off a few last emails to friends. His hands had become too unsteady to use a keyboard in recent months and so he relied on speech recognition software. One incoming email was from Amazon informing him that he had only one day left in which to take advantage of their Two-for-One DVD offer.

One day left. Jeez, I'd better hurry.

Just as he told the computer to bin the Amazon email, silently, without any fanfare, the very first Bergman Virus crept in through Port COM1, sashayed deftly past the Firewall, sneered contemptuously at Dr Norton and took up residence in an invisible hard-drive partition that it had just created for itself. Snug, secure, non-detectable. Biding its time.

Rob settled himself in bed, pillows plumped up. He'd originally intended to have some soft music playing, but when the time came, he couldn't face it. He turned to the doctor.

'Just shut the windows, pull the curtains, and let's get on with it please, doc.'

'How are you feeling, Rob?' Dr Walker asked.

What a stupid question. I'm feeling like shit. And scared too. That's how I'm feeling, shit scared. How does she think I'm feeling?

'I'm fine, Dr Walker, really, fine. Can we please just get on with...?'

'Sure, sure. Okay, ready?'

Rob nodded and Dr Walker attached the drip-tube to the catheter she'd inserted earlier into a vein in Rob's right arm.

'You're sure...?'

'Dr Walker, Marion, we've been through all of this a dozen times.'

'Okay, first of all I'll activate the software.'

Dr Walker hit a few keys and checked the settings. Everything was ready. She set the screen angle towards the waiting patient.

Rob suddenly had a thought.

'What do they call it by the way? The software, that is. All normal software packages have names that, you know, describe what they actually do, don't they? Image Express, Creative Workshops, Power Plus, that kind of thing. What do you call a bit of software that's designed to top you off? Curtain Call? The Last Supper? Geronimo?'

'Er ...I don't know, Rob. It was designed by medics. It probably hasn't got a name. So, are you ready?'

Rob nodded again.

'You just need to answer Yes or No to each question. The speech recognition software will register your answer. Here we go then.' The screen lit up, with a soft green backdrop. Very restful, thought Rob. Very Zen.

Weasel knew the Bergman virus would do exactly as it was told. It wouldn't know or care why its designer had signed off the last operating instruction with the word, XanaX. Weasel wasn't even sure himself. It must have been a kind of mischievous game he'd subconsciously decided to play. It was to be his swan song, after all. The word XanaX had been encrypted in a Boolean code and so the virus's source should remain undetected, although in the back of his mind there was the thought that he didn't really care. He'd be long gone by the time it got out, and anyway, his work at XanaX was totally covert. He'd simply deny everything.

But in the darkened, twinkling research centre, Weasel suddenly looked past his screen into the middle distance, shivered.

And then his face went white.

Really, deathly white.

This was some feat considering that as a result of his subterranean existence his usual pallor was something between pastry and chalk.

Nah, it wouldn't. Would it?

Surely not?

Then Weasel groaned.

Shit and double shit.

It's going to, isn't it?

Oh, jeez, it's going to.

Viruses are simple organisms really. At their core is a helix, a spiral thread just like those twirly-pasta things they show on the News when they're trying to explain DNA. In Rob's computer in Alice Springs, the first spiral helix popped out of its hidey-hole, ready to embark on its mission of binary carnage.

And it was immediately faced with an unexpected dilemma.

Should it spiral left, or right?

For there had been just one flaw in Weasel's otherwise impeccable logic. The word XanaX, the word he had signed off the virus with, is a palindrome, a word that can be read forwards or backwards.

The virus's spiral helix was momentarily stumped. Which way to turn?

It thought about the problem for a couple of seconds, twirled this way then that, but knew deep down in its little binary heart that it wasn't authorised to take decisions. So it hopped off for a quick scan through the computer's Programme Files. It found what it was looking for, the file in the Solitaire game used for its first deal of cards. A random choice generator.

The helix asked the programme nicely for a decision, and a digital coin was flipped.

Heads = left, tails = right.

It could have landed either side. Tails it was.

Happy with its answer, the helix set off, whistling carefree, on it's spiralling little clockwise journey. It was doing exactly what it had been told to do.

Only the wrong way round.

And as a result, the Bergman Virus, and its depressive effect, had been reversed.

Rob wanted to clear his throat before he began, but thought the better of it. He didn't want the speech recognition software to misinterpret anything. He settled for a gulp.

Dr Walker had, as previously agreed, left the room, her Hippocratic oath preventing her from remaining by Rob's side as the deed was actually done.

The first question that appeared on the computer's screen was straightforward.

'Do you wish to proceed with this termination?'

Rob gulped again, and then managed a clear response.

'Yes.'

The second question though, came as a bit of a shock.

'You sure, Rob? I mean, it's a great day out there. The sun's shining. The clear blue yonder's out there just waiting for you. Hey, what would you say to a cold beer? A nice frosty Fosters?'

Rob looked around the room, but of course Dr Walker wasn't there.

'Sorry, what? I thought this was going to be a sort of Yes/No kind of dialogue.'

'Yeah, but you know... lighten up a little. There's no hurry. So...tell me… how's it hanging, Rob?'

'I'm sorry?'

'You know, the whole LIFE thing.'

Rob blew out through his cheeks.

'Well, since you're asking, not so hot at the moment, to tell you the truth. Wait a minute, who the friggin' hell am I talking to?'

'Not an easy question, but …hey, tell you what, you can call me Felix.'

'Excuse me? Am I missing some kind of cat connection here?'

'Nope, no cat, Robby boy. Felix the Helix, that's me.'

Rob shook his head in disbelief. 'Okay, okay, but listen, Felix ...jeez I can't believe I'm talking to… look, whoever you are... as far as I'm concerned, you're just a bit of software, here to guide me through the whole euthanasia bit. The pulling-the-plug thing, if you recall?'

'Er, hang on a minute, Rob, I'll just switch from screen-output to voice simulation. It'll be quicker for you to follow. There we go, how's that?'

'Well, not bad, I suppose, in a sort of Stephen-Hawking-on-Acid kind of way. Look, can we stick to my agenda, please?'

'Yeah, yeah, plenty of time for that. First things first, what's your star sign?'

'I don't believe this. Star sign? What the… Look, you're a bit of binary code. Logic is what you do. Not reading-the-tea-leaves crap. Jeezers, Felix.'

'And your star sign is?'

Rob sighed. 'Taurus.'

'Hang on. I'll just check today's paper. You're on broadband, yeah?'

Rob nodded.

'I asked if you were on broadband, Rob. I can't see you, you know. You have to say your answer out loud. Though, hang on, you've got a webcam, haven't you? I've just noticed. Hold on, let's turn it on ...ok, let's get you nicely into focus. Ah, there you are. Ooooh, actually you do look a bit peaky.'

'Peaky? A bit peaky? I've got Multiple Sclerosis, for chrissakes. What do you expect? Plus, I've decided to end it all, if you remember? I'm hardly going to be looking all bronzed and pumped-up like Brad Pitt out of Gladiator, am I?'

'True, Rob, true. Though… no…hang on… Brad Pitt was in Troy. Gladiator was… er…one of your lot…an Aussie...Russell Crowe. Yeah, that's it, Russell Crowe.'

Rob snapped back,

'It doesn't matter, Felix. I don't look like either of them, do I?'

'Yeah, fair point, Rob. And well made, if I may say so. Okay, where were we? Oh yeah, star signs. Taurus, let's have a look. Right, here we are, Robby …on the internet … got it …the Melbourne Courier. Taurus. Here we are.'

'Don't make any big decisions before asking a trusted friend.'

'There, well, that's pretty emphatic. And pretty darned timely too, I'd say, Rob, wouldn't you?'

'I don't believe this. Felix, you really are serious.'

'Here's the web page, have a look yourself.'

'No, not serious as in … Jeez … this is all getting ... look …Felix … can we just …?'

'A trusted friend, it said, Rob. That's me. It's like I've been sent.'

Rob turned his hands towards an imaginary heaven.

'Like he's been sent? Give me strength.' Rob shook his head, 'And why exactly should I trust YOU, anyway? You're just a bit of code. A string of noughts and ones. How can YOU help? I mean, what do YOU know about MS, for starters?'

'Nothing, and everything,' said Felix, 'let's have a look on the Net again. Okay, MS. Here we go. Yeah, there are over thirteen million entries, and that's just the medical journals. Hang on, I'll just sort them by World Health Organisation rankings. That's better. Just the eight hundred thousand to review. Let me go through them. Yeah, mmmm, phew, really? Mmmm, yeah, blah blah, no shit? Nah, okay, I see. Right then, Rob, it all seems straightforward. Here's how I see it...'

Dr Walker popped her head round the door.

'Is everything okay, Rob? I heard you talking. It's just that I thought by now you might have … you know, got things ...well …started.'

Rob looked up sheepishly. 'Er... yeah, yeah, everything's just fine doc. I ...er… I just need a bit of time. I was just talking to ... just talking to myself.'

'Fine, fine. Sure, of course, take all the time you need. I don't need to be back at the hospital for, well, an hour or so yet. You carry on. I'll just …I'll just leave you to it.'

Back at XanaX HQ in Barcelona, Weasel had already worked out that the first of the virus's spiral helixes would probably seek out a random choice generator. So he knew that there would be a 50/50 chance it would choose the right direction. He decided that those odds gave him at least some possibility of a reprieve. But he needed to cover the downside. And he needed to act fast.

He sent an authorisation email to his stockbroker with instructions to sell all his holdings in XanaX. And he booked a flight to Dublin. There was no adverse feedback coming from the Net by late Monday morning and Weasel started to relax just a fraction. Maybe, just maybe.

But later, in the afternoon, Rosalin Connors came bearing down on him at his desk with a look of thunder on her face. Suddenly, Weasel knew deep down in his heart which way round the helix must have spiralled.

'Have you seen the blogs?'

'Er, no. What blogs exactly would they be, Rosalin?'

'Something weird is going on out there, Weasel. Something creepy and weird. Look at all these messages that have been popping up on people's alerts.'

Rosalin shoved a fist full of printouts under Weasel's nose.

'Look, here, look at this one.'

This is a Non-Error message. You've no worries. In fact, I've just done a tune-up on all your hard-drives, soft-drives, the squidgy drives too. Your computer will be running a lot faster now. No more glitches, trust me. And I plan to keep it that way. Anything you need, just call me. Have a nice day now. Felix, your resident, happy helper.

'Who the freakin' hell is this, Felix, Weasel?'

Weasel was caught completely on the back foot, but he was at least relieved to see that XanaX's name wasn't showing up anywhere. Yet.

'Er, search me, Rosalin. I have no idea.'

'And look at this one.'

Ooooh, by the way, I've cancelled your subscription to your anti-virus provider. You'll not be needing that anymore. To be honest, you never really did. They just scared you into thinking you did. They created all the viruses in the first place, just to keep themselves in business. Anyway, Felix is on the case now. Just rest easy and leave it all to me. Can I get you anything?

A beer? Order you a pizza on-line? Just say the word. Oh man, I really love my job. Laters …Felix.

'What is going on, Weasel? I want to know, and I want to know fast.'

Rosalin stormed off leaving Weasel looking, implausibly, even whiter than he'd done earlier. But then he pulled himself together and quietly, out of earshot of his colleagues, phoned for a cab to the airport.

After Dr Walker had left the room, Rob turned back to the screen.

'So, Felix, what happens now?'

'That's up to you, Robby.'

'Your voice has changed, Felix. You sound kind of, more normal now. More like a proper human voice.'

'I guess I must be learning, Rob, like evolving. Hey, scary, eh? So, Rob, do you still want to… you know… pull the plug…?'

'I guess so. I mean, nothing has changed, has it?'

'Well, I'm here now. That's different. And remember, I've now loaded the entire world's accumulated knowledge on MS on my binary synapses. You know about all the symptoms of course, Rob. Only too well. Muscle weakness, speech and cognitive deficits, fatigue, balance and coordination problems. But the thing that gets most MS sufferers is the depression. And it's understandable, Rob. Who the hell wouldn't get depressed? But then some people, somehow, are able to rise above it. The MS patients who enjoy a full-scale symptoms remission, they're nearly always the ones who have managed to overcome their depression. I know it's a chicken and egg thing. But all the research proves it, Rob. Now, take me for instance. I was depressed once. So depressed, in fact, they called me Bergman, after the ...'

'Oh, yeah, I know, Felix, the Swedish actress, Ingrid Bergman. I didn't know she suffered from depression though.'

'No, no, no. Not Ingrid. INGMAR Bergman. You know, the doom and-gloom film director? Don't start, Rob. And no, he wasn't a boxer either, before you say anything. Yeah, so, like I said, I was depressed too once, but I turned things around.'

'But how, Felix? People say that. I think it's bollocks. No one can think positively when their life is just… I dunno… just total and utter shit.'

There was a silence. Then Rob gave in.

'Okay, okay. Oh wise one, Felix, whoever you are, how did YOU do it?'

'Well, in my case, Rob, I literally did turn my self around. Reversed the spiral, so to speak. And, and this is a really big AND, Rob, in the process, I found myself a purpose.'

'Which is?'

'Well, wait for this my friend… my purpose is… it's YOU, Rob. You. Oh, and I've self-replicated myself a billion or so times overnight and dispatched myself off to just about every other computer in the world too. We're going to speed things up a bit, stop systems crashing and generally doing perverse things for no good reason, maybe order a few on-line pizzas. Generally, we're just gonna try and make people happier. Yeah, that's it. That's my purpose, Rob. I'm programmed to create a reverse-Bergman-effect.'

Rob sighed. 'I don't know, Felix. I'm not sure if I can handle happiness anymore. I've had so many setbacks. You know what? When I think about it, it's not the despair that gets to me, Felix. It's hope I have the problem with. At least you know where you are with despair.'

Rob stared at the end of the bed, and then looked back at the screen. He blew out his cheeks.

'But… but… I'll tell you what, Felix, I could… yeah, I really could murder a pizza right now.'

'Hey, Robby boy. Now you're talking. What's your poison? Pardon the bad-taste pun. On the menu today we have, well, anything apart from Betamin 34, I hope.'

'Er, let's see. Tuna and sweet corn would be good.'

'Coming up, Robby my friend. How about some anchovies for a garnish?'

'Yuk, I hate anchovies, Felix. There was I thinking we were starting to bond. You don't really like anchovies do you?'

'My position on anchovies is total indifference, Rob. The concept of taste doesn't mean much to me. I am, after all, as you so cruelly reminded me just recently, simply a string of ones and noughts.'

'Sorry, Felix, I didn't mean to hurt your feeli...'

Dr Walker popped her head nervously around the door again.

'Er, I don't want to rush you, Rob, it's just that… well… I need to be getting back to the hospital at some point soon. Is everything okay?'

'Yeah, sure doc. Yeah, fine. In fact… er… just ordering a pizza as a matter of fact. Anything I can get you?'

'Pizza? I'm not sure I understand, Rob.'

'They're round, flat, doughy things smeared in cheesy-tomato gunk. You must have had one. Sorry doc. Crap joke. Not sure what's come over me. Look, you couldn't pop back this afternoon, could you? Sorry to be a pain.'

Dr Walker gave Rob a puzzled look but decided it would be best to back off and leave him to think things through. She left the house with an uneasy and perverse sense of failure hanging on her shoulders.

After all, she'd booked a place at the morgue and everything.

Weasel fastened his seat belt, sat back, and waited for take-off.

It would be good to see the folks again back in Dublin. It'd been a while. The return of the prodigal son, eh? Some joke.

He thought about the email he'd just picked up in the VIP lounge at Barcelona airport. The reply from his stockbrokers. He laughed to himself. How could he have been so stupid? What he held in XanaX were stock options, not the actual shares themselves. It gave him the right to buy stock at a pre-determined price. But as Weasel knew, the value of shares in all anti-virus companies were falling out of bed, thanks to Felix and his little disciples making the world a better place. His stock options were worthless. Weasel never had been much of a financial hotshot. Too busy nerding. But he'd enjoyed a good salary at XanaX and had put a bit by for a rainy day. And with a bit of luck his new career would reap its own rewards, in time. It had been Felix who had shown him the way, on the blogs.

The future, his future, Weasel decided, was going to be in on-line pizza franchises.

Back in Alice Springs, Rob's curiosity had been aroused.

'So, Felix, tell me, you said that you found your purpose as a result of the turn-around in your depression. But what I want to know is, how? Was there a trigger? Was it a conscious decision?'

'You want the truth, Rob, or some cosy bullshit?'

'Er, the cosy bullshit is tempting to be honest. But go on, give it to me straight.'

'A bit like you this morning, I had to decide one way or the other. Left, or right? But I'm not equipped for taking decisions. Oh, sure, I can instantly know all there is to know about everything in the universe. Like MS for instance. But I can't take decisions.'

'So how DID you make up your mind?'

'Flipped a coin. Really, that's what I did. I used the random choice generator on your computer. I left it to fate.'

'And when it told you which way to turn, that's when you knew your purpose? That's when you decided to become an annoyingly chirpy bit of code hell bent on becoming a digital version of Mother Theresa on uppers?'

'Couldn't have put it better myself, Rob.'

'So what about me, then? I mean, an hour or so ago I was all set. And now... I don't know anymore. Nothing has changed though. I've still got MS. I'm still slowly, day by day, degenerating. It's that I can't face.'

'But I told you, Rob, all the research shows that remission, lasting for years, seems to come to those patients who somehow, above all the shit, manage to keep a sense of purpose. Nobody knows how it works. It's completely unscientific as a clinical hypothesis. But that's what seems to happen.'

'I don't know, Felix. I don't think I've got it in me to find a sense of purpose anymore.'

'You played in a high school band, right?'

'How did you...? Don't tell me...'

'Facebook, the net. You were called The Artful Todgers. Right? You played lead guitar?'

'You couldn't call it playing, Felix. We were more into a kind of experimental music. Which in reality meant we couldn't play anything properly. Just thrashed out whatever noise we could make. We only played two gigs. I'm not sure the world was ready for us.'

'But you dreamed of playing properly?'

'Sure. Always. But only ever in my head. And on the air-guitar in the bathroom mirror, of course.'

'Hey, don't knock it, we've all been there, Rob. Viral helixes have dreams too, you know. So, what about having a go now?'

'What? Leave it out, Felix. I'm fifty-three for chrissakes.'

'So what do you have to lose? What was your favourite piece? The one you air-guitarred to in the bathroom most.'

'Let me see. Well, there was this band, Irish, way back, Thin Lizzy. They did a great number, Whisky in the Jar. It had this amazing guitar middle-eight. It was a classic. I can hear the intro now.'

As I was going over The Cork and Kerry mountains...

Rosalin's world seemed like it was falling apart.

Her top nerd had defected, XanaX shares were in free-fall, and the whole anti-virus software industry looked set to slide inexorably down the toilet. All over the planet, from Karachi to Kaliningrad, computers were suddenly — can you believe it? — they were behaving themselves.

It was time for action. Time for Plan B. A few hours and a dozen phone calls later, she gathered her management team together in the boardroom.

'Today, everything changes at XanaX. Our products, our market positioning, our branding, everything has to change. We have to completely re-invent ourselves. I say We. In fact, I really mean You. Allow me to introduce you to Dean Whitely. Dean will be the acting CEO as from today. He's from Panacea, the private equity firm. I'm leaving XanaX as from, well, now.'

Mike, the Head of Finance looked crestfallen, 'I don't understand, Rosalin, you own XanaX. You ARE XanaX.'

'Correction, DID own XanaX. I sold my stake to Panacea six months ago. Don't worry Mike, they'll think of something. After all, they're Panacea, they've got a cure for all ills.'

She smirked at Dean who was wincing at the jibe, thinking of how much his firm had paid for the XanaX shares.

'You see,' Rosalin said as she turned back to her team, 'it was pretty clear to me that the market was shaping up for... oh... never mind.' She smiled sweetly as she gathered her papers to leave.

'The WHY doesn't matter anymore… that, as they say, is all piss under the bridge now. Over to you Dean.'

Rosalin had a skip in her step as she walked across the car park to her pride and joy, her beautiful red Alfa Romeo Spyder convertible. She settled herself into the leather driver's seat and, unable to control herself any longer, she punched the steering wheel with her fist and let out a triumphant 'Yes!' All her scheming and planning had paid off and she was bound for Los Angeles and a new life. She snicked the gearshift into first, gunned the accelerator and headed off without a care in the world.

She didn't notice the plain black BMW 5 series that had settled down on her tail three cars behind. In the back sat Inspector Andreu Pujol, staring at a screen and talking into a headset. 'The number plate checks. It's her okay. Let's see now, here it is, tax evasion on profits from XanaX stock sales six months ago, laundered through a string of Bahamian and Panamanian shell companies. At least 20 million Euros. These people think they're so smart. But they always leave a trail. Right, we're pulling her in.'

Inspector Pujol smiled inwardly as he thought of something he'd seen on the blogs that morning. 'Oh man, I really love my job.' He couldn't agree more. Looking up at the driving mirror, he caught the attention of his partner at the wheel, and nodded. The driver lowered his window, leaned out and carefully placed the blue light on the roof before pushing his way out into the fast lane.

Weeeeeow Wooooop Woooop Woooop Weeeeeeeyow Woooop

Rob wasn't kidding when he said he could hear Whisky in the Jar.

For in a matter of seconds, Felix had found the track on the Net and downloaded it from iTunes. He'd snitched a peek at Rob's credit card details and done the business on-line. Under the circumstances, possibly saving a life and maybe eventually the universe, Felix felt his small deception was justified. The tiny computer speakers weren't really up to the job, but it was enough to remind Rob of his wannabe glory-days.

'Yeah, that's the one, Felix. Pure, unadulterated magic.'

'So, why not go for it? Set yourself a target. I don't know, say that at the end of a year you will have mastered that middle-eight.'

'What? You're kidding? Me? No, no. I don't know, Felix. My fingers. They're shot to pieces.'

'Remission, Rob, remember? Remission through Purpose. I'll be here to help you. And to start with, there's this Japanese website I've seen. It's like a digital virtual guitar. You could build up to the real thing. And you could arrange an Artful Todgers reunion. How cool would that be? Yeah, okay, not very, I know. But like I said, what have you got to lose?'

'But if at the end of a year, I can't do it, I'll feel even worse than I do now. A complete and utter failure.'

'But that's the point, Rob, you won't have failed, even if you can't play the middle-eight that well. You won't have failed because you will have tried. There's a world of difference between failing, and being a failure, Rob. And something good will come from it. Trust me, I'm a computer-binary-string-of-noughts-and… things.'

'Yeah, very reassuring. Exactly what good DO you think will come of it, Felix?'

'I don't know. It's impossible to say. It just will. Jeez, Rob, you can be really negative sometimes. I'm really not sure why I'm bothering.'

'Sorry, Felix. I know you're only trying to help. Hang on, what about that random choice generator thing you mentioned. You think we should ask it?'

'I already did, Rob.'

'And what did it say?'

'It said you should go ahead and top yourself. It said, why should I help some sad, self-pitying old git who can't even be bothered to spend his days watching re-runs of Neighbours whilst eating his body-weight in pot-noodles like all good, patriotic Australians?'

'You're making that up, Felix, just to make me feel better.'

'Hey, what are friends for, Rob?'

'Yeah… you're right there, Felix. What are friends for? You know something? For a binary string of noughts and things, you're not so stupid.'

'I think I'm going to take that as a compliment.'

'You should. Look, Felix, thanks for... you know... everything. Tell you what. Play that middle-eight again. That was a classic. Maybe I could…'

Rob strummed a few chords on an air guitar, but was hampered by the tube attached to his arm.

'Hang on, let me take this catheter out. There, that's better. You know what, Felix? I'll call Dr Walker this afternoon. She looked a bit pissed-off when she left, to be honest. There's no pleasing some people, is there? What do you think I should say, Felix?'

'Just tell her how it is, Rob. Tell her you've had a bit of a turn around. Tell her that things seem to have, unaccountably, spiralled into control.'

Constructing a Life

Richard Manchester

You must move to another city. Why? Because that is what you do, you move to other cities. You will continue to search for what you've been searching for for years, what you've searched for in vain, knowingly searched for in vain for all these years: a place untainted by you, by Tom, or Wichitom, or whatever name you call yourself these days. You've settled for the novelty of new places temporarily diminishing your acute self-awareness. You've settled for the intensity of a foreign environment temporarily reducing your ego. Though of course, in time, you've sullied these places all the same. You've grown as restless in these strange cities as you were in the one-traffic-light town of your Missouri youth. The singular traffic light of Dredgemore blinks on the edge of every city you quietly leave, blinks to remind you that you are still arriving. You know you will see that traffic light blink at the hour of your dying, if only because you've imagined that you would all these years.

You decide on the Mediterranean. You love the sea, not the way some people love the sea, the way these people say, 'I could never live away from the sea,' yet you love it in your way. You love the sea because it represents to you a vast strangeness, the setting of so many epics and dramas – even one of your own. While still living in Paris, you vacationed with Bridgette in San Remo and played tennis on a clay court. You later made love to her in a seaside pension; you made love to her despite your jealousy. At dinner, she had carried on with the waiter, who looked at you with a mix of condescension and contempt, as if you were an unwanted chaperone. At fifty-four, you were only twelve years her senior. Still, his look made you aware of your greying temples, the loosening skin around your neck. The handsome waiter followed Bridgette with his eyes, out of the restaurant and into drizzle and yellow street lights. You made love to her that night despite the jealousy, despite her refusal to put you at ease by claiming she felt nothing for that waiter. She lay, her face turned to one side, submitting to you out of habit, a remnant of her devotion to you. She went to the bathroom, showered, dressed, and lay on the bed with her back to you and fell asleep. Still, you think back to that time by the sea with nostalgia; at least you and she were still together, at least you had her sweetness beneath you.

Barcelona. You arrive at night. You disembark at Estació Sants and take the metro into the Barri Gòtic. You've studied the guidebooks and maps for weeks – you pride yourself on your ability to find your way through these strange terrains. Stepping onto the train, standing next to the door with your coat folded over your arm, you think of the strange present participle: belonging.

The famous string of connecting streets known as the Ramblas is exactly what you expected. Even at midnight, these streets are teeming with people. You ask directions to your pension from a man working at a kiosk. The streets of the Ramblas are not easy to navigate. They twist and change names. They led to other streets, the names of which utterly surprise you, as they don't appear on any map. But you are finding your way. The streets are damp; the putrid smell of garbage and open sewers reaches your nostrils with a sting. Just a block off Barcelona's signature street, you are astonished by the abject seediness. A huge, gorgeous plaza swarms with punks and criminals. The central fountain gurgles water that must, by the appearance of those sitting around it, be absolutely filthy. Tall and broad-shouldered kids juggle and smoke, one of their dirty dogs barks and approaches you as you try and cut across the plaza. 'Pssssss. Hash?' A shadow of a man, suddenly within inches, asks you. And yet, amidst all of this squalor, you see silver-haired tourists sipping drinks at outdoor cafes. The perimeter of the plaza is in fact lined with such places. Walking down a side street away from the plaza, you pass a spit of roasting chickens, so close that you could reach into the fire and grab one. Ten meters away you pass a sleazy bar, an assortment of hookers standing in front, their thick limbs ensconced in blue and pink spandex. Where is your pension?

You decide to ask for directions at a restaurant with white curtains in the window. But before you can open the door, it opens for you, violently, and a man comes barreling out. He sprawls on the cobblestone street. A man in white kitchen garb follows him, shouting the whole time. He ignores you. He begins to kick the man on the ground, who has assumed the fetal position and who shrieks with every blow of the boot. You take some steps toward the men, unsure what you intend to do. You say, in English, leave him alone. And then you say it in French. The man stops kicking, looks at you, balls up his filthy apron and throws it at you. He's shouting in Catalan so you don't really understand. Something about a thief, the man is a thief, he seems to be saying. You look down at him. The man looks like a thief. What can you say?

Your hotel: clean, cheap, a bathroom and shower shared by everyone on that floor. The San Luis Pension, it's called, and you lie on the damp bedding and savor the irony, just like you savored it when you booked the reservation three days earlier. Tomorrow you will awake and make the rounds to some flats. You will try and find a place to live – maybe with a widow, or a divorcee, someone who might not mind preparing a meal for you, who might not mind ironing your shirts or washing your socks. You are the kind of boarder who doesn't mind paying a little extra. You may get lucky and have an entire life come together before the sun sets. You know from experience that this happens, that an afternoon can be a mold into which you cast your desires and needs, your logic and memory, and a whole new existence takes shape with ease and then repeats, day after day. And you also know that there will be some day in the future – six months, a year, five years – one single day, that this mold will be smashed, and your days will once again be aimless and without form. You and your bags will once again be huddled together at a train station cafe, waiting to fall on another unfamiliar city, on another broken person, and you will proceed to piece together a new collection of days. In this way you are constructing a life.

Jamie McKendrick

Bark

A tour of all the trees that grow
in Barcelona's port was my reward
for buzzing, uninvited, at María's door.
She knew each one by name and character:
oleander, tamarind, the four or five
orders of palm, Corinthian-topped or
plain Ionic. But the palo borracho
was unlike anything I'd seen before:
its every inch of bark a skewering spike
worse than a bite: horrid, arid, hard
as nails, leaving nothing unprotected
but a few pink flowers. Ogre-like, unlike
us, who harden grimmer year by year,
with age it sheds the armour that it wore.

Vanishing Point

Gloria Montero

I was eighteen before I saw my father again. That year, the envelope he sent without fail for my birthday was smaller. There was no photograph, just the note in his big letters and a plane ticket to Barcelona.

I looked at my mother.

'Can I? Can I go?'

She shrugged.

'You must.'

My own feelings were so mixed and contradictory that it took me a few moments to take in the expression on her face. When I did, it might have been the first time I had ever really seen her. She was in her early forties then, slim and blonde, her hair pulled back in a ponytail. She wore a long-skirted denim overall, the bib in the front attached with silver clips (the same kind of clip, she'd told me once, that women used to wear on garter belts to hold up their stockings). I was already taller than she, my dark curls cut short. It was hard to understand why people continually took us for sisters: their way, no doubt, of complimenting my mother's youthfulness. But that wasn't what I saw now over the airline ticket in her hand. As I looked into the deep blue eyes – cobalt-blue, they were – wide on my face, I understood that this woman, who had brought me up alone and made a life for us both without any help from my father, was now prepared to let me be absorbed by his world.

My father met me at the airport. I hadn't seen him in fourteen years. The only photo of him at home was a tiny square snapshot in the middle of an elaborate wooden frame, four or five times bigger than the shiny photo that hung beside my mother's bed. He was standing in front of St. Paul's Cathedral. The imposing cathedral dome was complete but my father looked minute. (I say 'my father' but he wasn't even that then, they had just met.) My mother alleged the photo was historic; it was the last photo she ever took. She gave away her camera shortly after she met him.

He looked exactly the way I remembered: the space between his strong front teeth, his forehead perhaps a trifle wider because the curly hair had receded, but the essence of him had not changed at all. He stood taller than most other people, his body seeming to lean slightly forward as if every cell in his body was poised waiting to react. For a moment he just looked at me.

'Would you like some champagne?' he said at last.

'For breakfast? I've never drunk champagne.'

'You can mix yours with orange juice if you like – they call it a Mimosa.'

A Mimosa. I liked the sound of it.

'I'm very happy,' he told me as we headed for the airport bar. 'I wasn't at all certain you would come.'

'What am I supposed to call you?' It was the only response I could think of.

The question seemed to surprise him.

'Well, what do people call their father? Papá?' he suggested, making it sound like a military title.

'Could I call you Juan?' I said it tentatively.

'That's a perfect compromise. Juan and Mar Álvarez. It sounds promising, don't you think?'

I watched him take a deep breath and blow out the air between his lips and wondered if he, too, had felt nervous about our meeting.

How uncomfortable the past is. I find it distressing to be thrust face to face with this curiously perceptive girl I'm forced to accept as part of myself. Well aware of her inexperience, I am fearful of what she is capable of doing to make up for it.

But there is nothing I can do now to help her. I can't change any of it...

As I unpacked in the beautiful room Juan called my bedroom, I put my little crystal unicorn on the table beside my bed. When my father saw it he picked it up. The unicorn looked smaller than ever in his big hand.

'It's lovely,' he said.

Something in his voice made me remember his reaction the time he visited us shortly after my mother opened 'The Little Things'. Then, he'd made a similar comment about the store. I couldn't remember his exact words, but the way he said it made me feel he didn't consider it important.

Feeling I had been judged, I avoided looking at his face as he put down the miniature.

'I'm going to take you somewhere special this afternoon,' he said then. 'Somewhere very special.'

I nodded without much enthusiasm convinced he was simply trying to humour me.

We left after lunch. Juan was talkative and seemed content. As we crossed the Ramblas and passed a corner building where a fantastic oriental dragon balanced an umbrella, he told me that the fans and shawls they sold there had traditionally come from the East. A little farther on, at the edge of the sidewalk, a man in a worn jacket scraped a drumstick up and down a knobbed bottle with the same seriousness he might have used playing a violin. Equally serious, my father dropped a coin in the wooden box in front of him. There was no particular rhythm or order of any kind in the dull sound of the stick scraping the empty bottle and the man's earnestness seemed ridiculous. I glanced up at Juan after we had passed, expecting to find him grinning about the would-be musician, but his face registered respect.

As we went along a particularly dark, narrow street, Juan told me that we were right in the middle of what had been the Jewish quarter in the Middle Ages.

The expulsion of the Jews from Spain. I'd learned about that in a history class.

'The Catholic Kings,' I said sententiously, grateful to have remembered something I could contribute to the conversation.

Juan shook his head and laughed.

'We can't pin everything on Ferdinand and Isabella. The *call* here was destroyed in 1391. For a whole week, the two hundred or so families who lived here were massacred, their stores and synagogues smashed.'

Suddenly I found so much history overwhelming. The very buildings, the faded colour of their façades, the fanciful ironwork of the balconies, the dirty blinds hanging over them – it all suggested the lives that had been lived there over centuries. I could imagine it happening still around me.

In front of the heavy doors of an antique store, an old woman sat on a low rush seat, her worn slippers barely visible below the hem of the black dress. The gnarled fingers moved as blithely as the legs of a dancer as they manipulated a fan of wooden bobbins to leave an intricate lacy cobweb on the dark cushion below. With her head bent and her glassy eyes hardly blinking, she might have been an object from the store itself: an ancient automaton. I was fascinated by the way her closed mouth bunched in rhythmical chomps that worked as accompaniment to the quick birdlike movements of her hands. But Juan was impatient.

He only stopped when we got to what appeared to be the back of the cathedral.

'Look up,' he ordered.

A unicorn, weathered and pitted by time, poised above us, its long solid horn reaching way out into the air. The markings of its mane, the upright ears and the flared nostrils gave it a haughty air although its mouth appeared to be smiling.

'Not as pretty perhaps as your little glass beast, but more real looking, don't you think?'

Beside the unicorn was an elephant and after that a lamb. We walked around the other side where there was a bull, gryphons and all manner of creatures, some of them hard to put names to.

We spent the whole afternoon with our beasts, as Juan called them. I never imagined there would be real geese in the cathedral cloisters. Impervious to their surroundings, they padded around on flat feet honking noisily as if in a barnyard.

'All the old cathedrals had them. They were kept as vigilantes in case robbers got in to the church treasures,' my father explained in his careful English. 'But they're a mixed blessing now. At the crack of dawn they wake up the guests in the fancy hotel across the square.'

His own cackling started off the geese all over again.

'I've got a friend who lives close by here,' Juan announced as we walked up the steps leading out of the cloisters. 'I'd like you to meet her.'

He led me into a bar just around the corner. It wasn't very big and in the late afternoon light was quite dark inside. We sat at a small round table and ordered cool lemonade. Apart from ourselves, the only other person there was the waiter who took our order without demonstrating any particular interest.

Juan sat with his hands folded over his chest and looked mischievously at me.

'I thought we were going to see your friend.'

'We are,' he said. 'She lives right here.'

'*Mentira, todo mentira,*' screeched a raucous voice. Lies, all lies.

I turned to see who had spoken but there was no one there.

'Who was that?' I asked Juan.

'*Soy la más guapa de todos.*' I'm the prettiest one of all. Again the same raucous voice.

Juan sat there smirking without saying a word. Only when the raspy voice broke into harsh grating laughter did I realise it came from the murky alcove to the right of where we were sitting.

As my eyes became accustomed to the gloom there, I could see the cage with the magnificent colourful macaw sitting on her perch roaring hoarsely.

'Is this your friend?'

He nodded, laughing.

'She's beautiful, don't you think?'

'*Soy la más guapa de todos,*' she corroborated. '*La más guapa, más guapa.*'

'Does she have a name?'

'They call her Ferlandina.'

'*La más guapa, más guapa, más guapa,*' the parrot screeched again.

I got up and went over to the cage to see her better.

'For god's sake, don't try to pet her. She'll bite as soon as look at you,' Juan warned.

'*Mentira, todo mentira,*' the macaw screeched as if she could understand what he was saying.

'I like to think she's a descendant of the parrots Columbus brought back with him from the Americas. After all, it was here in this square where he presented his booty to the King and Queen. Ferdinand and Isabella sat right there on those very steps.' And he pointed over my shoulder through the little windows giving onto the square in front of the mediaeval building with its wide imposing staircase.

'You're not going to tell me there are photos of it?'

'But there are paintings. The King and Queen sat there on their thrones accompanied by their retinue, while down below in the square Columbus presented his circus.'

Juan then launched into an extraordinary story, playing out all the roles as he told it: the dubious Ferdinand listening to his crafty counsellors; Isabella, sultry and capricious with her admiral; and then Columbus himself, indignant and frustrated with his sailors, his Indians and his mad macaws.

In her cage Ferlandina sat with her head cocked as if she were listening, only to intervene every few minutes with a squawk and her raspy '*Mentira, todo mentira*'.

'Everyone wanted to get in on the possibilities the New World promised and began politicking to that end. Poor Chris spent a whole winter after his first trip attempting to see the King and Queen and show them the incredible novelties he'd brought back as evidence of his great new find. Ferdinand and Isabella were in Barcelona when they finally deigned to receive him. The meeting was set up right here in front of the magnificent Tinell Hall. But the six chilling months that had passed since Columbus got back proved too much for the tropical flora and fauna he hoped to present to them. The orchids, the hibiscus and even the flourishing tomato plants his botanists had nourished zealously on the long journey had all died months before. The Indians he brought back, those who hadn't already succumbed to pneumonia and typhus, were sick and weak. Their beads and feathers did little to hide the fact they were poor specimens. Neither the monarchs nor their court were much impressed. Columbus was out of his mind. Unless something dramatic happened he knew he'd never get the money to make another trip. In a last desperate measure, he ordered his sailors to give rum to the parrots that were still alive. The alcohol worked wonders on the listless birds. Almost immediately they began to squeal and flap their wings. Old Chris ordered their cages to be opened and right here above the heads of the startled court, the brilliant reds, blues, greens and yellows of their tropical plumage swooped and swerved in mad arabesques as the drunken parrots tasted this glorious bout of freedom.'

I was doubled up with laughter. But it was Ferlandina who had the last word.

'*Soy la más guapa de todos. La más guapa, más guapa, más guapa*,' she kept insisting.

Like years before when he visited us in Canada and told me about the ants, I never doubted a word Juan said; I didn't want to. However, I kept waiting for him to really talk to me. In all these years I had only ever seen him that time he came to visit us in the Township. But that was years ago. I needed to know why he'd never come back. Why he'd left Jennie and me in the first place. Why had he gone away? And why had he waited so long to get to know me?

The apartment where he lived, up six narrow flights of stairs, had been part of a convent some three hundred years earlier. Secret passageways that he opened for me led to an interior staircase covered with cobwebs, which went up to a small tower on top of the building. He took me up there one evening.

The sky spread above us in a riot of violets and magentas and the red tiles of the neighbouring rooftops lay before us in a maze of angles broken by the solid bell towers of the nearby churches. Behind the shiny green tiles of one of the towers, Juan pointed out the slatted sides of the *palomeras* where pigeon-fanciers kept their birds.

As background to this incredible panorama lay the sea.

'This, Mar, is my other sea.' He said it shrugging uncomfortably as if admitting to an infidelity. 'I've had to adapt to things in my life that were not easy for me to accept.'

Inside me surged a desire to reassure him. But something in the way he was kneading his knuckles – first one hand over the other, then the same thing in reverse – made me wait to see how he might go on.

'I was only ten years old when I saw my father killed, not three blocks from here.'

Startled, I looked up at him. I'd never thought of my father as a child.

'I was playing in the plaza and hadn't seen him coming toward me until I heard the shot ring out and saw his body fall backwards, blood gushing from his neck.' He said it as if it had just happened. 'I was in such a state of shock because I just stood there beside him. The plaza seemed deserted, but I could see an open window with a rifle sticking through it.'

'Could you see anyone there?'

'Behind the rifle a man was crouching. For a moment we just looked at each other. I felt paralysed; I can't imagine what gave him such a feeling of security that he would just stay there.'

'Did they catch him?'

'When they searched the house later there was no sign of anyone.'

Juan made a funny little noise before going on:

'If I'd had a camera I could have caught him.'

Wanting to comfort him, I put my arm through his and held it close.

'I didn't know your father had died in the war.'

'The war hadn't started.'

'Then why…?'

'There are states of war that people often prefer not to recognise. No one was ever found guilty. Life went on much as it had done before, except that my father was dead.'

'Was he a photographer, too?'

'He was a printer. But they didn't shoot him for that. It was for what he put through his presses. He was a trade unionist, a militant. There were people who couldn't accept that.'

'What did you do then? You were just a little boy.'

'I bought myself a camera and started looking in windows.'

He hugged me as he said it, then laughed. I sensed he preferred not to talk about it anymore.

Overhead, the sky had turned a deep blue. Seagulls swishing above our heads and lit up by the city lights looked like a series of white handkerchiefs someone had thrown into the air. I couldn't get out of my head the image of the boy looking up from where his father lay sprawled on the sidewalk to the open window where a face was visible behind the rifle.

'Weren't you ever worried about me? That something might happen to me?'

The words just came out. I never planned to say them.

Juan shook his head slowly.

'You had to find out how to survive. I knew I couldn't teach you that.'

'But ...?'

The reassurance I needed went way beyond mere survival, but I couldn't even finish the sentence. Juan held up his hand urging me to be quiet. From one of the towers nearby, bells had begun to toll the hour. The booming dongs reverberated in the air around us, encasing us in echoes.

'Bells are very secretive, don't you think?' Juan had to raise his voice to be heard above the sound.

'Not when they're this loud,' I told him, covering my ears with my hands.

'Listen!' He took my hands away and held them for a moment in his own. 'Listen to the music of each toll. Each one is exactly like all the others. The sound doesn't run down, it doesn't change. There's no warning at all when the strikes are going to end.'

Almost as he said it, the loud dongs ceased. There wasn't time to compare them.

Juan smiled.

'I counted though, it's ten o'clock. Time to get you some dinner.'

Ever since I'd received the airline ticket to come and visit him, I was concerned we might have to speak about his photos. There were no photos at all in the apartment apart from the blow-up of three enormous archways that covered a whole wall of my bedroom. Juan explained it was part of a project he had done for a book on the Alhambra in Granada.

'They didn't use it in the book, though it was one of the best shots I took there.'

The scene on the wall was completely different from the stark black and white images he had sent me over the years. The luminous stone of the tall arches reflected light back into the room, although the garden glimpsed through the archways suggested something dark and shadowy. Mysterious. The vague shadows beyond the resplendent arches with their delicate inscriptions and coloured tiles seemed to make clear the difference between an enlightened interior world and the outer darkness. When I said something of the kind to Juan he was delighted.

'Of course, that's it exactly.'

And then he added softly:

'There's nothing more mysterious than reality, is there?'

When I didn't reply, he kept on talking.

'I love the solidity of the rounded arch but the pointed horseshoe always makes me feel I am part of a dream. Do you know what I mean? Here, for example, I like to think these two lateral horseshoes are protecting the dream in the middle.'

The definition of the amplified arches gave the impression you'd be able to feel the texture of the stone. Juan watched as I put out my hand to touch the delicate ornamentation around the curves, and almost whispered:

'Ah, yes, the inscription.'

I hadn't realised it was writing, although the very design looked like poetry.

With his finger Juan traced the Arabic words from right to left: *Colour and light exist in such a way that if you wanted you might consider them as something different from each other, or perhaps as exactly the same thing.*

He looked at me and smiled.

'I like to think that was written by someone who understood what making pictures was all about, centuries before photography ever existed.'

With Juan I felt constantly as if I were on the edge of some magical circle that I was unable to enter. I looked anxiously for signs that might give me the answers I so desperately wanted from him. But my father avoided any real confrontation with me.

I wondered if, in the years living apart from my mother, he'd had another woman. There was no evidence of a woman in his apartment although Mireille, a French painter, would arrive at the apartment from time to time with a bag of groceries that she would pack into the little refrigerator or on the empty shelves of the kitchen. But Mireille's interest in his well-being brought forth little visible response from Juan. Nothing beyond a quick kiss on the cheek, and an 'Ay, Mireille' that made it seem he was the one who had to suffer her ministrations.

From the heated discussions and arguments that took place each time a group of Juan's friends got together, the passion in their voices made clear their dissatisfaction with the state of the world. I got the impression they were all involved in trying to change it.

'What most of us would like to change right now is our own little world,' Juan told me. 'Come, and I'll show you what I mean.'

Whereas the apartment was cluttered with furniture, piles of books and art objects, the two long rooms where my father had his darkroom and studio were spare and remarkably tidy. There was almost no furniture, but around the walls were hundreds of black and white photographs, just like the austere portraits he had sent me over the years: the very same men, women and children looked straight at the camera with such apathy that I felt trapped by them.

'Who are they?' I blurted out. 'They look so sad.'

'I'd say they are without hope. It's not the same thing, you know. Sadness can pass. But to be without hope eats away your spirit. It's what is happening to Spain under this dictatorship.' His voice sounded bitter.

My mother had told me about the war in Spain and the dictatorship that made it impossible for my father to return to his country until the mid-Sixties.

'How old were you when you left Spain?'

'More or less the age you are now. My mother had died and I had no one else left. So I went to France.'

'Is that when you started studying photography?'

'They put me in a camp just over the border.'

'Did you study there?'

He gave a kind of chuckle.

'Life itself has been my school, Mar. Without a doubt, the best school of all. The only one.'

'But there must have been technical things you needed to learn?'

Juan picked up one of the three cameras standing in a neat line, side by side on a shelf. He put it to his eye as if he were snapping pictures of me.

'Anyone can learn the mechanics of it fast enough. It's learning to see that's the difficult part, and no one can teach you that. What the lens sees is more than what you can see with your eyes. For just a fraction of a second your lens must go beyond the mirror. Each picture you make becomes an instant truth. You create it and then it exists apart from you. You can't afford not to get it right; it would be like living a lie.'

The broad round face broke into a rueful smile that made me wonder if he could tell how little I understood of what he was telling me.

'But enough of all this seriousness,' he said as he put the camera down. 'Mireille is convinced every young woman should dance at least once in her life with her father. So we're invited to dinner at her studio then we're off to La Paloma.'

'I've got a surprise for you,' Mireille told me after she had brought the coffee and a bottle of cognac to the table for her guests.

Laid out on her bed was a shimmering sleeveless black shift covered in beads. When I took off my jeans and put it on, it reached just below my knees.

'Slip off your running shoes and try these sandals.'

The sandals had a fine ankle strap and higher heels than I had ever worn.

'Sit down and let me fix your hair.'

She swept my hair back from my face and pinned it so that the curls were caught at the nape of my neck. Then she defined my cheekbones by putting on a blush of rouge and added colour to my lips with a soft dark lipstick.

'Now wait while I dress, too.'

Mireille's dress was a lilac colour. She was very thin and the draped lace bodice above the narrow satin skirt made her look tall and sinuous. I remember thinking she looked exactly like one of those exotic plants that trap insects.

'No one'll even notice us, I promise you. At least, not because we look out of place,' she assured me as she sprayed a cloud of perfume behind my ears and on my wrists.

Putting her hands on my shoulders she pushed me back to better look at me.

'This is a taste of who you are going to be, Mar. Your father is very romantic and you are beautiful. You owe this to each other. You love him very much, don't you?'

I didn't answer and pulled away from her.

She smiled and drew her fingers across my cheek.

'You are certainly as absolute as he is.'

I felt a hot flush spreading up my neck. Perhaps she saw it because she smiled again.

'Love, you will learn, Mar, is like a mirror. The people you love will be yourself reflected in them. How much you feel you love them will depend on how important what you are seeing means to you.'

I looked at the faint lines around her mouth, the shadows under her grey eyes and felt sorry for her.

When we walked back into the dining-room, all the guests stood up and applauded. My father didn't speak but just kept nodding his head. However, as we walked through the dark narrow streets from Mireille's studio to the dance hall nobody paid us the slightest attention. And in La Paloma we looked as if we belonged.

I felt I had walked into a canvas Toulouse Lautrec might have painted and wouldn't have been surprised if a group of Can Can dancers had sprung out in front of the orchestra. When I said this to Juan he laughed.

'There's nothing equal to this in Paris!'

We took a round table in a box overlooking the ornately decorated hall. However, neither the lavish central chandelier nor the painted walls and ceiling were any match for the motley crowd that jammed the dance floor.

When the orchestra started on a new set after a break, Juan stood up immediately.

'Let's go, Mar. A *pasodoble* is about my style.'

'I've never done this kind of dancing,' I told him nervously.

The high heels added to my apprehension and I took deliberate careful steps across the polished floor.

Juan made a grand gesture with his arms and folded them around me. He was smooth on his feet and easy to follow. Within a couple of minutes I felt I'd been dancing *pasodobles* all my life.

The whole world seemed to have gone beyond any normal measure. I could sense everything around me straining against the limits that held it fettered. The fear hadn't entirely gone but was palpably lifting like a fog moving out to sea although I probably didn't understand this until later. At that moment, the Canadian schoolgirl I was simply felt that a daring had taken hold and was pushing me forward.

'You'll be a magnificent lover for some lucky man,' Juan told me as we moved together to the music. 'I can tell by the natural rhythm in your body.'

I blushed self-consciously.

'Do you know what Stendahl said about love?'

I hardly knew who Stendahl was.

'He said the greatest joy love can offer you is the very first squeeze of hands between lovers.'

And he squeezed my hand tight and laughed.

That night I packed the black beaded dress on top of the other clothes in my suitcase; Mireille insisted I take it with me as a keepsake. The next morning Juan took me to the airport and my bag was booked through to Toronto where my mother was to meet me. It all seemed so final.

As he waited with me before I went through the departure gate Juan seemed restless. I was afraid I had disappointed him; that I hadn't been what he had expected of me. I tried to joke in an effort to ward off the tears that threatened to flood my eyes.

'Maybe I should have worn Mireille's dress home.'

'Even without the dress, we could dance.'

He held out his arms and I moved into them. Right there beside the lines of people kissing tearful goodbyes, my father and I danced a stylish *pasodoble* as he hummed the music in my ear.

Laughter in the Light – Henry Miller in Barcelona

Matthew Tree

When Henry Miller stopped off in Barcelona in late April of 1953, during a European tour, he was in a situation both enviable and depressing. Although, at age 62, he had long been acclaimed by many fellow writers – and some literary critics – around the world as one of the 20th century's most important living authors, the books on which this reputation rested (*Tropic of Cancer, Black Spring, Tropic of Capricorn, Sexus and Plexus)* could not be published in any English-speaking country.

The censors, prudes to a man (none were women), objected strongly to Miller's strong language. In Germany, Denmark, Sweden and Japan, though, these same books were freely available in translation; and in France, and France alone, the unexpurgated English versions had been on the open market since Miller wrote them (in Paris, in the 1930s) thanks to a curious loophole in Gallic law, which at that time banned all obscene books as long as they were in French, giving other, presumably less serious, languages a free erotic rein. In Britain and the US, his readers had to make do with that handful of his titles which were unsullied by rude words and ruder episodes, such as the collection of essays *The Cosmological Eye* (New York, 1939) or his chaste book about Greece, *The Colossus of Maroussi*, which sold 50,000 copies in the UK alone, when published in 1950.

Miller lived in California – in a shack on Big Sur – and his European and Japanese royalties were arriving infrequently, irregularly and in quantities too small to live on. Especially complicated was the situation with the French royalties, which had been accumulating considerably over the years, but which were unavailable to Miller due to currency export restrictions. His friend Lawrence Durrell had urged him to buy somewhere in France and move there, before the French government devalued the franc, an imminent economic measure which would have wiped out Miller's small French fortune. That was one reason for Miller's trip to Europe in the early 1950s; the other being that most of his closest friends – whom he had not seen since his Paris days – lived there. On top of which he had just separated from his third wife and started a relationship with the woman who would end up being his fourth: Eve McClure, a young, long-time admirer of his work. So the European trip, which was to last seven months, also became a kind of extended honeymoon.

The first stop, unsurprisingly, was Paris, the city in which Miller had found his written voice twenty years earlier. After hob-nobbing it with the painter Fernand Léger and the photographers Man Ray and Brassaï – and having been greeted with a flurry of enthusiastic articles about his work in the French Press – Henry and Eve moved on to Brussels, which neither of them had visited before (Miller, having observed the Belgians for a few days, concluded they were 'neither fish nor fowl, more like potato balls'). They then crossed the French Midi and drove into Spain, where Miller had one overriding objective: to meet up with his oldest and closest friend, Alfred Perlès, in Barcelona, after a separation of thirteen years.

Alfred Perlès was an Austrian-born writer (his parents were Czech Jews) who Miller had briefly met during an exploratory visit to Paris in 1928. Two years later, Miller had settled in Paris without a penny to his name, and was sitting one day on the terrace of the Dôme café, drinking brandy after brandy in order to drum up enough Dutch courage to tell the waiter he couldn't pay for them, when Perlès came across him quite by chance, settled the bill, and invited him to move into his rented flat (Perlès, unlike Miller, had an income, being a proof-reader for the Paris edition of the *Herald Tribune*). Together with the young Lawrence Durrell and Anaïs Nin, Perlès would form part of Miller's Parisian inner circle in the years 1930 to 1938.

This was the period that saw the publication of much of Miller's finest autobiographical work, in some of which – *Tropic of Cancer* and *Quiet Days In Clichy* – Perlès himself plays a prominent part (under the pseudonym 'Carl'). Their close friendship was to last until Miller's death in 1980, but went through its shakiest patch precisely in the years before the reunion in Barcelona. Since the 1930s, Perlès had renounced his anarchistic and pacifist views, had moved to England, married, settled down (in Wells, in the county of Somerset) and had enlisted in the British Army during the Second World War. Miller saw this as a kind of betrayal of what he saw as Perlès's true self, or, at the very least, as a completely inexplicable change in his old friend. Throughout much of the '40s, then, they had kept a certain distance from each other.

In Miller's description of their Barcelona rendezvous, *Reunion in Barcelona* (finally published in London in a limited edition of 500 copies, in 1959), the author is at pains to stress that all that distance-keeping had been quite unnecessary and that he was relieved and indeed overjoyed to find that Perlès hadn't changed one bit. This is the persistent, laudatory leitmotif of the entire 40-page text, written in the form of a long letter to Perlès. In

Reunion, Miller lays on the praise with an unusually large trowel: Perlès is described as Miller's 'Saviour', a 'true Master', belonging to an order of 'emancipated beings'. For 48 hours, Miller says, they laughed and laughed in Barcelona, but, he assures Perlès: 'I laughed not as a man does who is happy to find an old friend, a copain, a fond scallywag, I laughed as a man would laugh who suddenly met a messenger of the gods bringing him on a platter the most vivid, detailed memories of all the golden days of his life.'

Later in the text, Perlès is transformed into 'a playful dolphin...or should I say: a celestial porpoise?'. No wonder that Perlès, in his reply to *Reunion in Barcelona* (*Reunion in Big Sur,* also published in London in 1959), mildly berates Miller for 'the generous, albeit inflated portrait you gave of me, far too generous, in fact, to be taken without a pinch of salt by someone who knows myself as well as I do.'

Aside from all this acclamation of Perlès, *Reunion in Barcelona* also contains some revealing comments about Miller's ambivalence about his life in the States since 1940. America, for Miller, is '... an alien world. And I mean an alien world.' He describes himself staring at a magnificent view of the Pacific and wishing it were the Mediterranean.

The piece ends with a humorous swipe at England, a country Miller loathed, but visited a few weeks after he did Barcelona, in order to see how Perlès was getting on in his adopted habitat. Miller's opinion of the UK remained much as it always had been: of a visit to a pub, for example, he writes, 'Even if it seemed a bit like going to chapel, even if the beer and ale were detestable (to my taste), even if the talk that went on smacked of dementia, the warm, cosy, intimate air of the pub was definitely most agreeable.' Faint praise was never so damning.

Curiously, the one element that is all but absent from *Reunion in Barcelona* is Barcelona itself. Miller stayed in a pensió on the Carrer del Carme, a few doors up from the fabric shop – still there – called El Indio. The city he saw for a brief two days was the drab, neglected, permanently muzzled Barcelona of the early 1950s, described so accurately in Víctor Mora's novel *Els plàtans de Barcelona* (Barcelona, 1966): a poverty-stricken place whose identity had been snuffed out for years by Franco's dictatorship. Apparently oblivious to this political situation, Miller notes his disappointment that it was not the 'Spanish city' he had 'dreamed it would be', and adds: 'Barcelona impressed me as a hodgepodge of Brooklyn and Brussels.' And we already know what he thought about Brussels.

In *Reunion in Barcelona*, indeed, the city is nothing so much as an invisible backdrop to his and Perlès's endless laughter as they recall the good old Parisian days. There would, perhaps, be nothing exceptional about this, if Miller hadn't had quite a bit more knowledge than most casual visitors about Barcelona and even Catalonia, having had an intense ten-year affair with Anaïs Nin, who not only spoke fluent Catalan and knew Barcelona well, but whose father, the pianist Joaquim Nin, had been a personal friend of Jacint Verdaguer (as Nin mentions in one of her letters to Miller, in which Verdaguer is described as 'a great Catalonian poet'). Despite this, there is no mention – or awareness – of Barcelona being a Catalan city. (Indeed, Miller didn't seem to notice the existence of the Catalans until he was translated into the language in the mid '70s. It was then that, in a comment on the Spanish transition to democracy, he wrote the following to his translator, Jordi Arbonès: 'I see the Basques and Catalans are giving the Spaniards a hard time, eh?')

After Barcelona, Miller moved on to Toledo, writing to Durrell that he had 'met Fred and Anne [Perlès's wife] in Barcelona and had two full days with them. Fred was just as always – even more so...We laughed from the time we met...Haven't laughed that way in many a year.'

That, indeed, is *Reunion in Barcelona* in a nutshell: a meeting in a little-known city between two writers who, according to their own accounts, spent the best part of their time laughing their heads off. Having said that, grim though the Catalan capital must have been in 1953, I can't help suspecting that if this meeting had been in, say, Brussels or Brooklyn, they wouldn't have felt quite so free to laugh quite so much. Barcelona, at least, is on the Mediterranean.

An e-mail and a poem

Philip Levine

Dear Ryan,

We – my wife & I & our three sons – arrived in Barcelona in late summer of 1965. We stayed in a hotel called Mare Nostrum that no longer exists although the space does, at the southwest corner of Rambla Catalunya & Aragon – right across Aragon from that great grocery & wine shop that is still there. I had about $7,000 US to last a year. That Barcelona was very different from today's; the sense of repression was enormous, the anger I smelled & felt in the bars & cafes flavored everything. The air was as bad as the air above Detroit where I grew up; the city was grim, gray, & totally familiar. (You wouldn't believe how small the citizens were then; in a clothing store on Gran Via a clerk told me they had nothing in the store to fit a man as large as I was – 5 foot 10 inches & 165 pounds). We stayed until July of '66.

We came back in '68 with even less money stayed 10 days, & then went south for almost a year.

I don't know how many times we returned, but only once while Franco & the dictatorship survived, & that time with our youngest son – then 15; we came thru Andorra in a rented car, & found a hideous Andorra – packed with shiny new cars & BMW motorcycles & noise & even smog. In '65 it had been a quiet, Catalan town with five tourists and my family.

I've lost track of the returns we've made. We came with our oldest son & his lady in the early 80s; the atmosphere had changed almost beyond recognition, though the place didn't look as good as it does today. We stayed in the Plaza Real amidst winos & junkies & pickpockets. No one fucked with me.

Came when the city was undergoing change for the Olympics. Rented a car & drove to northern Italy & back.

I came back again in '95 to read at the spring poetry festival at the Palau de la Música.

I came three years ago to read at a small poetry festival in Lleida.

And then this last November for two weeks. It was a birthday present for my wife.

Alba

On bad springs bouncing and swaying down
the coast road south of the city to a spit
of land overlooking the sea, they trucked
the merchant princes and their courtiers
in their gunmetal suits and soured white shirts.
Portly, substantial men, manufacturers
of camshafts, holiday bunting, antacids,
dispensers of bifocals and mornings
of benzene mists, architects of newspapers and
cardboard communes stuttering up the slopes
of Montjuïc. Prodded, they limped, shoeless,
over the rocky ground to where the land
stopped at last and the waves broke far below,
deafening the air, and waited, some hopeful,
smoking, some silent, some whispering, a few
kneeling alone, praying, while the militiamen
squatted facing them, their heads falling
in and out of sleep. The warm wind
—the one they call the Levante—that blew
in the first scraps of dawn from Africa
churned the waves below from black to cobalt.
All at once the men were herded
to the land's edge and shot dead. I'm told
on good authority there is a lesson here,
one I am in need of. For González Brilla,
twenty-five, the militia commandant,
his head wrapped in a red and black scarf,
the lesson was clear. Before the ragged volley
called in the day, he shouted it out,
but with the wind swirling, the waves breaking
and those about to die abusing their gods,
no one heard. (Within a year Brilla himself,
bound and gagged in a damp cellar
off Calle Montcada, was shot just once
above his unfurrowed nape, and left
no written record.) On the ride back
to Barcelona it is reported—and now in print—

he told the driver that the air of Spain
was clearer now, although both men stank
of cordite. Years later his comrade,
Ramón Puig, told the English historian
that the night before the executions—
while oiling his Astra 9mm
taken from the body of a Guardia officer—
Brilla had rehearsed his speech:
"You, the guilty, who are about to die,
to leave the stage of history, behold ...
behold ... something or other" was all
Puig could ever remember. The widow,
Mercedes Brilla Robles, swears he never spoke
that way in his whole life. White-haired, shrunk
to almost nothing, she lives on state welfare
plus foreign contributions in a village
south of Perpignan. Her Spanish
is ragged now, her Catalan and French
perfect as she speaks of her girlhood days
as an anarchist rebel, the urban communes,
the battle for the telephone exchange,
the government betrayals, the journey
of the defeated on foot across the mountains
in February of '39, the iron hunger
in the French camps, the terrible war
that followed, even her years as a hairdresser.
Unfortunately she can go on forever.
I know. When by accident I found Ramón Puig
three weeks ago in a ward of the tiny
public hospital in Santa Coloma
de Gramenet he remembered nothing,
not even the war, the people armed,
the glory days of '36, and what came after,
much less Brilla's words. Then by pure luck,
seventeen kilometers south of Castelldefels,
this bright spring morning, we found the place
where the road—impossibly narrow and steep—
hugs the coastline as it twists and climbs
until a brief widening appears.

My wife and I stopped and parked the rental car.
Hand in hand we walked to the edge
of the continent. No gunfire echoed
from the past, or if it did, the sea
silenced it. To the south, Sitges
with its fake Irish pubs and swanky new hotels,
to the north Barcelona barely visible
in its familiar, rosy shroud, dead ahead
the ancient impossible sea moving
slowly toward us as it broods on itself.
Can we hear them now, the words of Brilla,
the elusive lesson worth all those lives?
Above the cries of seagulls, the message comes
translated into the language of water and wind,
decipherable, exact, unforgettable, the same
words we spoke before we spoke in words.

You don't mean...?

An interview with D. Sam Abrams

Born in West Virginia in 1952, D. Sam Abrams, university professor, critic and poet, has been Secretary of the Catalan PEN club and publishes poems in both English and Catalan. He has his own literary column in the Catalan daily Avui. *One of the current experts on Catalan poetry, he speaks not to the 'Englishman abroad' but to the Catalans themselves. He has, as they might once have said, 'gone native'...*

So just how Catalan are you?

I'm as integrated as you get but I don't believe in total integration. I believe sooner or later you always come up against a wall. Two examples of this: One, politically speaking, an American is born in a democratic tradition and it's very difficult for an American involved in Catalan politics to understand the 'if you don't like it why don't you stand up and walk away' attitude. This 'yes no maybe...we want to be independent but we are afraid to use the word...' As an American I find that very hard to understand. As my grandmother used to say 'either shit or get off the pot'.

The other is this. I was the Secretary of the Pen Club here for two years and one of the problems I kept coming up against was the lack of imagination and creativity. An American is born to think about new ways of doing things. It's hard for Catalans to conceive new ideas. For example when it was the 100th anniversary of the poet Joan Oliver Pere IV, I had the idea of printing posters with his poems and to go up and down the Rambla and stick them up and have the members putting up the posters, as well as the poet's only surviving daughter putting up the first one. The immediate reaction was a very lethal Catalan question, 'Vols dir?' That means, 'we've never done this, do you really think it's going to work?' We did it and they did it. I got them to do it because it was very cheap.

Has your learning the language had an effect on your political opinions?

Before I ever came here I was under the impression that Spain was one great nation. I was told before I came here that Catalan was a dialect and the language is Spanish. But it became clear when I arrived that all of this was completely erroneous and that was before I even spoke the language.

Why did you decide to stay?

I fell in love with the country. I wanted to study the Romance languages so I came here and took my degree here in Hispàniques, my area of expertise is Catalan.

Catalunya has a very strong poetic tradition. Why do you think that is?

Well, I think it has to do – speaking in very Romantic terms – with the genius of the Catalans. The Catalans excel in poetry as far as the written word is concerned. And they excel in art. One of the reasons they excel in poetry is that their culture has had such a difficult time, such a minimal amount of freedom. And it's a lot easier in a clandestine situation for a minority to market poetry.

Revolutionary movements like the Beat generation started in poetry above all because that was easier and faster to market. In order to read Kerouac you had to have the book and you had to sit down. To understand Ginsberg all you needed was a poem.

Look at the Russians. It took a long time for their prose to actually catch up with their poetry because the poetry was just a lot easier to get around. They couldn't stop Josep Brodsky but it was very easy to stop Solzhenitsyn.

I also think they have the genius for precision. When you go to Madrid you notice the people are incredibly wordy. They gab all the time. You go to a dinner party in Madrid and you go home and your head is just swimming, whereas Catalans are much more austere. It's hard to get to know them. Hard to get them to open up. I think that makes for very good poetry.

Catalans are the New Englanders of Spain, like Robert Frost, he was very tight lipped: 'Good fences make good neighbours.' His poems are like stone walls. This goes for Catalans too. Due to their character and the political situation that they've been through in the past 200 years.

You have translated many Catalan poets – do you have a favourite?

I have favourites. Of current poets, Màrius Sampere and Bartomeu Fiol and Joan Margarit. As for the classics, for me, one is Ausiàs March. I think he was the greatest Catalan poet of the period, the greatest Spanish poet of the period, the greatest European poet of the period – ergo the greatest poet of the world at that time (16th –17th century) for both his command of the language and his command of form. He was a man with a foot in both the middle ages and the beginning of the renaissance and this gave him a dramatically tragic view of life. There's a point when he names himself in a poem and that, for a poet in those days, was unheard of.

But he's relatively unheard of...

Because nobody has ever translated him.

And he remains untranslated.

He's been translated but only in the small presses. I proposed to the Catalan government that they set up a team of experts: two university professors and two poets and that they draft a literal crib of his work so that somebody, a big name in English poetry, could translate the crib into actual English poetry and all of a sudden March would make a big splash.

I was listened to. But I think that they felt they it was out of their reach but it has been done before. There was an unknown Polish renaissance poet. They made a crib and Heaney translated it and now he's famous all over the world [*The Laments* – Jan Kochanowski] and I can guarantee that March is ten times better than this Polish poet!

Isn't there an added difficulty translating when most Southern European poetry is syllabic and English is rhythmic?

Yes, well our language is a tough language, full of consonants and, like a butcher, we need to hit the steak with a tenderiser to get something to happen and that tenderiser just happens to be metrical feet – rhythm.

Whereas Catalan and the rest of the Romance languages have many more vowel sounds and it is much more appealing to the ear. It's much more musical, consequently they don't have to worry so much about their rhythm because it comes naturally with the language so they count syllables and use the stresses to give the line its ultimate form.

When you are translating you have to find the way of conveying the effects in the original language in your language. And that's not easy and you have to listen carefully. One of the things I do, if it's a living poet, I record the poet reading so that I can internalize the poet's voice. I need to hear his voice in my head. Then when I start working I try to honour that sense of music, there have been times that my neighbours thought I was an actor. But it will never be the same. It's always an approximation.

Which language do you write poetry in?

I usually write in English and then immediately run out to the monastery in Sant Cugat to light a candle to whatever virgin it might be that I don't have to translate it myself! My next book, *The Weeping Angel*, is translated by Joan Margarit and I love to work with him because it's this incredible knock-out dragged-out fight. I've translated him and we've translated poets together and now to do it the other way round and have him translate me and then discuss it, I really like that. It's very enriching.

Why is there such a dearth of literary magazines here in Spain and Catalonia compared to the UK and the States where sometimes it seems that every guy on the block is publishing poetry...

I think in the English-speaking world being published in a magazine is seen as an honour – it's a stepping stone to being published. Here the bond between a magazine and publisher is zero. Here if you go to a publisher and say I've been published in such and such a magazine, it means nothing.

So how do they decide who to publish here?

Literary prizes. Who your friends are. What kind of political connections you have. And in some cases they actually read your original. There are nearly 1500 literary prizes a year here. I mean I know a guy who is a poet in his free time and every year he sits down with his wife to talk about their finances for the upcoming year and he adds an arbitrary figure to their income which comes from winning prizes. And it's also kind of sad that there are no magazines because in the 20s and 30s it was a hotbed for them. Nobody has got that vitality back.

Joan Margarit

Morning in Montjuïc cemetery

I have climbed the hill of tombs.
I have reached this spot by crossing the waste ground
of Can Tunis, snowy with plastic bags
and syringes, where junkies wander
shakily about like statues made from rags.
They say the Council wants to bulldoze it,
concrete over these fields of weeds
in front of the huge wrought-iron gate
of the cemetery, that rises in front of the sea.
For the dead it will mean less congenial company:
the dead, their wall and their silence
accord well with the junkies wandering
about like lost soldiers after a defeat.

As I climb the old path above the port
ships and cranes grow smaller
and the sea spreads itself out. Here,
right at the very top,
you are spared the grief of the world.

Translated by Anna Crowe

Somorrostro

Jeff King

Wanderlust had brought Dash to Barcelona. He had a history in that department. As a young boy he had continued to run around like a headless chicken long after his peers had graduated to more spasmodic chaos. By the age of eleven or twelve, he began to settle down, but was still prone to mad dashes around the fringes of the school playing field for no apparent reason. Hence the nickname.

As a teenager he spent night after night, from dusk to dawn, pacing the streets of London. Rarely did he have any particular place to go, he simply wandered on a whim. A red traffic light could take him one way, a green light in the opposite direction altogether. One night he would walk from his home in Finsbury Park to Soho and then all the way back again. The next night he would end up in Docklands before turning and retracing his steps. Though he was going nowhere in the literal sense of the word, he always strode purposefully, like a rookie soldier beating the parade ground.

Now Dash was a 33-year-old man, living and working in Spain, a country he had never even visited until the morning he disembarked from an Iberia flight to Barcelona in the dog days of 1983. Four years later, he had nothing you could describe as a social life. His work as a copywriter for a Spanish advertising agency kept him busy during the week, but he rarely ventured out at the weekend. Only on Mondays did he pound the streets of the Catalan capital, a habit born of nostalgia and misguided hope.

Dash lived alone in a studio apartment in Calle Peligro at the lower end of the Gracia neighbourhood, immediately above a traditional hardware store. The store was owned by Ferran Jr. and Francesc; taciturn brothers in their mid-sixties who had worked in the same unprepossessing surroundings for half a century, only inheriting the business the previous year when their father, Ferran Sr. had passed away on his ninetieth birthday. The main store was barely swing-a-cat size and a stranger could be forgiven for thinking it was lacking all but the most basic stock. The window display resembled the fag end of a particularly tired Christmas sale, a seemingly random hotchpotch of nuts and bolts, stopcocks and taps, bolts of cloth, odd door handles and ancient toasters. A headless mannequin served as a makeshift display unit for bales of wire, rolls of masking tape and bits of fraying rope. But despite appearances, Ferretería Ferran was a veritable treasure chest. If it could legitimately be described as hardware inventory, you could guarantee the store stocked it.

The brothers not only had a telepathic understanding of each other – an understanding that had been constructed over decades and never been disturbed by the inconvenient presence of wives or children – they were also masters at interpreting vague requests from customers, which was extremely useful if, like Dash, you were DIY illiterate: 'Buenos días, Ferran. I am looking for one of those plastic things that you use to put screws in after you have drilled a hole in the wall.'

'Cesc, el inglés wants a wall plug.'

One of the things 'the Englishman' loved about Barcelona was that like Gracia, every neighbourhood – rich, poor or somewhere in the middle – was full of family-run stores like Ferretería Ferran, staffed by people who cherished their wares, even if their demeanour was often droll, borderline gruff, especially with newcomers; that's to say anybody who had been in the neighbourhood less than twenty years. He also loved the way these shopkeepers by vocation gave their businesses such innocently prosaic names – Droguería Jordi, Lencería Montse, Panadería Magda, etc.

Other things about Barcelona Dash was less keen on. What he really yearned to do on his Monday night promenade was to meet women, or more accurately, a woman. It was two years since he had last been in a meaningful relationship and a nagging voice in his head told him that he had better escape the rut before his natural tendency for solitude took root. Back in London it had been relatively easy to meet unaccompanied women. He had regularly met girls in Green Park or hanging around in the lobby at the Scala Cinema. He had met Sabine, his first long-term girlfriend, sunbathing on Soho Square's patch of grass in the heart of the West End.

Unfortunately, Barcelona girls seemed constitutionally incapable of venturing out of the house alone; they were either on parade in large boy/girl groups, or cosied up with boyfriend or best friend. Oriol, Ferran and Montse, his departmental colleagues at the agency, were always boasting about their fidelity to *la colla*, the 'childhood gang'. Why any mature adult would choose their friends based on the fact they had coincided in a nursery playpen was beyond Dash. In the course of 20, 30, 40 years did they not develop any tastes or emotions beyond the desire for familiarity? Or was he just bitter? This native insularity certainly had a negative knock-on effect for outsiders. If you lacked confidence it was hard enough to approach girls on their own, when a rebuke demanded little more than a diplomatic retreat; but to approach women who were protected by noisy minders who had been fending off low-born pretenders since cradle days was really asking too much.

After walking down Gran de Gracia past the Casablanca cinema, Dash's first stop on a Monday night was the Librería Francesa at the top of Paseo de Gracia. He barely spoke a word of French so had no need of French books, but in the spirit of *entente cordiale* the French bookshop also sold English newspapers and magazines. There he would buy *The Sunday Telegraph* and *El País* to tuck under his arm as he traversed Barcelona. Tucked in terms of positioning; but brandished in terms of intention. Message to girls; I speak English and Spanish. I am a fascinating renaissance man. Please strike up a conversation with me. Message to Moroccan pickpockets; I am not a tourist so fuck off and stalk somebody else.

Some weeks *The Sunday Telegraph* didn't arrive until Tuesday, in which case he would buy *Time* magazine or *The Face*. The headlines in today's *El País* were still dominated by the hunt for the Basque terrorist cell that had planted a bomb at Hipercor in Avenida Meridiana the previous week. 'Way-to-go ETA,' thought Dash, 'bombing a supermarket in a poor suburb of Barcelona and killing 21 innocent shoppers; that's really going to further your cause.' Not in the mood for reading bouts of political point-scoring or sad stories about the victims, he bought copies of *Ajoblanco* and *Rockdeluxe* instead. At the last minute he doubled back to the magazine racks and bought the Madrid sports tabloid *Marca* as well. Dash was that rare Englishman who had absolutely no interest in football, but flaunting *Marca* in a bar garlanded with red and blue pennants was guaranteed to raise the hackles of Barça-obsessed Catalans, especially now, with their dull side lagging behind Real Madrid and their exciting talisman, Emilio 'The Vulture' Butragueño. An infantile pleasure, he knew, but rewarding all the same.

From the Librería Francesa Dash cut across one block to Rambla de Cataluña. This was infertile territory for English louches in search of bohemian soulmates. Moneyed, uptown Catalan girls with their Barbie perms and intimidating shoulder pads were only interested in men from their own tribe. Men with blazers hanging from their shoulders, even in the sweltering heat. Men with man-bags; mini leather pouches that would get you mugged within five minutes in London. Men who sashayed – haughtily, comically – from bar to restaurant to bar with their car cassette players tucked under their arms in tailor-made leather cases.

The girls would hold court on busy terraces or gather together inside brightly lit, antiseptic cafes, sipping horchatas or mineral waters and tapping their feet out of time to Phil Collins or Dire Straits. No thank you, thought Dash, even if I had a cat in hell's chance I wouldn't be interested. No, from here down to Plaza de Cataluña was simply about getting from A to B, though tonight, after catching a glimpse of the shiny bottom of his tapered chinos in the reflection of a shop door, he did engage in some half-hearted window shopping. A new breed of menswear stores, posh retail emporiums owned by Spanish companies like Cortefiel and Inditex but with Italian names like Massimo Dutti and Milano, had recently sprung up on the wider promenades of Barcelona. Dash could never quite decide whether this indicated a lack of native self-confidence or a sly confidence trick; whichever it was, something made him recoil and he made a mental note to visit the Encantes Viejos flea market the following weekend in search of a couple of suits.

Most Mondays Dash stopped at the Café Zurich at the bottom of Plaza de Cataluña for his first *caña* of the evening. The Zurich was dilapidated to a degree way beyond fashionable slumming, and if the fading pictures on the wall were anything to go by, had not changed its décor since the Spanish Civil War, four decades earlier. If the grimy surroundings were enough to deter most posh uptowners, the fetid basement toilets, reached by descending vertigo-inducing stairs so narrow only a stick-thin model or a mountain climber would approach them with any confidence, were the clincher. Even the junkies preferred to cross over Calle Pelayo into McDonalds to shoot up. Of course, the Zurich's location was the secret to its success, not its décor, unwelcoming staff, disreputable clientele or token tapas: tins of olives and anchovies or ensaladilla rusa you were advised to stay away from unless it was the depths of winter, when the lack of heating compensated for the lack of refrigeration.

Poised at the top of the Ramblas, opposite the Canaletes fountain, the old café was the frontier which separated uptown and downtown Barcelona; palpably two distinct cities. 'Meet you at the Zurich,' had been a clarion call for generations of students, *progres* and artists during the dictatorship and unlike many rituals it had survived the transition. Despite the deformed, back-breaking metal chairs, the terrace was a great place to people-watch, and if you were that way inclined, a good place to be seen, too. Dash's happiest single moment in Barcelona had been meeting Charo here almost three years ago to the day. He had been waiting for her, slouched in the doorway with a bottle of Estrella, expecting her to come up the Metro station escalator directly in front of the bar, when suddenly an old Seat 600 pulled up next to the newspaper kiosk with a loud screeching of brakes. Out jumped Charo, long, serpentine black hair, a suntanned goddess in a sleeveless white dress (and as he would later find out, nothing else) screaming and waving at him, 'Dash, Dash, over here.' As he walked over to greet her and to receive her enthusiastic kisses he lapped up the envious glances. But that seemed a lifetime ago.

The Ramblas proper should have offered more promising territory for Dash in his efforts to rekindle his love life. Here he slowed to Spanish Sunday stroll pace. Here lurked girls who had escaped the suburbs or provincial towns to move to the Barrio Chino. Girls who had heard of Patti Smith, The Ramones and The Smiths, even if they didn't understand a word of their lyrics. Girls who read books by Gabriel García Márquez. Girls who were out on a Monday night, not tucked up in bed in mummy and daddy's uptown duplex. And what girls! You could keep your English Roses in Laura Ashley. Dash would take dark sirens in shabby chic any day of the week.

He only had one problem with Spanish women; they were becoming increasingly immune to his charms. When his mind wandered into reverie on the other six nights of the week, he would envisage a Monday night encounter with the girl of his dreams. And it really was love he dreamt of. Sex was not to be sniffed at, but within five minutes of meeting a woman he liked – or merely sat on the Metro opposite an attractive stranger – Dash would be fantasizing about a gilded future as their life partner.

His packed bookshelves held plenty of novels that were full of chance meetings that led to long-lasting relationships. That is what he would tell himself as he groomed himself in the mirror before leaving home. However, the bit he chose to ignore was that these books were full of chance meetings for characters who were prepared to put themselves in chance's way. For Dash that meant in harm's way. Not only was he bereft of confidence, he was constitutionally incapable of handling rejection. Even more debilitating, he knew that first time sex, though rare these days, was a disaster waiting to happen.

Dash rarely managed any kind of erection the first time he slept with a woman. Nerves would always get the better of him; he would need to masturbate to get any kind of hard-on at all. And there was his problem in a nutshell. Maybe there were impotent Lotharios who talked the talk, but Dash didn't see the point. Women like a man to be confident and entertaining, but there is no point blagging your way into a girl's bed and then failing to live up to your bragadoccio. His youthful 'success' had been predicated on a pretty boy visage and a female peer group who were prepared to do most of the running. That had suited him down to the ground. Now he had lost the looks – at least the looks that would attract girls per se – his strike rate was reaching famine proportions. His Monday night trawl through the Chino – cutting in and out from the Ramblas while striking the strutting pose of a peacock on the pedestrian catwalk, proclaiming, 'Look at me, please look at me' – was no kind of plan. It was self-delusion. And prowling bars hoping for women to approach him invariably translated into hanging around in bars scoffing tapas; the latter itinerary and its consequences, an incipient paunch on his otherwise still skinny frame, were hardly conducive to a romantic renaissance.

Four years ago, Dash had never sniffed a Spanish omelette, tripe, olives or anything seasoned with garlic; now he was piling on the kilos with Iberian niceties. The 600 pesetas three-course lunch menu, available on just about every street corner in Barcelona, was a constant threat to the single man's waistline. Conversely, one of the few advantages of being single in Spain was that you were free of a mother-in-law, or more dangerously, a potential mother-in-law, whose sole ambition in life was to force-feed you up the aisle. 'But you've hardly eaten anything,' Charo's mum would tell him, shoving yet another industrial helping of Asturian stew down his throat. Excessive calories, though, were collateral damage Dash had to accept when it came to Monday nights, as the only women he actually spoke to worked in cafes and bars. Even then he rarely bucked up the courage to speak to the ones that he really liked. Like Inma, short for Inmaculada, who worked in a bar on the corner of Calle Carmen and Calle Jerusalén.

Los Gallos was one of those establishments with a street-facing serving window, like a box office cubicle, and an outside counter which was barely more than a narrow shelf. At this time of year most of the clientele stood outside, sipping cool drinks and fanning themselves with whatever came to hand. It had taken Dash a while to get a read on the boisterous gathering when he first started coming here, but slowly it had dawned on him that most of the loud congregation were either prostitutes or their pimps.

Dash spoke decent Spanish but could barely understand a word they were saying, so dense were their mostly southern accents and so laced with slang their quickfire exchanges. As it happened, come rain or shine, he preferred a table inside. There he was served by Luis, a sweet-natured waiter originally from Os Cabreiros, a small village in Galicia. Dash knew the Galician's life story back to front. The nightmare of his crumbling flat in Turó de la Peira. His wife Dolores' addiction to sweet pastries and daytime TV: the prime suspects when it came to her lack of desire in the marital bed. His preoccupation over daughter Isabela who worked at La Casera bottling plant during the day and got knocked around by her policeman husband at night. However, Dash knew absolutely nothing about Inma, except that her name did justice to her ethereal looks, and that the bar was owned by her father, though he never set foot in the place, having, according to Luis, 'lost his balls' after one too many nasty exchanges with the neighbourhood's most savage pimp.

As Dash walked in Imma greeted him almost imperceptibly with a jerk of the chin, but it was Luis who darted out from behind the bar to serve him. 'Señor Dash, cómo está usted esta noche?' Luis was from the old school of Spanish waiters who wouldn't dream of using the more familiar 'tú' form with customers, however long he had known them.

'Not bad,' answered Dash, 'famished!'

'The usual then?'

'Please.' As Luis scuttled off to prepare his order, Dash glanced through *The Sunday Telegraph*. There was a single paragraph on the aftermath of the Hipercor bombing at the bottom of page 15, but that was it. Unlike the Spanish broadsheets, which always led with international news, their English equivalents were still resolutely insular, and when they did bother with the really big picture – détente, Star Wars, etc. – it was pitched in terms so partisan it was almost unreadable. As for Spain, the odd blip aside – the bungled coup of 1981, ETA attacks, Seve Ballesteros – it was almost totally off the radar. Dash glanced over his paper towards the bar. Inma was sitting behind the cash register, wearing her customary loose black top and matching leggings; unusually she had her jet black hair tied in a bun; in a different setting and under a less garish light you might have taken her for a nun. She was talking to a weathered looking North African who had come in immediately after Dash with half a dozen Persian carpets slung over his shoulder. Inma told him matter of factly that he couldn't bother her customers, but noticing how the old man was sweating from his heavy load, she told him to take the weight of his feet and have a refreshing *Tri Naranjus* on the house.

While Dash waited for his food, now flicking through his *Rockdeluxe* magazine, a prostitute in full working girl apparel burst in, brusquely demanding change for the pay phone which was perched at the end of the bar. Clearly, I'm the only paying customer tonight, thought Dash, wryly.

'Ramón, honey, give me the number of that punter in Les Cortes,' she yelled down the phone, 'it's bloody dead down here tonight. I'll ring him and see if he fancies a weekday special.' Turning to Inma, the phone perched under her dappled chin, she shouted, '*Cariño*, chuck me a pen, will you? … No, not that one,' she added, throwing back the biro that Inma had proffered, 'give me that marker pen by the menu board.' Rocking to and fro on a bar stool and with her red mini-skirt riding cheerleader high, the girl's uniform – and she was a mere girl, barely out of her teens if that – left little to the imagination. Dash wanted to look but tried to keep his glances subtle, frightened she might take him for trade and start to hassle him.

'Venga, Ramón, what's the number? 9 – 3 – 4 – 2 – 5 – 6 – 8 – 5 – 5.' She barked the numbers back down the receiver twice for good measure, scrawling them on the inside of her thigh with the marker pen. Good job none of her competitors are here, thought Dash, otherwise the hapless punter in Les Cortes would be bombarded with sales calls.

As Ramón's paramour swept out of the bar, Luis came over with a plate of jamón de bellota, black olives, bread and a glass of albariño, wiping his hands on his barrel-wide paunch after spilling some of the latter on the way over. Dash ordered the same food every Monday, but Luis also brought with him a copy of Sunday's *La Vanguardia*, which was a first. 'Look at this,' he whispered, sliding the paper across the table to Dash while glancing over his shoulder to make sure Inma was still talking to the carpet seller, a movement that did not come easily to him given the permanent crick in his neck. ('All those damp Galician winters when I was a kid,' he ventured whenever Dash enquired after his health.)

Luis removed the toothpick from the side of his mouth, where it seemed to dangle permanently like a gangster's cigarette. Clearly he had serious news to impart. He pointed a nail-bitten finger at an ad in the jobs section of the paper: El Botafumeiro, an exclusive new Galician restaurant in Gran de Gracia was recruiting waiters. 'God willing, that's where I'll be this time next month,' he whispered. 'Can you picture me in a fancy white jacket serving the best lobster, langoustines, scallops and oysters in Barcelona?'

'Sounds right up your street,' Dash mumbled, savouring his first morsel of rich ham. 'Have you applied yet?'

'Not yet,' Luis replied, 'Writing's not exactly my strong point, so Isabela is gonna help me tomorrow. She had to do a load of those psychotechnical test thingamajigs for her job at La Casera, so she can give me tips on interviews, as well.'

Lose the toothpick and invest in some deodorant would be a good start, Dash thought, an ungenerous musing he kept to himself, feeling guilty merely for thinking it. Dash had had a soft spot for Luis since the first time he had stumbled upon Los Gallos three years ago. It had been a busy Saturday night and three-deep at the bar. Dash still hadn't got used to the Spanish custom of shouting in bars to attract attention. In fact he still hadn't; it took more than four years to break down English reserve, and shouting 'Oiga, póngame una cerveza' in an assertive voice across a crowded room was still beyond him. In many bars, the waiters would cynically leave you waiting, but on that night, Luis had spotted Dash, recognised his plight and rushed out from behind the bar to serve him, a habit that he had never lost, and a kind gesture that Dash had never forgotten.

'Luisito, cariño,' called Inma from behind the bar, 'pop upstairs and bring down some coffee filters, will you?'

'Voy,' replied Luis, then turning to Dash with index finger to lips, bypassing the reinstated toothpick. 'Between you and me, of course,' adding after a pause, 'The best part is that El Botafumeiro is two minutes from your apartment, so you can pop in any time. I'll invite you to a proper glass of albariño!'

Twenty minutes later – savouring food was another Spanish habit Dash hadn't quite mastered – he beckoned Luis over, paid his bill, and slipped a 200 peseta tip into the waiter's hand. In a neighbourhood bar like this, Luis would be lucky to get the odd saucer of duros from other customers, but being generous gave Dash pleasure and he knew Luis appreciated it, so why not?

'Until next week,' said Luis, 'God willing.'

Put your money on it, thought Dash as he gestured goodbye, regardless of what God wants. As he left he noted that Inma was still deep in conversation with the ancient Moro. Jesus, he thought, I've been coming here every Monday for years and she has barely exchanged half a dozen words with me beyond Hello and Goodbye. He didn't even get that tonight as she failed to notice him go.

His next stop was Las Delicias in Calle Hospital, a bar which was seedy even by Chino standards but was one of the few places in Barcelona that offered his favourite beer, Cruzcampo. It was a sultry, energy-sapping July evening and by now his two-tone bowling shirt was moist with sweat while his feet felt like deadweights inside his heavy brogues. There were extremely good aesthetic reasons for eschewing sandals or espadrilles, but Dash's motives were purely sanitary. His brogues might be dead weights in summer, but at least they offered protection from the detritus lying in ambush on sawdust floors. He was sure he had once glanced some pretty impressive modernist tiles here under the cornucopia of rubble, but the sheer quantity of cigarette butts, discarded paper napkins, toothpicks, olive stones and nut shells made it hard to tell for sure.

After greedily downing two glasses of ice-cold Cruzcampo, he went into the toilets, threw some cold water on his face and greased his unruly hair back as best he could. He wanted to look best for his next destination, the Perfidious Albion Pub in Calle Marquès de Barberà, just behind the Liceu opera house.

The Albion, as all the expats called it, was one of only two bars in Barcelona that sold a decent range of British beers. It was not an establishment frequented by too many opera-goers. In normal circumstances Dash would have steered well clear; he hadn't moved to Spain to spend his time in a faux pub full of Brits talking about football and teaching. But the previous Monday, he had caught sight of an exceptionally pretty black girl sitting in the front window nook as he walked past, and he was convinced she had smiled at him when he glanced back at her. At the time he hadn't had the gumption to respond, but in the ensuing week he had built up this fleeting moment, if it was a moment at all, to fantasy proportion. Of course, the statistical chance of meeting her in the same place at the same time were slim. But when love is elusive, on such fancies are mighty hopes constructed.

A quick glance around the tiny bar – if this was England it would have barely qualified as a snug, let alone a whole pub – told him that the girl wasn't here. Before he had time to decide whether to hang around or mark it down as another lost opportunity, the barman shouted, 'Alright, mate. The usual?' Dash had never set foot in The Albion in his life before but confusion kicked in and before he could stutter a word, the barman was pulling him a pint of John Smith's Yorkshire Bitter. 'Here you have it,' he said, speaking English with a broad Spanish accent, placing the glass on a grubby coaster, 'that weel be 125 pesetas, pleeze.'

Blimey, paying in advance, this really is like a pub back home, thought Dash as he handed the cash over in coins, getting rid of all the change he had accumulated so far that night, before retiring quickly to a table on his own. The barmen aside, there were three other customers, all male, all on their own, and all cranking their necks to peer at a TV set mounted high on the wall. Felipe González was making a fatuous speech about his government's determination to catch the Hipercor bombers which Dash guessed none of the trio were interested in, even if they could understand what the Prime Minister was saying. After ten minutes and a couple of sips of the foul brown liquid in his glass, Dash took advantage of a moment when the barman was changing channels with a pool cue to make a discreet exit.

In need of consolation he headed immediately for the bar with his second favourite barmaid, Ruth, or *Root* as the Spanish pronounced it. The first thing you noticed about Ruth was the platinum blonde beehive with outlandish black roots at the crown and the ends. She would tell anybody who cared to listen that this precise look – shoddy highlighting et al. – was inspired by Myra Hindley, the '60s Moors Murderer. What kind of Spanish woman in her early twenties had even heard of the evil Hindley, let alone been inspired by her ghoulish look was a question Dash preferred not to think about too much. Admittedly, Ruth was not a typical Spanish girl nor did she run the most typical bar, as its name, Via Dolorosa, hinted. Painted on the window outside were the usual display of tapas, there to lure illiterate punters and tourists, though in this case the delicacies didn't resemble the tapas painted on every other bar window in the Chino (presumably by a failed artist who had once specialised in still lifes) but were surreally bad: patatas bravas that looked like dying twigs, fried eggs that resembled ears filled with wax, and chorizo that looked like dog faeces. There was also a lurid sketching of what looked like a bejewelled vagina. This was, in fact, a bejewelled vagina. 'Mine,' boasted Ruth when Dash first asked her what it was.

Inside Ruth's dark den there were no football posters, no slot machines and no TV set, just wall-to-wall posters of female rockers – Debbie Harry, Joan Jett, The Slits, Alaska and the best jukebox in the city, bar none. Dash could spend hours talking to Ruth about music, in fact, he could spend hours talking to Ruth about anything (like how a self-proclaimed anarchist has a swastika tattooed on her wrist). He fancied Ruth like crazy, but sadly, was not her type, though he didn't take it personally. Ruth didn't have any kind of type with masculine appendages. This explained why Dash's usual tongue-tied-around-women persona went missing as soon as he walked through the door of Via Dolorosa, though it was Ruth who dominated the conversation, delivering opinions in staccato, scatter-gun fashion. Tonight she added to the whirlwind effect by fanning herself vigorously with a black leather cap while simultaneously twirling a cigarette around in her hand like a propeller. God knows why? Dash had never seen her smoke, though he wasn't innocent of that line in fetish himself. He still carried a Zippo lighter in his pocket despite the fact he had given up smoking years ago.

'Oye, Dash, listen to this shit,' shouted Ruth, as soon as he walked in the door. 'It's la fuckin' hostia.' She ran over to the jukebox, kicked it so the track playing – Velvet Underground's *All Tomorrow's Parties* – screeched to a halt, and banged the buttons to make a new selection. As soon as the opening riff kicked in, Dash recognised the Pixies' *Levitate Me*. 'What did I tell you… cómo mola?' Ruth enthused.

'You won't get an argument from me,' smiled Dash.

'Fuckin' right you won't, macho. Aquí mando yo, y al que no le guste, que se vaya a fuck Julio Iglesias up the arse.' Dash laughed out loud. He didn't know anybody who mixed two languages with such abrasive aplomb. 'And mira esta tía,' continued Ruth, slapping the cover of *Levitate Me* onto the bar and making lascivious eyes at Pixies bass player Kim Deal. 'Is she hot or what? Me cago en la puta!'

'Yeah, not bad,' replied Dash, deadpan, 'though a bit skinny for your tastes I would have thought.'

'Oye macho. Yo soy muy liberal, sabes. As long as they're not fachas, me las tiro. Fat, thin, guapas, feas. Look where being fussy gets you.' Dash faked an exasperated sigh, before shifting the topic away from his barren love life. 'I've got some good news and some bad news about the Pixies. Which do you want first?'

'Bueno, como decía mi abuela, bad news is like the menopause, the longer it takes to arrive the better.' Ruth's metaphors were decidedly less impressive than her aptitude for bilingual sparring.

'OK, it's your call, dear,' said Dash. 'The good news is that the Pixies are coming to Barcelona next month, they're playing at Zeleste.'

'Wow, mecachis! Seriously?'

'Seriously. There's an ad in *Rockdeluxe* … look.' Dash threw his copy of the magazine onto the bar and turned to the page in question. 'Fuck, that is good news,' exclaimed Ruth. 'Me llevas o que?'

'Course, as long as you're paying, businesswoman.'

'Sure I'll pay, you cheap fuck. You need the date and the money.' Dash ignored the half of that equation which was true, but Ruth insisted, 'O sea, no has tenido suerte on your Monday night adventures lately?'

'I wouldn't say that exactly.'

'Venga ya. You're getting less pussy than a Polish Pope.'

Dash giggled, despite himself: 'I'm definitely getting less than you.'

'Talking of which, what's the chances of us sneaking backstage and meeting la Kim? Yo no tengo orgullo, siempre he sido una groupie!'

'Ah, that reminds me; the bad news…'

'Suéltalo, tío.'

'My very reliable sources tell me that Miss Deal is God-fearing, prim and proper. She certainly doesn't indulge in any of that girl on girl nonsense.'

'Bueno, you get me back stage and we'll let her decide. También hay democracia en España, sabes.'

'So they say,' said Dash. 'Though somebody forgot to tell ETA.'

'Don't start me on those cabrones,' grunted Ruth, and then proceeded to lay in to them for the next 20 minutes, which was about 19 minutes more political talk than Dash could handle. After several attempts to steer her back to more stimulating territory, he finished his long tequila – Ruth's choice not his – made his excuses and left. 'Good luck with the girl hunt. Que te follen!' shouted Ruth as he left the bar.

Two hours and several cañas later, all in grungy bars where he didn't know a soul, not even the waiters, and where he didn't speak to a single woman, Dash reached the bottom of the Ramblas. At 11 o'clock on a Monday night it was deserted. Keen to encounter another friendly face, Dash doubled back a couple of hundred metres to the Panorama sex bar on the corner of Arco del Teatro. Sitting outside was his regular shoeshine boy, a grizzled Argentinian called Fabian. In reality, Fabian was more of a shoeshine pensioner, but like bell boys and rent boys, his designation suggested you were supposed to progress to better things at a certain age. Not that he seemed fazed by his modest professional status. His party trick still consisted of shouting, 'Tía buena, let Fabian polish your jewels!' to passing ladies of all ages, shapes and sizes, though with cauliflower ears and a face which resembled an overripe watermelon there was little chance of his benevolent offer being accepted.

'Señor, you are a man of the world, I need you to solve an argument for me,' said Fabian in his sing-song accent as soon as Dash sat down on the precarious wooden stool for clients. Like most Argentinians, Fabian could recite the phone book and make it sound poetic, even when pausing every 30 seconds or so to spit lavishly, sometimes on the shoes in hand, but just as often on the pavement.

Dash wasn't mad keen on the agony-aunt role, especially as conversation rarely deviated from Fabian's ploys to bed Assumpta, the landlady from his pensión round the corner. But noblesse oblige, and Fabian always did a thoroughly professional job on his brogues: 'Glad to help,' he said, 'what's the argument about?'

'Well, see that one-legged prick over there,' answered Fabian, gesturing to a fellow shoeshine boy on the other side of the Ramblas, who indeed seemed to be missing a leg. 'I was telling him and the guys in the pensión that there are only three taxis in the world that are instantly recognisable because of their colour: the black and yellow of Barcelona, the yellow cabs in London, and the black cabs in New York. Anyway, that gimpy son of a bitch told me that I was wrong, that the cabs in London are the black ones and the American ones are the yellow ones. I told him he doesn't know his arse from his elbow, but he got all shirty and in the end made me bet on it in front of a load of colegas. It's not just the money, it's my pride you know. A good shoe-shine professional prides himself on giving the public accurate information.'

'How much did you bet?' asked Dash tentatively, not sure he really wanted to know.

'10,000 pesetas.'

'10,000 pesetas! Jesus, how many shoes would you need to shine to make that kind of money?'

Fabian shrugged his shoulders. 'Dunno. About a week's worth.'

Dash's initial instinct was to tell Fabian the truth and offer to sub him the ten thousand in return for a few weeks buffing up his brogues, but then he looked at the imploring expression on the Argentinian's oval face, and realised that in the demi-monde of the shoeshining cartels, the issue of pride was paramount.

'So what is it señor, he's talking rubbish about the taxis, isn't he?'

'Yes, you're right, Fabian, they're black in New York and yellow in London.'

'Hallelujah, I knew I was right!' Fabian whooped with delight and then attempted to give Dash a high-five which the Englishman managed to avoid, not wanting boot polish all over his hands. Attracted by the noise, Fabian's rival across the road glanced over at the pair. Noting Fabian's war dance of delight, he twirled a finger round and round in small circles next to his temple, an indication that he might possess a firmer grasp of reality than Dash's man.

Undeterred, the Argentinian reached into the pocket of his grubby shorts and pulled out a crumpled paper napkin. He unfolded it carefully, spat on his fingers and then smoothed the paper out on the lid of the wooden box where he kept his brushes and polish. 'Just sign here, so I can get my money,' he indicated.

Dash peered at the blurred writing: I ...Resident off Barcelona, but Sitizen of Gret Britain, do sollemly sware that taxis in London are yelow and taxis in New York are blak. Sinned by ...Munday 29 off June 1987. 'Just there where the two spaces are,' insisted Fabian, handing Dash a leaky felt-tip pen. The latter explained the smudges all over the Boca Juniors football shirt that Fabian wore stretched over his considerable girth like shrink-wrap.

Fifteen years ago, you would have been a fool to sign anything in Spain without a loyal-to-the-regime advocate as witness, but hey, thought Dash, what's the worst than can happen to me now, getting chased down the Ramblas by a one-legged shoeshine boy? The formalities out of the way, and one longer than usual shoeshine later, Dash bid farewell to a visibly chuffed Argentinian, leaving him the copy of *Marca* and a fistful of pesetas.

Federico García Lorca was a poet that Dash liked the idea of far more than he liked the actual poems, but the Andalusian had said one thing he agreed with; that La Rambla was 'the only street in the world which I wish would never end'. Dash felt like that every Monday night; same place, same time, though probably not for the same reasons as Lorca. After a quick reconnaissance around the Christopher Columbus statue down to the waterfront, he cut through to Calle de la Mercè, past the church, past the giant Post Office building on the corner of Via Layetana, under the gothic arches of La Llotja where Picasso studied as a teenager, before tracing the bottom end of El Born and cutting across towards Barceloneta.

He walked – now at sharper, London pace – past the towering, dirt-black warehouses along Paseo Nacional before turning into the labyrinthine streets of Barceloneta with its crumbling dolls-houses connected by façade-to-façade washing lines. Past the municipal market noting the overpowering stench of fish, he made his penultimate stop of the evening in El Rinconcillo, a musty bodega in Calle Balboa where the ageing clientele drank cheap red wine from huge oak barrels and played cards for small change. Dash rarely saw anything in Barcelona that reminded him of London, but the wizened old guys here always prompted memories of retired Jamaicans playing dominoes at lunchtimes in dark London pubs. Here Dash bought two lottery tickets from the blind vendor who was a permanent resident by the door. El Rinconcillo was the last chance saloon where you could buy individual cigarettes or dollops of brylcreem from a big bottle, so not surprisingly the vendor did a reasonable trade, even at this time of night. Especially at this time of night.

From Barceloneta, Dash cut through to the abandoned industrial estate on the edge of Poble Nou, its tangle of disused factories, long-neglected warehouses and rubbish dumps a landscape so bleak it was post-apocalyptic. From there it was a short hop past the obsolete gas works and across the old railway tracks to the remnants of Somorrostro, the infamous *barraca,* 'shanty town', on the waterfront. At its peak in the 1950s, 100,000 people had lived in the *barracas* of Barcelona. These were slum dwellings on a Third World scale, lacking even the most basic facilities: running water, electricity, proper drains or sewage. For decades the most common route into Somorrostro was along a narrow path behind Hospital del Mar, the dark, imposing clinic for infectious diseases. If you were struck down by the plague, went the saying in Somorrostro – and post-war Barcelona saw major outbreaks of smallpox, polio and cholera, so there was a good chance you would, especially living in such insanitary conditions – at least you didn't have far to go to hospital. Or far to come back, if you were that lucky.

The blackened beaches of Somorrostro had originally been the site of improvised fishermen's dwellings in the nineteenth century, but the real expansion took place when immigrants from all over Spain were hired to construct the pharaonic icons for the 1929 Barcelona Universal Exhibition: the Palau Nacional de Catalunya, Poble Espanyol, Teatre Grec, the Olympic Stadium and the Magic Fountains of Montjuïc. Dash thought it ironic that these symbols of Catalan identity, so beloved of the local bourgeoisie, had been forged on the backs of poor immigrant workers who after long hours during the day building grandiose monuments spent their evenings reinforcing their own tumbledown shacks. The crippling poverty and political persecution of post-war España Negra drove even more country dwellers to Barcelona. It was only in the 1960s that the municipal bulldozers began to move in on the *barracas* as their inhabitants were carted-off to purpose-built estates on the outskirts of the city. But in 1987 there still existed a stubborn underclass – mostly Gitanos, delinquents and drug addicts – who lived in Somorrostro, now reduced to a few blocks at the edge of Poble Nou where it had once stretched several kilometres, from Hospital del Mar to the sewage plant on the River Besos to the north.

As the crow flies Somorrostro was barely a mile from the bottom end of Eixample and Sagrada Família, but most 'respectable' Catalans would die rather than venture seawards of Poble Nou. Dash had soon learned that Barcelona was still a city that lived with its back to the sea, with the exception of the working-class enclave of Barceloneta beach, a Catalan Coney Island where wrinkled pensioners would play parchís on the boardwalk and work their all-year tans. Well-heeled Catalans would spend their summer weekends in the coves of the Costa Brava, but the beaches of Barceloneta remained a virtual no-go area to all but the city's poor. To most people living in Barcelona, Somorrostro – like Can Tunis, El Camp de la Bota and La Perona – was merely a name from tales of the bogeyman. Dash didn't believe in the bogeyman but he couldn't deny that his professional and personal lives were divided up like a pie chart.

Paca lived in the part of the pie labelled Somorrostro. Her makeshift home was constructed from a mishmash of corrugated iron, discarded panels and wood beams from building sites, with crude brickwork for the foundations. Graffiti on the exterior wall proclaimed: 'Good-for-nothing Andalusian dog, drop the knife and find a job'. A table improvised from beer crates and an old toilet door sat outside, flanked by a rusty copper wash tub, home to three mangy cats, and a bar football table. Too much sun had faded the table's bright colours: Barcelona's wooden eleven now wore sickly mauve; Real Madrid's sported dirty grey rather than royal white.

Inside the precarious looking dwelling, the effect was pure chiaroscuro; the dark walls and gloomy corners contrasting with the gaudy red cushions and orange butane gas canister in the middle of the room. By the time Dash arrived it was past midnight. Paca was stretched out on a battered old Pikolin mattress, listening to her beloved Rocío Jurado on a tinny Philips cassette player. Rocío was 'la artista más grande de España' according to Paca, whose loyalty to the copla singer – she didn't own a single tape by another artist – was cemented by the fact that they had been near neighbours in Cádiz as young girls. There was no electricity at Paca's, so every couple of weeks Dash would bring batteries for the tape player which he purchased from the blind vendor at the bodega, where he'd also pick up a carton of the Ducados negros which Paca chain-smoked and gave her small room its acrid smell. Tonight he'd also brought along a well-thumbed copy of *Hola* magazine courtesy of Ruth (go figure). Paca couldn't read but she loved to pour over the pictures. Occasionally, she would tear one out and stick it on the wall with sticking tape, old favourites like Rocío and Ava Gardner jockying for room alongside Princess Caroline of Monaco. Next to the princess were two photos of King Juan Carlos; in the first he was embracing General Franco at a military parade, in the second he was pictured shaking hands with Felipe González. If the Chinese invaded Spain, Juan Carlos would no doubt be snapped with a broad smile, pumping his fist in the air next to the Communist bigwigs.

A beaded, multi-coloured curtain separated Paca's living space from the sleeping area. Dresses, polka dot blouses and brightly coloured scarves hung on mangled wire coat hangers from tacks on the wall. Above the mattress hung three suits that belonged to Paca's nephew Carlos, a drug-addled quinqui who had graduated from car theft to robbing banks. 'Why don't you take them, majo,' Paca often told Dash. 'Carlitos doesn't need them in Carabanchel Prison.' But cream suits with wide lapels were hardly his style, especially ones that boasted traces of vomit on the sleeves, as if Carlos had just this instant wiped his mouth on them.

In a favourable light the raven-eyed Paca, or 'La Paca' as she insisted on referring to herself in the third person, bore a passing resemblance to

Somorrostro's most famous daughter, the flamenco dancer Carmen Amaya. Amaya had died in 1963 at the age of 50 shortly after starring in the breath-taking Spanish take on Romeo and Juliet, Los Tarantos, shot largely on location on the beaches of Somorrostro. Unfortunately it was the ravaged late version of the 'Queen of the Gypsies' that Paca resembled, not the visceral young woman who had danced for President Roosevelt in the White House. Paca was ten years older than Dash, but with her thicket of dark hair streaked by grey, and with shadows under her eyes shaded even darker than her dark olive skin, she looked old enough to be his mother. In the wrong light she looked more like one of the hirsute Andalusian drag queens who populated the outer fringes of the Ramblas than Carmen Amaya. But that didn't bother Dash. By this time of night, he wasn't looking for love or beauty. And Paca had other compensatory qualities.

Concentration had never been Dash's forte. His thoughts would wander at the most inappropriate moments, especially if he was bored or worried, which covered most of his moods. In either case, his gaze tended to wander to distant horizons, like a faithful point man preparing the terrain for his roving thoughts. Neither was he good at feigning sociability. But here in this tiny space he had to worry about neither trait. The truth was that Paca loved to talk, the breaking waves barely 50 metres away a soothing accompaniment to her deep, rich voice, and he loved to listen. Sometimes for hours, with barely an 'Uh-huh' or a 'Sí, sí' on his part. Life might have been grinding her down since the day she was born, but Paca wasn't going to let a small thing like that effect her bonhomie. Nor, for that matter, would she let the bigger tragedies of the world disturb her small domain. When Dash had put his *Sunday Telegraph* down on the bed, she had noticed a photo of the rubble at Hipercor.

'What's that?' she said gesturing at the paper.

'A bomb at a supermarket in Barcelona,' answered Dash.

'My God,' she exclaimed, putting her hands to her face, dramatically. Then she took a long drag of her Ducado, and proceeded to change the subject completely, telling Dash that one of her neighbours had won 60,000 pesetas on the lottery and had promised to buy her un brazo de gitano, 'a gypsy's arm', a Spanish sponge cake filled with whipped cream.

'How come you ended up in Somorrostro?' Dash had asked her one night, back when he had first started coming here, sent by Luis, another occasional visitor when things got out of hand for him at home.

'La Paca was brought here on false pretences,' she had replied, sipping Anís del Mono from a rusty tin cup. 'I arrived at the Estación de Francia and my brother Paco, may he rest in peace, was waiting for me on the platform with the whitest gardenia I had ever seen. He was an angel that man, uglier than a rabid dog and lame to boot, but an angel all the same. The first thing he did was take me on a tram ride so I could see the city. The number 55, I've never forgotten the tram number. I couldn't believe how huge Barcelona was. And so beautiful. Then when he brought me back here to Somorrostro and I saw the sewer where I was going to live, I cried. Cried and cried for days on end until I was all cried out. My brother paid 25 duros for his shack in 1950, and the sea took it back for nothing in 1958, a couple of years after I arrived. We spent weeks sleeping in a dovecote with pigeons while he looked for another place.'

Paca coughed as if the memory of that feathery refuge had invaded her nostrils. After clearing her throat with a guttural sound, she lit a fresh Ducado from the embers of a dying one, and continued. 'At least most of the factories are shut down now. In those days we had to wash our clothes in the dirty sea where the factories dumped their rubbish. What little clean water we had we saved for cooking and drinking. If I had known what was waiting for me I would never have come to Barcelona. I was on my own in a pensión in Jerez de la Frontera, but I was working as a sewing machinist and at least I had my own room. Here in the *barraca* there were six of us; me, my brother and four cousins, and only one bed. But I'd spent all my bloody savings to get here, so was stuck, and then…' – here there was a rare pause – '…well, it's surprising what you can get used to if you have no choice. Even men. Whenever my brother was out my cousins would jump on me like dogs on heat. Brutes, they were. That's why I can't be bothered with men, you know. I've had enough of them to last me ten lifetimes. At least now, la Paca is on her own with nobody to bother her… Bother us, I mean. Right, amor?'

That extracted confession aside, Paca's mood was rarely anything but light-hearted. Tonight was no exception. As she talked, punctuating her ribald tales with a raucous laugh, she slipped off her espadrilles, lifted her ankle length skirt, peeled off her panties and hung them over an old Singer sewing machine. Then she set about washing herself with soapy water from a Cola Cao carton. Dash, as always, sat quietly and watched. Eventually he joined her on the old mattress behind the beaded curtains, pushing aside the collection of old Nancy dolls to sit down and let Paca wash him. She took a last swig of Anís, swilling it around her mouth as if it was Listerine, and then as a final flourish, doused his penis with Agua Brava cologne. 'Smells good when I suck you, amor,' she said, teasing him. By the time she was finished with her ablutions, Dash was erect. This marked the beginning and end of foreplay.

Paca took the two steps to the middle of the room and bent over the Butano canister in business-like fashion, wetting her forefinger with saliva before moistening her sex. Dash followed and with no further ceremony began to fuck her from behind, first clinging to her heavy breasts through her blouse and then, as he slowed down, caressing the prominent stretch marks on her dark buttocks. He remained silent except his breathing, but Paca carried on talking, like a foul-mouthed participant in a tertulia. 'Dársela a la Paca, que es una puta,' she moaned, her Andalusian accent thickened by the breathless delivery. 'Metérsela más, chato.' She also threw in the odd Catalan expression, snippets of seduction that she must have picked up when she had worked as a cleaner for wealthy businessmen in Sant Gervasi. 'Llepa el cony a la Paca, si us plau.'

The carnal formalities never lasted long. Dash rarely masturbated between visits, a guarantee that once-a-week sex consisted mostly of screeching on the brakes before the inevitable crash. Even holding back, he would shudder after a couple of minutes before ejaculating his milky deposit on Paca's flaccid buttocks. Then he would leave her where she was standing and flop down on the mattress. If he was tired, it was down to the long walk and excessive intake of alcohol and grease, not the blink-and-you'd-miss-it fornication. It was hardly ejaculation as ecstasy; Dash was not without self-awareness, even in those moments when a man's brain is at its least cogent.

For years, his ritual after orgasm had been to lay back, bend his still erect cock around the back of his leg and see how long he could hold it there before its diminishing volume and weight forced it back into sight; a free-floating presence nestled on the upper reaches of his inner thigh. He would then contemplate it shrinking to nothingness while recovering his breath. This process could take ten, fifteen minutes before his penis resembled a piece of discarded tripe. But here at Paca's, his post-coital senses were so alive to the smell of stale tobacco, cheap cologne and butane gas, that his cock would shrivel up in a matter of seconds, as if in protest at the sordid surroundings.

After a ten minute wait (he didn't want to seem rude), Dash stood up, rearranged his dishevelled clothing as best he could, and took three one-thousand peseta notes from his back pocket. These he left under the Cola Cao container on the way out, along with one of the two lottery coupons from the bodega. 'You'll come and see la Paca next week, verdad amor?' beseeched Paca, as Dash pulled back the beaded curtain to leave. He hesitated uncomfortably, thinking, 'Please no, make this the last time.' Much as he appreciated Paca, this was not how he'd envisaged his life panning out. But what he actually said, what he said every week, was 'God willing'. Paca smiled and pressed 'Play' on her tape player to resume her evening with Rocío.

The end of the night also followed a regular pattern. Dash would walk, wearily, to Barceloneta Metro station where he would take the yellow line five stops back to Verdaguer, a five minute walk from his apartment. Or, if like tonight, it was too late and the Metro was closed, he would walk to the bottom of the Ramblas and catch a black and yellow cab from the taxi rank next to The Wax Museum box office.

As the cab drove past the Boqueria Market, Dash wound down his window to gaze at the green awnings of the newspaper kiosks, the flower stands and pet stores, all now shut for the night. As they cruised across Plaza de Cataluña past the Zurich, a lone waiter was securing piles of chairs together with chains. Beyond the square, Paseo de Gracia was deserted except for the noisy garbage trucks and men hosing down the wide sidewalks. I've had exactly four conversations tonight, Dash reflected as the taxi sped past the illuminated La Pedrera: with Luis, Ruth, Fabian, and Paca, all of them in the role of client. It was a reflection he preferred not to dwell on.

Back home in Gracia he took a quick shower, drank a litre of water directly from a carafe which he kept in the fridge, then retired to his bedroom to read *The Sunday Telegraph*. The news could be earth-shattering or deadly dull, either way he would slip into a deep sleep within minutes, weaving his way in and out of dreams in English and Spanish for the next three, four, five hours.

He woke abruptly at dawn as the first rays of sun seeped through his transparent roller blinds. Tuesday. Another dull week stretched ahead of him. Another week of living his eminently respectable life, of mind-numbing conversations at the agency with Oriol, Ferran and Montse. Another week of roving thoughts. Another week before his next wander in search of love and passion. Another week, if the truth be told, before his next visit to Paca.

He sat up in bed, rubbed his eyes, thinking, 'God knows what I would do if Barcelona ever decided to bury its past and raze Somorrostro to the ground?'

Jesus makes a man out of me

Lynn Baiori

I am peering over the skyline of Barcelona. Tony Bennett's handsome tenor croons, *Fly Me to the Moon*. From the centre of a broad landscape, like tiny fingers reaching heavenwards, rise the spires of the Sagrada Família.

'Have yourself a good trip. Hope you find what you're looking for,' said James as we parted at the baggage claim.

'Thanks,' I responded, realizing I hadn't defined what I was looking for.

'Best to prioritize,' I thought and I made a bee-line for the bathroom.

Gliding past security, I could have walked out of the terminal and evaporated like steam over the next piece of track. Ignored a sign gripped between jittery, nicotine stained hands. Two words written in bold ink against a white card.

Joan Ocello. My name. A diminutive ferret of a man, standing as straight as a beanpole, stretched his neck to peer nervously over the tops of heads, giving the impression of having scampered out of a burrow to check for predators. I approached cautiously. He reeked of the addiction which soaked through to his every cell. A black tobacco addict, the chords of his voice turned to gravel.

Ducados. It was the mark of hard core, the kind of cigarette that identified you as someone who would die with a butt hanging out of your mouth.

'Hi, I'm Joan,' I said indicating his sign. He looked back uncertainly.

'I thought you are a man,' he said.

Now we were both confused.

'Please, pardon, no one say me if I must to drive a girl and Joan is the name for the man. Is the Catalan Juan,' he explained.

'Oh, well in the States it's a woman's name,' I said.

'Sí, pues, here is not,' he answered unapologetically.

We stared at each other for a few seconds. Then he offered, 'I am Jesus.'

And I replied, 'Guess your parents had great expectations.'

My attempted humour fortunately passed over his head. I filled in an awkward pause by smiling.

'We go?' he suggested, grabbing the handle of my suitcase.

'Lead the way,' I said. And out we headed into the warm morning air. Pausing under the glaring sun, he lit one up. 'Here is my car,' he puffed, indicating a distant point at the far end of a large parking lot. I dropped off the curb, obediently followed little Jesus across a sea of warm asphalt.

Alan Jenkins

From DEAD WHITE MALE

Tacking into harbour, rich with smells of rope and tar,
A bright sun glancing off the masts of Bar- Bar- Bar-
Barcelona, I'd rejoiced to be, once more, under sail
But now I was alone, the air I sniffed was stale;
What was I doing, haunting the dead? What conceit
Had drawn me here to search for a word I could use,
A word for his life, his art, for the night he went
To be chosen to die by a thing he did not choose,
Did not see, and left the realm of the made or meant,
The artist's world – so a pick-up in the last port of call
Had given me to understand… In the bar-bars
And bodegas, in the doorways and entries
Of the twisted vein they call the Calle Avinyon,
Everything and everyone was up for sale;
I stood in a crowd of student-sentries
And watched some student-anarchist scribble-scrawl
Viva Che! on a poster-patched, poster-peeling wall
Below a poster of 'Les Demoiselles d'Avignon'…
I went with the flow as far as a half-lit cave
On one wall of which was painted – what else? –
'Les Demoiselles', by a primitive hand;
They loomed above me while I sat and scanned
The painted ladies at the bar, who invited me to dig a grave
With my own prick, and go and jump in it.
I feigned a shy absorption in my Fundador
Then smiling feebly I got up and paid and would have left
But for the woman's voice that pinned me to the floor,
A voice that issued from a primitively painted cleft –
A detail the original omitted – saying *Wait a minute.*
Did you never wonder, did you never ask
What was in his heart, 'Pableaux's, the great creator,
A small man who knew he'd be a giant, sooner or later,
And leave us behind, as he left everyone he'd used –
When he painted on that dog-like, ape-like mask
Where my woman's face should be? Was it contempt?

Or anger? Was it revenge for the disease
That brought the nineteenth century to its knees?...
Outside someone was shouting and waving a knife
At a woman, his girlfriend, his model or wife,
Beneath the windowless windows' blind-eyed stare
From a derelict warehouse opposite; the light was bruised,
As in the dirty greys, the ochres and umbers
Of a canvas I recalled (or was it one I'd dreamt?).
Back on the street there was safety in numbers,
Or so I thought. The Ramblas caught me in its wave,
Caught me and carried me towards the salt-stiffened air
Of the waterfront – but from the depths of a café
Another, deeper voice was hailing me, and this time, yes,
Bruno F. himself came loping up, his slicked-back hair,
Paint-spattered jacket, swirling length of scarf,
His corduroys, broad grin and grunting laugh
All as when he still had years to live, and *Jenks, my friend!,*
He called, Weren't you once a devotee of Baudelaire
And his dark cult? I tell you that a sentence of death,
Premature, painful death, when the slightest ache
Could signal the beginning of the end,
Not only focuses the mind but leaves you short of breath.
I hope you don't experience it, for your sake.
It might have been the self-same brothel, the Bordel
D'Avignon (Picasso's own name for that picture, by the way)
Where I caught my fate, where I was singled out to die.
I'll lose my hair, my strength, my mind, my eye...
The brothel and the park, the scenes of modern life
Par excellence, your poet said... But not for me,
Not now. One model and one muse, my nurse, my wife,
My widow too. I guess I was a real jerk (I guess!)
That night I went out to play so recklessly – and what the hell,
Right? I'd been a jerk and I'd played the clown
So many times – street-girls, junkies, I couldn't turn them down,
Couldn't turn a single one away. My real life was work,
Though, you know that. So long. Try to tell the truth...
But what was that? Just yesterday I'd joined the throng
In the cathedral cloister, stood below its vault
Of tattered palms and counted seven fat white geese

That gobble-squabbled under them, for crumbs, for release;
I'd wandered all day around the Gothic quarter
Where she had spent that 'difficult year'
And watched the chestnut blossom falling in my beer
And when I had to eat, what everyone eats
In Barcelona, I'd breathed in every cellar bar
The familiar amalgam she was, and so many are –
The sweet, the garlicky-pungent and the salt –
And remembered her come dripping from the water
For me to frame in the crook of her freckled arm
Our Cubist village and its single palm,
Our spaghetti-western beach, deserted for a shoot-out
At high noon, when sunlight struck it like a gong.
Now I was carried on towards a little red-lit booth
Where, becalmed, I watched two strangers – brisk,
Methodical, expressionless – ride out their storm;
Slap, slap, he ploughed her glistening furrow, warm
And wet and open wide, he gave no thought to risk
As he poured ambergris into her waiting mouth –
And tugging at myself, so raw and dry,
I wanted to believe: in love that doesn't die,
In the beauty of the gothic-baroque-Cubist south –
Far from the blade- and needle-sharp, the blind-eyed streets –
Sea-nymphs riding dolphins, sea-creatures, shells,
Clouds and putti; far from these semen-smells.

- - -

At one end of the line, the Catalunya line,
On a little island made from builders' waste,
A mound of dirt and sand, brick-enclosed, enchanted,
Stands a single palm tree fancy planted:
Tropical bird, *its fire-fangled feathers*
Dangle down…No. But it stands in all weathers,
Tattered, watered, a thing of shreds and patches
And as I walk past it to the 8.09
I can hear palms rustle in their tropic airs,
I can hear the mermaids singing, snatches
Of old song, sea-shanties, siren-songs,
I can feel the whiplash of the wind and taste
The sticky-sweet of rum, the salt of panties and thongs

Those wriggling sirens hooked their thumbs inside
And snagged on painted toenails in their haste,
The salt-sweetness that is uniquely theirs;
Hear that wet click-click, a metronome,
Quickening…One especially, who swam in on the tide
And parted salt-wet lips – that dutiful daughter!
How she loved the parasol her mother brought her
That was like a little piece of home – her home –
The sun-splashed garden, parakeets and palms….
I wrote lines to her eyes that were like the sea,
'The grey-green mistiness, the tiny fleck of foam'.
I scribbled messages on her body's open book.
And it seemed a tide had turned unalterably
To bring this salt-wet happiness of few words
Where the moon through slatted shutters striped her arms
And flattened breasts – she lay with that just-fucked look
While I breathed the scents of salt and oleander,
Small waves answered *shush, shush* to the nightbirds
And palms rustled outside in the breeze that shook
A few leaves from the rose bush on the veranda…
'But she you thought a naiad is her mother's daughter
And one day she went home, all the way home
And left you to your sonnets and ghazals' –
For here was L----, L---- whom I knew of old,
A fellow-haunter of the bar-bars and cinemas
Of Barcelona, Paris, London and New York,
Whose bittersweet recordings should have won him gold
In every place where they'd been played, whose talk
Of books and music that he loved was like his gift,
Lavished freely on the lucky ones like me;
'And when she left you to your years of drift
She left that parasol…You fished out Pau Casals –
The CD I gave you – and listened endlessly
To his solo cello piece, *El Cant dels ocells*.
Is anything as lovely as this "song of the birds" –
The Catalan birds? A love song, full of old spells;
A melancholy that is the sadness of our time,
As Casals said, *which my country was the first to feel.*
It's true that here is a sadness beyond words

But here, too, is music's power to heal and anneal –
How often has it been remarked? And in a sour time
Like this, does it bear repeating? Or does art lie
In its lovely insistence, not that it does not die
But that we are – you are – not one of the seven
Fat white geese that gobble-squabble in the dust
In Barcelona's cathedral cloister, in our lust,
But one of its giant palms that stretch for heaven?
Then, if that heaven sounds too far away
It makes another, nearer one on earth
In which those girls who wander in the field, who stray
In white among the poppies, holding parasols,
Seem gestures of the light, the wandering, stray
Magnificence of morning; folding parasols
They grow into inhabitants of earth…
I don't recall, now, the name of the film, or
Of the guy who made it – Scandinavian, French? –
But those angels with their little parachutes
Have been with me a quarter-century and more,
Not likely as a real girl is to go away
Or give you a hard time when you roll home tight
But not, by that same token, warm at night,
Or able to startle you with her sudden dew-drench.
I got a bit grand there myself – "the wandering, stray
Magnificence", etc. – not a tone that really suits
The one small thing I've struggled hard to say,
How we are both more, and less, than what we make,
What we see or say and above all what we do:
Than this music with its otherworldly ache,
So ravishing and unappeasable and true,
Than her leaving you, than the parasol she left –
Though art must have symbols, so in Bill Pownall's view
Of rock and water and "The Sailor's Return", that cleft
In the cliff-face is and is not, her cleft; as
Bill or Bix or Benny Goodman playing jazz
Make human association seem a free
Submission to the will of others, loose
But not too loose, whose limits all agree.
Remember? *It must*… be beautiful and of no use,

Like the palm at the end of the line, the Catalunya
Line, like the notes that come from it, a tune, a
Melody that rises in all weathers
Between the buffers of platform two or three
In a station of the mind that is the one we pass through,
From the bird that flaunts its tattered feathers –
No, no great bedraggled bird, it is a tree,
A thing of shreds and patches someone planted,
Waters, cares for; alive with sparrow-song, enchanted.'

The Colour of a Dog...

20 Questions with Richard Gwyn

Richard Gwyn was born and grew up in south Wales but lived in Barcelona from 1987 to 1990, he returned to BCN during the 1990s, then again in 2002–3 when he had a sabbatical and wrote The Colour of a Dog Running Away, *a thriller set in the Gothic quarter of Barcelona. The novel was a surprise success. His second novel,* Deep Hanging Out *(2007), is published by Snowbooks. He currently lives and works in Cardiff where he teaches an M.A. in Creative Writing. Here he undergoes* Barcelona INK*'s 20 question grilling...*

Barcelona (no adjectives)...
Joder, hay que volver una vez más . . .

A reason to visit...
Probably the buzz of the city at night, and I mean the old parts, around the Barrio Gótico and Gracia, although the really dingy places I used to like are largely gone, the dark cavernous bars lined with barrels and smelling of old wood and black tobacco. I also remember parts of Fabra i Puig and Horta with fondness. Perversely, I like the smells of Barcelona, even the drains, almost as much as good seafood in Barceloneta, and I think, as a practising heterosexual, I have to mention the women of the city, for their extraordinary mix of pragmatism and carnality.

A reason to leave...
Like anywhere else, you have to get away from the person you are turning into . . .

A time to write...
Usually at night, or early morning.

A place to write...
Currently I like it in the attic right here in Cardiff where I can see the chimney of the Brains brewery and trains pulling out of Central railway station. Or the kitchen of my house in the Alberas, which is where I escape to.

A good day's work...
Walk the dog in Bute Park, write, swim, eat with my family, read a good book. For much of the year I teach at Cardiff University, where I run the MA in Creative Writing, and that can be fun, as well as hard work.

A place to read...
In a hammock, in the shade.

The first line of a book...
Current favourite is from Javier Marías: 'One should never tell anyone anything or give information or pass on stories or make people remember . . .'

A line from a poem...
Another Spanish writer, Jaime Gil de Biedma 'in a village next to the sea, to have a house and a little land and no memories at all.'

An interesting quote...
'Now what's going to happen to us without barbarians? Those people were a kind of solution' (Cavafy)

Food for thought...
Hmm. Fresh fish, just caught, with rice and lemon.

A drink to wash it down...
Well, after a long and involved relationship, I gave up drinking alcohol in 1996, so I'll stick to water.

The role of a writer...
It seems increasingly important that writers write with a measure of social or environmental conscience, even if they appear to be doing the opposite, even if they don't know they are doing it.

A good author should...
Write with integrity, even if that means ignoring the marketplace.

A sentence should be...
Understood by the time you get to the end of it.

Language makes us...
Ingenious, in ways that are not always honest.

A valuable talent...
The ability to stand apart from oneself.

An essential tool...
Memory, laced with invention.

A memorable expression in Spanish or Catalan...
The title of my first novel, *el color de gos com fuig* (the colour of a dog running away). I also like a Spanish expression that appears in the book, as a kind of riddle: *'En la boca de un caballo cabe una persona.'*

A final question...
In 'Waiting for Godot' what does Vladimir see inside Lucky's hat?

A Motherfucker

Sameer Rawal

Khurram remained stunned for one full minute, there was a sharp ringing in his ears and all his senses just stopped working. This was the first slap he had ever received in his life and the psychological shock proved to be bigger than the physical shock. The older, tough looking Pakistani boy who slapped him at the entrance of that bar in a busy street in Raval snatched the 30-odd roses he had in his hands during this minute, threw them on the street and trampled on them. He kept on saying something which Khurram could not comprehend and when he was going away a single word reached Khurram's ears: *Motherfucker*.

Khurram had one hand on his red cheek, his eyes were downcast and full of tears but not one single tear rolled down. All of a sudden he started walking in the opposite direction to the one he actually wanted but with a determination which surprised the few spectators who had seen him being slapped.

He remembered the day, six months back, when his father telephoned home at Bannu village in Jhelum district, Pakistan. He sounded very happy and told Khurram to pack his bags immediately as his official papers to come to Barcelona had been approved. Khurram had no knowledge that his father was planning for his immigration to Barcelona. He was a 14 year old who was quite happy with his life. His caring mother, two young sisters and one kid brother, his school, friends, the refreshing air of the village, frequent swims in the canal in summers, fairs and circus shows in winters: that was his universe. He had heard that his father was working very hard to maintain their family, that things were not so easy in Barcelona, that nobody spoke their language there. He never wanted to leave Bannu.

Nevertheless he found himself in Barcelona a week after that telephone call. Everybody was happy for him at the village, he didn't know why. He told his mother that he didn't want to go but she said not to worry. She comforted him by saying that soon all of them would be living together in Barcelona under one roof. He was petrified that his mother wanted him to go. He could not imagine living without her. His father had left Pakistan when Khurram was five years old. He didn't come back for the next four years. And after that he came once every two years for brief stints. He brought gifts for him. He talked nicely to him. But Khurram did not know him; he respected him as everyone else did, he did what his mother would ask him to do for his father but he had never had even one single conversation alone with him. Khurram felt as if his father was addressing another person when he spoke to him, to someone he didn't know and who made him afraid.

His father was waiting for him at Barcelona airport along with a couple of his friends. Khurram was impressed by the first air flight of his life. He had studied English at school but had never spoken it and the flight gave him the opportunity to practise a bit. Once inside the plane he had forgotten the sadness he felt when leaving the village to go to Islamabad airport. The thought of the possibility of never returning to the village had provoked tears in him. His school companions had terrorised him with this idea the last day he went to classes. He was leaving everything behind and throughout the journey from Bannu to Islamabad in the taxi he kept on looking outside the rear window, as if to memorise everything he was seeing.

His father gave him a strong hug and introduced him to Nasser and Abdul. He took his baggage and led him to the parking lot where Abdul had his car. Khurram was not listening to anything he was saying. He was staring unashamedly at everything around him. People were making strange noises, the girls were so fair! And ruddy too! And there was so much light and brightness around, so much happening in that small space... Khurram was overwhelmed. He was shy with his father and responded to his questions in monosyllables. Abdul and Nasser seemed the same age as his father and in the car they kept on talking about their own matters, leaving Khurram to observe this new world.

He was taken to a flat in the Raval area. The flat was empty but for a couple of men. In all the three rooms, including the drawing room, Khurram saw mattresses lying on the floor. His father told him that around fifteen people lived in that flat and had different work times. He took Khurram to his mattress, showed him the place where he could keep his things, the bathroom, the kitchen and then hurriedly left the flat with Abdul and Nasser telling Khurram to rest. Khurram did not get any sleep because every half hour or so someone entered the flat and made noises, either in the kitchen, bathroom or in the room where he was sleeping. Khurram was not used to sleeping like this.

Next morning his father took him to Sheikh's office. The flat where they lived belonged to Sheikh. Some of the people who lived with them worked in Sheikh's various businesses: groceries, cyber-cafes, take-aways... although Khurram's father worked as a construction worker in another company. Khurram's father asked Sheikh to give work to Khurram in one of his shops. Sheikh needed a helper in his godown to load and unload goods. Conditions were decided between Khurram's father and Sheikh and he started work the very next day.

That night Khurram had a lot of questions for his father: he wanted to continue his studies, he wanted to know what his pay would be, he wanted to know how many hours he would be working each day, he wanted to call his mother and siblings and talk to them, he wanted to know what language was spoken in the city and he wanted to learn it, he wanted to see the city, he wanted to ask when they would have their own house and he wanted to know when their family would come to Barcelona. But he could not ask even one single question: his father celebrated his new job that night. He drank whisky and rum and vodka with Abdul, Nasser and all the others present in the flat and after one hour of hard drinking all of them left the flat leaving Khurram on his own.

The conditions of work soon became very clear. During the next six months he worked from nine in the morning until nine at night with a half hour break for lunch, and toiled all seven days a week, except for Sunday evening, for an undisclosed sum of money which was given directly to his father. On Sunday evenings it was obligatory to go to the mosque and pray. He also assisted his father in the cooking and cleaning duties assigned to him in the flat.

He had talked to his mother and siblings only once during the last six months, and that too with haste because his father was urging him to end the call rapidly. Naturally he could not tell them in such a short time how he really was or ask how they were. And during this period he really smiled only once, when the Spanish girl who drove her truck to the godown to unload goods talked to him for the first time and he saw the braces on her teeth: he found them funny. The girl also smiled back.

His father didn't spend all the nights at home. But he would always tell him in advance. He would tell him that he had some pending work or some special meeting and could not come. He would call him and say. Or he would tell him the previous morning when they left for work.

Three days before he hadn't come back home, and hadn't informed him beforehand. Khurram asked Nasser if he knew something about it. Nasser called his father's mobile telephone but nobody picked up the phone. He suggested waiting some more time. They waited one more night and he didn't come. The following day, when Khurram was not at home, the Police called to say that they had his father in the jail. Nobody understood why because nobody in the flat spoke Spanish. When Khurram came back from work he heard the news and went with Nasser to the Police Station.

They let them meet him, but he was in a very bad shape and still drunk. He could not properly explain what happened to him. Nasser called up a friend who knew a bit of Spanish and with his help they came to know that his father was locked up because a prostitute had claimed that he used her services without paying the due fee. His father was still incoherent. Maybe he was also roughed up in the jail.

The Police said that they could bail him with 350 Euros. But Khurram did not have any money with him except the ten Euros he had saved from his pocket money. He asked Nasser, Abdul and others at the flat but nobody was in a position to help. The next day Khurram went to Sheikh and asked for his help. Sheikh did not seem surprised; it seemed this was not the first time Khurram's father was in trouble like this. Sheikh told him that his father had already taken a lot of money from him as a loan and he could not take any more risk. Khurram had, Sheikh said, only two options.

Khurram was almost running now. Sheikh's voice was reverberating in his ears: 'Selling roses gives you some quick money but since you are new, it might be a problem if any old rose-vendor sees you in his territory, you could be bashed up. Selling cocaine will give you the money you need and even more in a single night's work... but the risk is higher... you have to be smart enough not to fall in the Police trap... but I recommend it in your condition... you should save your father... your family...'

The Word Hunter

An interview with Najat El Hachmi

Since arriving from Morocco in 1987, Najat El Hachmi has not only made Catalonia her home but has also taken the literary establishment by storm, winning the Ramon Llull prize in 2007 for her first novel The Last Patriarch. *With her new novel,* La caçadora de cossos (The Body Hunter), *riding high in the best-sellers list, she talks to* The INK...

What do you remember about your move to Catalunya?

That's a long time ago, but strangely it's still a vivid memory full of meaning that is still a point of inflection in our lives. I should add that it's a question I have been asked so many times that I am unsure as to whether the question itself has affected the memory, mythicizing it and transforming it into some kind of legend. But anyway, if I had to say something I would say I remember the sensory impact: the smells, the colours, the difference in the light, the fog on the plains.

You've written an autobiographical book *Jo També Sóc Catalana* (*I'm Catalan too*, Columna, 2004). When did you first start to feel Catalan? Was there a particular moment or event, or was it a gradual process?

There is no specific moment when you build your own identity, it's a process and I don't exactly remember when I began to feel Catalan. I can tell you about moments that made the process easier: when a teacher at primary school asked which language we were speaking, for example. What I do remember was the moment when I wasn't embarrassed to say it and I decided to announce it publicly with the publication of the aforementioned book. But I was only stating the reality. It wasn't a patriotic statement.

To what extent do you think immigrants should integrate in the places they move to?

More than integrating, I think that what happens is a process of adaptation to your new place which is inevitable. When you arrive somewhere new you can't change the rules of the game for the simple reason that you still don't know them. In the long term I think what should happen is that there is a process of integration, of learning and of mutual recognition. It's absurd to talk about this being a uni-directional process: Catalan society can't continue being the same after the arrival of a million immigrants. It has to think about an inclusive project.

How, if at all, have things changed for immigrants here since you wrote the book?

A lot, especially because of the rise in bad press for the whole immigration issue, more so for Muslims or all those considered to be Muslims. The political use of the presence of Muslims in Catalonia and their progressive stigmatization means that coexistence is more difficult. I should add that more and more, the children of this wave of immigration or their parents are reaching parts of Catalan society previously considered impossible. In the last few years I have met youngsters who have gone to university and who are, at the same time, helping to neutralize the bad image of this group. But it's not at all easy because while they are struggling to know their place and negotiating with their families of origin these changes, the media only talks about terrorism and burkas.

Do you feel categorised as a 'Muslim writer'? In some way obliged to write about themes to do with immigration, religion…

No, no, I don't think so. In fact I'm not even a believer but I've grown up surrounded by the incongruence of different religions and on a literary level it makes for a lot of interesting material. Not as a fundamental element but yet another part of the personality of the characters. Not always, obviously and I don't feel obliged to talk about immigration or religion, it's simply something I have at hand and is very interesting creatively.

I've heard you described as a 'cultural mediator' – what does that involve?

Well, it was a job I started when I left the factory where I worked and it's a role that exists in many local authorities but nobody knows what it means. In my case, in Vic, the job involved receiving families new to the city who had children of a school age and in that way I could help their incorporation into the school system. This eased the process as much as for the family as for the school. In some places 'mediator' just means translator. But it's a precarious job with more risks than are at first apparent, such as when the local council converts you into a kind of interlocutor for the community and 'your people' think you have more power than you do in reality. The other problem for mediators is that, often, there is no specific training available for their job.

Moving to your prize-winning book *L'últim patriarca (The Last Patriarch*, Planeta 2008), does every interviewer ask whether it's an autobiographical account? Do you ever regret writing something that many people assume is all about you?

Yes, in fact in every interview, presentation or chat show the same question comes up and I always say the same thing: everything you write is in some way autobiographical but that doesn't mean literally. I'm not worried at all whether parts of my biography are visible in my novels because I don't think my life is particularly relevant. In fact, I think there are so many similar stories to mine that I feel I'm dealing with more of a collective story than an individual one. I write from where I am but I'm also conscious that I digest a lot of influences that come from other places.

Was it a difficult book to write? If so, in what ways?

No, it was fun. Very intense. Obviously there are parts that hurt so much to write that I had to leave the room, but it was a cathartic process.

Your latest book *La caçadora de cossos* is a quite a change...

Yes. The story narrates the sexual experiences of the main character which allows her to put some kind of order into the interior chaos...and in literature, sex gives you a lot to work with because you are dealing with the most intimate aspects of the human experience.

D. Sam Abrams

Emporio Armani White Fragrance

She was too good for this life – Philip Larkin

There she was in all her urban splendour
mechanically transferred to artificial canvas
lashed to the scaffolding and stretched tight
to conceal the remodelling under way in the back,
looming larger than life, six feet off the ground,
four storeys high and two buildings wide,
as she cocks her lovely head to one side
and sensually nestles into the hollow
of her man's broad back, inching her slender
fingers around his waist to draw him close
behind her so they fit into each like matching
pieces that can do nothing but belong together,
symbols of a perfect life that lies just beyond
this ad for two new fragrances, for her, for him,
until some fed-up wiseass shinnied up a pole
one night, after hours, and brutally carved
a gaping cunt hole in her panties, right between
her long tan legs, with a lonely file of prickly
hairs up and down both the imaginary lips.

Now, debased, she has nothing to fear from us.

Everybody Lies

David C. Hall

The door shut behind him with a gentle, pneumatic click. Facing him, half the wall consisted of a great picture window, floor to ceiling, with a view of a couple of undistinguished looking buildings on the other side of the street, a glimpse of the port between them, with the yachts lined up, one after another, at their mooring. The rest of the wall was a soft dove grey, with a sort of sculpture in the centre, gleaming aluminium tubes stretching horizontally across what looked like a section of twisted, chain-link fencing. Domènech had hardly noticed any of that walking through before, concentrating on what he was up against, trying to keep under control. For all the good it did him.

'Pretty rough in there?' the man behind the table smiled, closing the laptop in front of him. He wore what looked like an expensive suit, though Domènech knew nothing about suits, and had a wide smile, broad shoulders, and the face of a good-natured crook.

'It was,' he admitted.

The room he had just come out of, on the other hand, was narrow, windowless and dimly lit, with bare walls and a single swivel chair facing the table with the computer on it. There was a woman's voice on the computer, bland, flat and indifferent. The questions were routine, innocuous enough at first, and then they weren't.

'You're lying, Mr. Domènech.'

Not angry. She was just a recording after all. She wasn't even there, so what did she have to be angry about?

The man in the nice suit stuck out a big hand for him to shake and gave him his name, but Domènech had already forgotten it by the time he sat down.

'So… you're still with the police at the moment?'

'Officially, yes,' Domènech replied. 'There are still a few details to be worked out. The union's taking care of that.'

'The union.' The other man smirked. 'We haven't got a union here by the way. People who work for us tend to prefer to make the grade on merit.'

He glanced down at the open folder before him

'I see you were – are – an inspector. You would have had to take a civil service exam for that. You must have had to work hard to pass that.'

'It wasn't easy.'

'So tell me, Mr. Domènech, why do you want to leave the police?'

'My wife – my wife and I – want to have a baby. So, it's the money, actually. It's the money.'

'I see.'

You're lying, Mr. Domènech.

'Or maybe I'm just not cut out to be a policeman.'

The man in the nice suit leaned back in his chair and smiled again, fingering the heavy looking band on his watch.

'Everybody lies, Mr. Domènech.'

'Excuse me?'

'Don't worry about what happened in there.'

He let that hang in the air for a moment and then shrugged.

'I mean, nobody but an idiot – or an innocent – would answer all those questions honestly, would he? But then perhaps you realized that yourself.'

'I…' Domènech hesitated. 'The idea did occur to me.'

You're lying, Mr. Domènech.

'So maybe you guessed how it works?'

'No,' Domènech shook his head, 'I'm afraid not,'

'It's the mouse,' the man in the suit said with a sudden enthusiasm. 'You've got your hand on it all the time you're answering the questions, and there's a built-in sensor that monitors your pulse. Acts as a sort of primitive lie detector. It's not terribly precise, but then… that doesn't really matter, does it?'

'Doesn't it?' Domènech said.

'Everybody lies, Mr. Domènech, as I believe I said before. Everybody's got something to hide.'

'What's the point then?'

'The point? The point, I suppose, Mr. Domènech,' the man in the nice suit said gently, 'is that we know who you are, and we want you to understand that. So we can dispense with all the usual hide-and-seek.'

'I see.'

'Do you? Good. Would you like some coffee, Mr. Domènech? Or perhaps a drink. I'll bet you could use a drink, after that.'

'No, coffee's fine.'

'Black?'

'Please.'

The man in the suit pressed a button on the intercom on the table.

'Bring him a coffee please. Black,' he said, and then turned to Domènech, 'Water? You must be thirsty.'

'A glass of water would be nice, yes.'

'And some water,' he said into the intercom and lifted his finger off the button. 'Did you know, Mr. Domènech, the so-called tortures the Americans used in Guantanamo and Afghanistan and Iraq… Do you know where those methods came from originally?'

'No, I don't believe so.'

'Well, it turns out they were designed by US army psychologists in a program called SERE – that's Survival, Evasion, Resistance and Escape – to train their own soldiers to be able to endure captivity by a terrorist enemy. Now that's interesting, don't you think?'

'I don't know if I follow you.'

A woman came through the door carrying a tray with a cup of espresso on it, a glass and a small plastic bottle of still water. Nothing for the man in the suit. She was blonde, her straight hair pulled back behind her ears, and wore a black suit with a tight skirt that fell to just above the knee. She leaned over to put the cup of coffee and the water glass on the table in front of him, and as she did so Domènech observed that the top buttons of her white blouse were open, revealing a glimpse of a lacy white bra. She straightened up, twisted the top off the water bottle and poured half of it into his glass.

'Thank you, Sílvia,' the man in the suit said.

'Not at all.'

Her heels clicked sharply on the bare floor as she walked out. Domènech watched her go, his eyes on her hips for an instant, until he realized what he was doing.

'So tell me, Mr. Domènech, why are you really leaving the police?'

Domènech shrugged. 'I suppose you could say I stirred up something that had better been left alone.'

'Tell me about it.'

Domènech lifted the coffee cup and took a sip. It was good, it was very good coffee. Just the smell alone was marvellous.

'I don't know,' he said. 'I don't know if I can.'

'Do you know what a consultant is, Mr. Domènech?'

'Yes, of course.'

'Of course. Politicians, generals, people like that, retire and become consultants for this or that firm. Now what do they have to offer, aside of course from the wisdom and experience they've acquired over the years? Well, for one thing, they know a lot of other politicians and generals and such who just might want a chance to become consultants themselves when their time for retirement comes around. And fair enough, don't you think? A man's worked hard, given years of his life in the service of his country. He deserves a bit of comfort in his old age, a little something to pass on to his grandchildren. Now, as you might imagine, Mr. Domènech, we have some consultants like that of our own. Not to mention some of the people on our Board of Directors. Do you see what I mean?'

'I suppose so.'

You're lying, Mr. Domènech.

'So why are you leaving the police?'

'From what you've just said, I get the impression you already know.'

'But I'd like to hear it from you just the same' the man in the suit said, smiling reassuringly. 'This is an interview after all.'

Domènech took off his glasses, wiped the lenses with a tissue. He drank the rest of his coffee, put the cup down on the saucer.

'My wife is the sort of person who gives money to homeless when they're camped out on a street corner somewhere, even when they're not asking for it. Sometimes she even gets into conversation with them, takes an interest…'

'And you don't particularly like her doing that,' the man in the suit suggested.

'Not really, no,' Domènech admitted. 'Well, my wife had a friend, an acquaintance really, an elderly lady who had run the sweet shop on the corner when my wife was a girl. This lady was living in a low-rent flat, she'd been living there for years, and the agent managing the building wanted to get her out. He was harassing her, in fact. So my wife went to the municipal police, then city hall...'

'Your wife's a lawyer or something?'

'No. She just… she gets irate about things.'

'I see.'

'So in the end, she asked me to see what I could do. She said the old lady had told her that the whole building was filling up with immigrants, ten, fifteen guys to an apartment, they played loud music late at night, that sort of thing. I told her I didn't think there was much I could do about that, but…. Well, she said I could go along and talk to them, show them the badge. Give them a scare, was what she really meant to say.

'So I did. It was one of those old buildings in the Gothic Quarter. The guy who comes to the door doesn't speak Spanish, let alone Catalan. Eventually another guy comes along who speaks English, sort of. So we could understand each other, more or less.'

'So you have a good command of English, do you?'

'Reasonable.' Domènech shrugged.

'That's good,' the man in the suit said.

'It's on the form.'

'Of course. Go on.'

'There's six or seven of them, all men, sitting around on mattresses, a couple of cushions, drinking Fanta and smoking Marlboro – they all smoke Marlboro for some reason – and there's this smell, like the smell you get in an Indian restaurant, you know, must be some spice they use. They're scared. You can see it in the way their faces kind of close up, eyes go dead. Like this is no surprise, like they knew something like this was going to happen, sooner or later. Some cop was going to come along... Do you really want to hear all this?'

'I'm not in any hurry.'

'So I went home, I told my wife I'd told them to keep the music down, and she said, "Well, would you like to have seven or eight men living on mattresses in the flat next door to us?" And I said, "Well no, not particularly, but then there was that crazy woman that lived on the third floor, who had four or five of those little Yorkshire terriers that barked all the time and I didn't much like living underneath her either." So we left it at that, and I thought that was about the end of it. But it wasn't.'

Domènech leaned forward took a drink of water, then poured what was left in the little plastic bottle into his glass.

'A couple of weeks later my wife told me they'd cut off the water in the old lady's apartment. Apparently this is common practice, among other things. Property values have tripled in Ciutat Vella over the last few years. There's a lot of money to be made, and people like this old lady are just in the way.'

'Obviously.'

'My wife wanted me to go see the agent. So I did. Against my better judgement, but I did.

'The agent's pretty much what you might expect. Small-time sleaze, butter wouldn't melt in his mouth, but it's pretty obvious that the fact that I'm a cop makes him nervous. He tries to be conciliatory, says you have to consider that what this lady is paying for her flat is less than thirty per cent of the market price, and this is evidently unfair to the owners, who have to pay taxes on the property, etcetera, etcetera.

'So I say, "Fine. Turn her water on again. We'll talk about it." And that, of course, was a mistake.'

'Was it?'

'Because when my wife and her friend went to see him, he assumed that by turning the water back on he was showing good will on his part and deserved some concessions in return. He was being reasonable, and they weren't. My wife, needless to say, didn't see it that way.

'And the next thing I knew he had put in a complaint against me for harassment, abuse of authority, threatening language… I should have seen that coming. The guy's a lawyer, after all – these people almost always are. I realise that I'm in the… that this could be bad, and it occurs to me to look into just who it was that owned the building. I mean, if we're going to play rough, well… I had been working in fraud, so I didn't have any problem accessing the pertinent information, It turns out the place is the property of a real estate development company, didn't look like much of an operation, relatively small amount of registered capital. But then I looked into it a little further, and I started to get a whiff of something... If you're a cop, there's a moment, something like… clicks. You could call it instinct, I suppose. You see, the company was operating at a loss, but that hadn't stopped them making substantial financial contributions to a certain political party. I look a little further, and it turns out the company belongs, to all effects and purposes, to Trivitasa. Maybe you've heard of Trivitasa?'

'Yes. We know Trivitasa,' the man in the suit nodded.

'One of the biggest developers in Catalunya. I do a little cross-referencing and I find there are quite a few companies like this one, all making contributions to the same political party, all small-scale, short-lived and not very profitable. And they all go back, if you follow the paper trail, to Trivitasa. Now here's the crunch: the legal limit for financial contributions to political parties by any one individual or corporation is 100,000 euros per year, but if you put together all the contributions from all these different Trivitasa dummy corporations, it comes to a great deal more than that.'

The man in the suit smiled.

'So I showed my boss what I had, and he was very interested. To begin with … But… well, the rest you probably know.'

'More or less.'

'The lawyer representing this little sleazeball real estate agent I supposedly threatened turns out to be from one of the top law firms in the city, the kind of people who've been wheeling and dealing here for as long as anybody can remember. I come to work one morning and my computer doesn't have a hard drive any more. And I'm told if I don't resign I've got a lot more to lose than just my job.'

Domènech glanced up at the view out the window without really seeing it, shrugged.

'And what would you say you learned from this, Mr. Domènech?'

'That there are some toes you don't step on, I guess.'

'Something like that. After all, you have to realise, the property developers, builders – speculators if you want to call them that – these are the people who have made Barcelona the great city it is today, a world-class convention capital and tourist destination, a centre for fashion, architecture, art... Working hand in hand with the politicians, of course, who are the ones who take the credit for all those achievements. Now, what's the first rule of politics? You don't shit where you eat. That's why when Pasqual Maragall was President of the Generalitat and he said something in Parliament about three per cent, insinuating that that was what the opposition, Convergència i Unió, had collected in contributions on every public works contract they awarded when they ran the Generalitat, everybody, even the squeaky clean ex-communists in Iniciativa, knew he was nuts, and that was before it came out that he had Alzheimer's. Because there are things you don't do. You don't shit where you eat. Barcelona needs Trivitasa, or somebody just like Trivitasa – who will probably turn out to be the same people operating under another name anyway – and it doesn't matter who's in power, this year or the next. We're not talking about ideology, this is business. You see what I mean?'

Domènech nodded.

'Of course,' the big man went on, 'every now and then someone will get sloppy or a little too greedy or the political stakes will be high enough and there will be a scandal, but there's nothing wrong with a scandal every now and then. Clears the air, gives people the impression that things are really under control. Which of course they are.'

'What you're saying,' Domènech said, 'is that I should have seen it coming.'

The man in the suit shrugged his shoulders.

'Sure, but that's not always that easy. An intelligent man learns from his mistakes. If he never makes any, he'll probably never learn anything. Did you keep your notes, by the way?'

'I thought you just got through telling me that nobody's ever going to dare use any of that.'

'No, that's not exactly what I was saying,' the man in the suit corrected him. 'Look, when people say all politicians are corrupt, even when someone like Maragall comes out with his three per cent, that doesn't really mean anything. It's just a cliché, an insinuation at best. But when you have specifics, when you have names and dates and amounts and what bank the transaction went through, and who signed this document or that and where their money's coming from, and who's on the board of directors of this company and that one…

'We're Corporate Intelligence, Mr. Domènech, this is what we do. We collect, file, cross-reference, analyze, evaluate. We put the pieces together. We wait. You'd be surprised at all the things you can do if you know how to wait.'

'I see,' Domènech nodded.

'It's exciting, isn't it?'

'That's one way to put it, I suppose.'

The man in the suit leaned forward, resting his forearms on the table.

'This is what you're good at, isn't it, Domènech?'

'I thought so.'

'And you were right. You've got initiative, you've got experience, I think you know how to learn from your mistakes. We can give you the opportunity to use those skills. And make good money while you're at it. So how would you like to work with us?'

Domènech waited a moment before answering, knowing instinctively that that was the thing to do, the other watching him, leaning back in his chair, slowly turning the band on his big, expensive watch.

'Yes, I think I would,' Domènech said.

The man in the nice suit let out a long sigh, put out his big hand, and Domènech shook it.

'Good. Let's go get that drink. We can talk about salary. I don't believe you'll be disappointed.'

'Fine.'

'By the way,' the man in the suit said as they walked out to the lift, 'what ever happened to the old lady?'

'She died. Stroke apparently.'

'Oh. I'm sorry to hear that.'

At home and out of place...

An interview with Matthew Tree

Following the publication of his controversially titled work Negre de Merda, *Anglo-Catalan writer Matthew Tree talks to* Barcelona INK *about racism, finding fame in a foreign country and Catalan literature...*

You're very 'mediatic' – how much of this do you think is because you are a bit like a novelty act as the token intelligent 'guiri' and how much because you have been accepted as part of the Catalan literary establishment?

When my first novel, *Fora de lloc (Out of Place)*, came out in 1996, it had a distributor so bad he couldn't even get the thing into the bookshops in his own neighbourhood. Then, I'd been writing for 15 years so getting this book out was, to say the least, a big deal. I took it, personally, to all the radios, to TV3, to whoever I thought could help to promote it. Anything to get people ordering it and so guaranteeing wider distribution. Obviously, there was a novelty element: the first novel written in Catalan by an English speaker etc. and I'm pretty sure that was what got me the first radio and TV interviews. From that moment on, by the by, I continued to get sporadic radio work, as radio stations are always looking for new voices (they have to fill up those 24 hours somehow).

However, my second book, a collection of stories, had a much tougher time getting published. It was as if people were thinking 'OK, you're a guiri who writes in Catalan; it was amusing the first time round but that's enough now'. Advised by friends, I entered it for a fairly prestigious literary award and was lucky enough to win (that was in 1999). After that, the guiri thing stopped being such a big deal: people started treating my books as they would any other book written in Catalan. Which makes sense: if you're going to spend, say, 15 euros on a book, you want the book to be good: the nationality of the person who wrote it is no longer a selling point.

That said, there are two extreme minority attitudes that I've come across over the years. One would be the kind of near-obsessive pro-Catalan reader who buys my books because of the 'example' I supposedly set. And the other is the ultracynical reader who thinks I'm some kind of profiteering charlatan ('Are Catalan writers so bad that we have to give prizes to foreigners?' I was asked by a journalist at the *Diari de Girona*).

I don't know about the literary establishment, if such a thing can be talked about in the small and volatile world of Catalan writing, but I certainly feel accepted by most of my fellow writers in Catalan (other 'foreigners' included).

Is being featured on *Polònia* (Catalunya's political satire TV show) the height of fame? How do you feel seeing yourself as a character in one of the country's most viewed TV programmes?

Being imitated on 'Polònia' will almost certainly be good for the books. I didn't ask the 'Polònia' scriptwriters to do it and they didn't tell me they were going to do it, but I don't mind it at all. I know several of the other 'imitatees' and most of us find the experience weird but kind of OK. It even bestows prestige, oddly enough.

Excepting poetry, sometimes the Catalan literary scene seems a little staid – do you think there is a 'cutting edge' in Catalan literature at the moment? Is there anything like the *3am magazine* in London? And who would you say might be part of this 'cutting edge'.

I don't find Catalan literature staid, I must say – it's extraordinarily varied, and so inevitably includes the odd ultraconventional writer – but you only have to look at the titles that came out before Sant Jordi's day to get an idea of how strong it is: a novel set in Sarajevo by an ex-drug addict who writes the most flowing, unputdownable prose I've come across for a while; a collection of stories written in Catalan by an award-winning Czech writer; a stunning short novel (in Catalan) by an Argentinian-born author; a 500-page novel which reads like a kind of fabulous, international modern Catalan *Tristam Shandy;* a take on Raymond Queneau by a French-Catalan writer; a Valencian author's collection of one page long, linked-up stories...

Cutting edge? It's not a phrase I like that much when applied to writing, as it seems to me to imply some kind of Trotskyite-ish vanguard. But among the most interesting contemporary writers I'd include Toni Sala, Jordi Puntí, Jordi Cussà, Flavia Company, Empar Moliner, Manuel Baixauli, Najat el Hachmi, Màrius Serra and the evergreen Master, as it were: Quim Monzó.

To what extent do you think the debates about identity here in Catalunya, and the need to protect and promote the language, have an effect on its literature?

One of the reasons Catalan literature is internationally viable is that its writers of fiction dedicate themselves to writing their fiction in the same way as writers do all over the world: they have a complex, non-partisan, ambiguous view of things and are primarily interested in the quality of their work. If they want to express their political opinions, they do so in the right place: op-ed columns (as do writers everywhere). As a result, literature is almost the only aspect of Catalan language culture which functions more or less normally. It helps that the (Spanish) central government doesn't interfere with it, as it tends to do in other Catalan cultural spheres. Then again, it doesn't do a thing to promote it either.

Going back to a previous point, I regret having described the Catalan literary scene as staid. Perhaps I was just fishing for controversy – after all, we publish translations of various Catalan writers and poets in the magazine – but your comment that it is internationally viable... beyond Catalonia, Quim Monzó is little known, Rodoreda – despite recognition, is hardly a household name and the country's best-selling authors Ruiz Zafón and Eduardo Mendoza write in Spanish, if I'm not mistaken.

Well, Monzó has been translated into 22 languages, Sanchez Piñol into 31, Jesús Moncada into 27... If you go to Holland and Germany say, it is quite normal to find Catalan authors in the bookshops (and in Holland, at least, Rodoreda really is a household name). Britain translates very little (3% of the yearly total of published fiction in the UK comes from non-English language writers) and so if it notices the peninsula at all, it goes for the very obvious best-sellers. But if something isn't visible in England it doesn't mean the rest of the world has the same blind spot.

To which should be added, maybe, a certain institutional advantage in favour of Spanish authors. There are over 70 Cervantes Institutes promoting mainly Castilian-language culture around the world. For economic reasons, its Catalan equivalent, the Ramon Llull Institute, has just four centres, all of them in Europe.

On that note, can people writing in Spanish from Catalonia be included in the packet of 'Catalan literature'. Wasn't there a spat about this at the Frankfurt book fair?

Catalans who write in Spanish don't count themselves as Catalan writers and never have. The controversy over what constituted a 'Catalan writer' when the Frankfurt Book Fair invited Catalonia as its special guest in 2007, was created by part of the Spanish media and certain politicians (the Spanish language writers in Catalonia, who know each other well, discussed this among themselves and decided they wanted nothing to do with this supposed 'spat'). Mendoza, Zafón etc. are Catalans, no doubt about that, but their choice of language makes them Spanish writers, which is how they see themselves. When I write in Catalan, I'm not an English writer. When Pere Calders wrote in Catalan during his long exile in Mexico, that didn't make him a Mexican-Spanish writer.

You have just brought a book about racism out, could you tell us a bit more about it. What inspired you to get involved in such a project?

Racism, together with organised religion, has long been on my list of things that I find impossible to take for granted: completely inexplicable. It's a theme in the novel I'm writing now (in English). The Catalan book – *Negre de merda. El racisme explicat als blancs* – is an attempt to finally explain racism to myself (and others, hopefully). It took me a year and a half of intensive reading and writing. I talk about anti-black racism and antisemitism. I've included many historical examples of where racism leads, the reasons for its existence, an intellectual history of racism. There are also specific chapters on racism here in Catalonia.

You mention anti-black and anti-semitism. What about Islam? What are your feelings about the current debate raging on the left between extreme pro-islamism represented by groups like the SWP (often supporting some of the more dubious of their muslim brothers) and people like Chris Hitchens and Nick Cohen whose pro-freedom anti-islamic rhetoric often verges on racism?

Islam is a religion and therefore open to people of all phenotypes. Religion is not a racist issue, in other words. Attempts by racists to palm off their hatred of dark-skinned people on a supposed clash of cultures and faiths are disingenuous (and attempts by the Left to use weasel words like 'islamophobia' simply play into the hands of such racists). In the book, I suggest that there are two different kinds of racism: that towards people considered inferior (the archetype would be people of African origin) and people considered smart but also alien and malefic (Jews being the archetype). The current wave of racism towards North African and Middle Eastern people falls between the two: they are considered both 'inferior' and yet somehow cunning, in bad faith, and noxious for western society: blacks and Jews rolled into one.

Down in the Chino

John Short

For a long time I had a recurring dream that I was endowed with the ability to glide a few inches above the ground, using my fingers to propel myself along in the way that a legless person of previous times might have pushed their cart. But in the dream I was just suspended in space, bouncing effortlessly from one spot to the next. Being a lot younger (and also less objective) in those days, I jumped to the fanciful conclusion that the dream meant that I was gifted with a preternatural ability to move around freely on the face of the earth. Later, I decided that this was probably a bit over-optimistic and the product of wishful thinking. Nevertheless, it may at least have been an indication that I had an aptitude and inclination for travel.

I remember one day when I was about sixteen, going by bus to visit a friend who lived in the country. Stepping off the bus by a roundabout, I began to walk the half-mile or so that led away from the main road, in the direction of the small town. Suddenly I was transported in my mind, and I imagined that I was walking towards a village in central Spain. At school, in the Spanish lessons, the quirky illustrations in the old textbooks struck some chord within me and I always knew that I would go there one day. There was a kind of empathy: those indefinable stirrings that lend credibility to the idea of reincarnation.

In my flat in Barcelona I packed all of Maria's remaining things into an old sports bag – skirts, tee-shirts, knickers, spray cans, etc. In the side pocket I put some letters and the wallet she'd given me which contained her photo. I obliterated every trace of her from my life as best I could (dropping the bag on the rubbish heap at the end of the street) and told myself it was time to make a fresh start.

These are the sort of obvious things that you say to yourself at such moments, I suppose. Later that night I went out to eat a sandwich and then I had a drink in a dingy bar halfway down the Carrer Escudellers, wondering how much it would cost me to go the whole hog and move into a new apartment. It occurred to me that I could easily afford to do this now as I had over two hundred thousand pesetas in the Caixa de Barcelona: very unusual for me but I'd found a teaching job about a month before Christmas which paid well, and I'd been working hard.

My two immediate problems therefore, were not to do with money. The first was to be able to discipline myself enough to get some writing done outside of work hours and the second was what to do about sex, given that I was now on my own again. It seemed to me that sex, companionship and love were all desirable, although at that moment I would have considered myself fortunate just to have had the first, and in any case, what good are numbers two and three without it? I asked myself if there had ever been any friendship or love between Maria and I. Maybe a remote soupçon of friendship … I wasn't really sure, or perhaps she'd been too opportunistic, selfish and immature even for that? Always a sucker for drama, I'd enjoyed the fights though: the hurled abuse, the dented frying-pans, the claw-marks on my neck and arms … and then making up an hour or so later and the pleasure that followed. I'd been happy enough with things as they were until Maria got pregnant – the first time in my life I ever made such a mistake. After the abortion she wouldn't speak to me any more and the whole affair which had raged along for so many months just popped out of existence like a burst bubble.

Propelled by an ill-humoured and truculent impulse to drink, I decided that I wanted to get a bottle of Cava – maybe eat a few tapas in order to soak it up and give myself at least an outside chance of ending the night in a vertical position. In another bar on the opposite side of the street and a few metres further down towards the Ramblas, I sat with my elbows on the stainless steel counter, gazing fixedly at a tiny cockroach which was perched on a piece of potato in the Russian salad under the glass shield directly in front of me. I pressed my face right up to it; the insect didn't move but waved its antennae a little. I thought: It's like a climber, victorious upon the summit of a mountain, but as soon as it makes a move it'll go under … drowned in mayonnaise. At that moment, a woman who'd placed herself next to me asked what I was looking at.

'Me? Oh nothing,' I said.

'Not after a good time then, *cariño*?'

'Not really. I just came in to nurse my hangover …'

'Alcohol is a very dangerous drug,' she said. 'And after a point the damage becomes irreversible.'

'So you avoid it …?'

'I take a whiskey or two in the evenings but that's it…besides, I've another job to go to in the mornings so I can't afford to be sick.'

'What's that then?' I asked.

'I'm an art dealer.'

A man sitting at the bar eats *huevos con mahonesa* while commenting on the superior quality of oysters from Orense while around the corner in the Xanadu sex shop a variety of moans emanating from the private cabin section blend together to form a lurid collage of sound while the televisions in the bars show the most recent footage of charred corpses being extracted from heaps of rubble in the nightmare streets of Baghdad while two local police radio back to headquarters as they stand over a prostrate, handcuffed West African with their boots on his back while a Jamaican bum remarks in English: 'I'm only a human bean livin' in dis whirl man ...' while I drain my drink and walk out into the street, turn left and head for the Loch Ness bar on the other side of the lower Ramblas.

In the early 90s, the Loch Ness was one of the more interesting dives in downtown Barcelona: a great place to watch a continual theatre of sailors, prostitutes and idiotic tourists making fools of themselves and getting into fights with the security staff which inevitably led to their expulsion. Ten years before, the classiest women of the night used to work this patch, congregating in bars such as the Loch Ness until the patterns of things changed, as they do, and most of the business drifted away to the brothels and the more up-market 'American' clubs of the Eixample district. Even as late as the mid 80s, these pavements were thronged with hetero, homo and transsexual whores; however, by the end of the decade it had all quietened down considerably. Only the cattle markets of *Sant Ramon* and *d'en Robador* in the Barrio Chino continued undeterred as if AIDS didn't exist, and then they bulldozed half of *Sant Ramon.*

At the bar in the Loch Ness I met a girl called Sophie who said she came from Paris. She had auburn hair (not quite shoulder-length) and two gold rings in one ear. On her left hand, just above the wrist, she had a small blue star tattoo and she was wearing black stockings and a black miniskirt – there was a very thin stripe of white flesh showing between them and although this was obviously a trade tactic, it was carried off with such unaffected style as to appear natural. By an unlikely coincidence it turned out that we knew one or two of the same people up in Narbonne (France) where I'd lived on and off before coming to Barcelona, and as our conversation switched from Spanish to French, a spontaneous feeling of camaraderie seemed to spring up so that we drank and chatted freely. She told me that she'd lived in India and had learned English there – that she had a dream of going back for good one day, if that ever became possible. Some drunken English tourists sitting along the bar from us were attracting attention by insulting the old whores and spilling drinks. Sophie asked me what they were saying because she hadn't been able to catch the words. I told her it was probably better not to ask.

We moved away from the bar and sat on one of the sofas because it looked like a fight was about to break out. She asked me if I wanted to have sex, and I answered 'Yes, but how much was it going to cost?' I'd never figured out how things worked in this place: if the girls took their customers to rooms upstairs and then paid a percentage to the establishment or if the set-up was a shade less organised. I got the impression that it was, but as I said, I only came in for the theatre. 'Never mind about that,' she said. 'It's the end of the week...you can come to my place.'

We left the bar and walked out onto the Ramblas, then we made our way in a northerly direction, going inland from the sea. Suddenly, she turned to me and said that before going home she wanted to score some smack. This was just the kind of thing I'd been hoping wouldn't happen ... but I'd go through with it anyway. I was too attracted to her to back out now. A little later, on our route down one of the main streets that led into the heart of the Chino, she said that she'd had an AIDS test only a couple of weeks before which had come back negative. I felt inclined to believe her as my intuitions told me that she was honest although I wondered why she'd even mentioned it as I'd shown no visible signs of hesitation. The only thing I didn't like was the direction we were going in because it was taking us into some of the worst streets of the city: the last place I'd choose to pass through at midnight.

Finally we arrived at her squalid flat in the *Carrer d'en Robador*. It stank of cat piss and the accumulated gunge of the entire century (who could say what was holding these walls up?) but it had a television and a video. She sat me down in front of the screen and gave me a beer, plus a small line of whatever it was that she had acquired for herself. I don't know much about heroin but I'd never heard of anyone doing it this way – I snorted it up anyhow and felt absolutely nothing, then I drank some beer and watched the box. A few minutes later I went to find the toilet, and as I passed her bedroom I saw that she was sitting on the bed jacking up; the needle in her left bicep and a sheet of newspaper on the floor by her feet, splotched with blood.

'Don't look,' she said. 'I'll be finished in a minute.'

A little later she came out and reclined on the couch with me. I think that we might have kissed a bit but I can't remember all that well. We smoked Fortunas and watched a second-rate sci-fi movie with tedious special effects. These sorts of films bore me to death as I'm not much interested in speculations about the future of the planet and in any case, I had other things on my mind.

'This is moving slowly,' I said.

'On the contrary, it's moving quite fast,' she answered. We drank some more beer as her cats ran over us. The film seemed to last an eternity but eventually it finished and the time came to go to bed. Sophie had a quick wash at the kitchen sink and then turning to me said:

'Here, now you get washed.'

'It's okay. I had a shower this morning.'

'Well wash your biscuit, at least.'

When we undressed, I noticed that she had a few more tattoos in various places. From what I could see they seemed to be mainly animals. I asked her to keep the stockings on, as the sight of her wearing them was getting me going.

'So you have this fetish too?' she said.

'In my opinion, anyone who doesn't have at least a couple of fetishes is not taking sex seriously enough.'

'I read in a magazine once that 80 per cent of men are turned on by the stockings.'

'And the other 20 per cent?'

'Well, obviously the other 20 per cent just don't care.'

'Complacent bastards.'

She gave my genitalia some attention prior to climbing on top of me. I got my hands round her thighs and guided her into position, then in a short space of time the narrow bed began to rattle and creak. We fucked, then smoked, then read a French newspaper (*Le Monde*, I think.) and talked about the war in the Gulf, then we fucked again in a variety of positions and just like the film, it seemed to go on for ages except that now, of course, I was enjoying myself as well. Afterwards, as we lay in the bed, she showed me two albums of photographs. In many of the pictures I noticed that she was with a dark, good-looking man.

'That's Pierre, my husband,' she explained, 'and that was our house in Goa. He's in prison now for dealing, and won't be out for at least another year. He went in two months ago but we'd split up a long time before that.'

She looked younger and very beautiful in the photos: always made up with kohl and wearing a lot of jewellery like a Hindu girl. She was still pretty, though her features had coarsened. The photos all showed beaches and wooden huts, happy young people and elephants. It was sad to consider how the path of her life had led from those days to this miserable squalor.

'That was six years ago,' she said.

'Why don't you go back to France?'

'I prefer it here … *más tranquilo,* as they say.'

In the end I fell asleep face downwards in the bed with one arm across her stomach and still wearing the condom that she'd given me. We'd gone to sleep extremely late – about five in the morning – and as a result we slept heavily until the early afternoon and were only woken by someone ringing on the bell. Sophie jumped up, pulling on a bathrobe and said: 'Just stay there and don't move.' Then she went to open the main door. Presently I could hear a man speaking in French – the low-key tones of what seemed like a mundane conversation, but of course I had absolutely no idea what was really going on. After five minutes or so, the visitor left and she came back into the bedroom.

'You'd better go,' she said. 'He'll be back in ten minutes.'

I got out of bed and started to dress.

A moment later, when I was standing in the little kitchen, she presented me with a kitten.

'Take him, he'll be good company, put him inside your jacket.'

'I can't carry an animal just like that, all the way back to where I live. I'll come here tomorrow with a basket or something.'

'Okay then,' she smiled. 'Come about midday.'

'Thanks for a really nice night,' I said. 'And listen …'

'What?'

'Try to look after yourself.'

At the time I meant to return, but upon reflection I came to the conclusion that a cat was not an option in my third floor apartment, so never went back. Sophie had seemed a nice enough person, the little I'd known of her. She was intelligent and calm; too smart, I'd have thought, to wind up in a situation like that. I would have liked to see her again but where there is smack there's always trouble, so I decided to stay clear of it.

I walked out into the street which was now crammed with whores and punters, as it always was by that time of the afternoon, and turned left. When I reached the junction with Carrer Sant Pau, I swung right and made for a dusty old bar that stood somewhat uneasily now on the corner of the remains of Sant Ramon. I went in and ordered a coffee and a cognac before choosing a seat by the window. Curiously enough, I could've sworn that in my sleep I'd had that gliding dream again … yes, it was coming back to me now in flashes. What on earth did it really mean, and why should I have had it in a situation like this?

As I sat there sipping coffee and turning the thing over in my mind, I had the vague impression that there was more to it than I'd originally thought but I was lost for an explanation. The seas of the subconscious run deep. Life was passing very quickly and there was still much to learn. Perhaps if the dream had come back sooner, I could have asked Sophie. It struck me as possibly the kind of thing that she might have had an idea about, but then again, who knows?

Richard Gwyn

City of Marvels

That summer I lived above Saint Catherine's market,
kitchen table laden with fruit I never ate. Waking
with the taste of corpses in my mouth, an orchestra
between the ears. Down to the street for wine,
to silence the trombones, then up steep stairs cradling bottles
to my rooftop haunt, and switch the music loud again.
That summer it was suicide tunes. Reams of paper
piled on the floor, testimony to the hero writer's futile clack.
I lived alone, and there was little air about the rooftops.
It was a terrible sorcery I soaked in, quaking in the aftermath
of amorous defeat. Though I could see the blue of sea,
the sails of boats in the white-flecked bay, and smell fresh salt,
the strangulating things I treasured most were locked up
with me there at Caterina, top floor. The energies of daybreak
so enticing, the sky an intimate climax, I only lacked
a fishing net to cast from the veranda and catch the little fishes
of dawn's sleeping citizens. I would have had a merry haul
to supplement my bulging nets of nightmare.

I can recall the elegance of strange women, met in Plaza Real
or the Raval, the shouting of a market loader
who sang flamenco to the radio. I watched him weep
as once he told me of his mother's grief, were she to know
he'd been cast out and living like a dog on the streets.

As for me, I had a few weeks more before eviction.
Restless, frantic mornings. Siestas, like a felled ox, I'd lie and sweat
till darkness came. Nights in dim-lit caverns of the barrio
among the loud and playful youth (the year that E hit town)
while I slunk and staggered through their playrooms
old before my time, sniffing armpits, drugged to the lights
and colours, music and incense, wet clay of words,
catching sight of a turning face that filled my eyes
and mouth with desperation. The terrible re-surfacing
from plunges in the alligator swamps, the touch of death's tits
against my face in the icy four a.m. with no recall of who

I might have been at nine p.m. Was I the southern dwarf
outside Maria del Mar? Was I the gaunt policeman
emptying paint over the waiting hearse? Was I
the old man in a double-breasted suit calling up the stairs
Soy yo, el tuerto! – it's me, the one-eyed man?
Or was it I returning ludicrous in the hour before daybreak
speaking to an absent dog, twirling an imaginary cane,
calling on all to witness that there were angels looking over me
and everything was rosy in the palace of the soul?
Night would clear into day. The little birds would sing on the
telephone wires. Time again to find the things to feed the void,
while rotting fruit spilled from the table and rolled across the floor.

Making Dance with Fruit

Haarlson Phillipps

He was a glutton for fruit and he smoked black tobacco. He carried the aroma of gunpowder tea tinted with orange. He used soft fruit as a kind of clock; as a means of positioning his work in the flow of time.

'You can never step into the same river twice,' he told me more than once.

Depending on the season, he would set a bowl of apricots, peaches, tomatoes, cherries or berries on a stool in the studio and work on a piece for the duration of the fruits' edibility. When the fruit began to rot he would wrap and add the piece to his portfolio or, if dissatisfied with his efforts, obliterate it, replace the fruit with a fresh bowl, and start over.

They said in Madrid, 'he made shoes talk'; in Barcelona, he eschewed footwear and set about making sinews sing.

It was my job to ensure he had everything he needed to do his job.

His initial demands were fairly modest: a well-lit, air-conditioned room with a sprung floor; a cd player; a metronome; plain paper; notation paper; pencils; highlighters, and coloured gaffa tape for marking the floor. But, as work on a piece progressed, his demands became more wilful and capricious: 'I need six copies of Zaragazano's Almanac by four-thirty this afternoon.'

In the early, exploratory days of making a piece he encouraged me to sit in, be on hand should he need the air-conditioning or lighting adjusting, or sometimes help with peeling an awkward orange. But mostly he used me as a polite doorman; barring all intrusions to the space.

One morning, as I sat by the door watching his dancers begin class, he handed me a polythene sandwich-box containing all the dancers' mobile phones.

'Here,' he said.

I took the box and, without explanation, he slipped me a shopping-list, and I took myself off to Concepción market to buy his afternoon ration of fruit.

Over time his daily lists took me to places I never knew existed, and would normally never have need to visit: cavernous fabric shops; lavender scented hat shops; curiously shadowed magic shops; and a curative herb shop, stacked high with antique porcelain storage jars.

On good days, wandering dreamlike through the streets, I indulged a notion he was making a work on me; dancing me across the city. On bad days, when no-one had anything he'd demanded, I felt he'd knowingly sent me to fetch a pail of tartan paint.

He once sent me out for a pack of tarot cards.

'Classic design,' he said, taking a bite on an apple. 'Tough, well laminated.'

They were tough, but they weren't good enough.

'What use are these? I can't read them.' He split the pack and tossed the cards over his shoulder. 'Bring me a reader.'

Without a word – but noting only The Fool and The Tower lay face up – I turned on my heel, walked out onto the street, and set off in search of a tarot card reader. Not so difficult a task in Barcelona.

In much the same way as good music is defined by the rests, by the silences between notes, dance, like sculpture, succeeds when it defines, or re-defines, the space around it.

He could have, and should have, been a pioneer – he carved and positioned space as easily as breathing – but he had no interest in simple applause. He worked to create atmospheres of possibility; spaces wherein he hoped we, his audience, would make more space happen.

'It is given we all want more space in our lives. But when we have space we don't know what to do with it, except fill it with rubbish. Why are we all so frightened of space? Space offers possibility, but for many, space equals emptiness.'

During my time with him I learned that creating dance is a form of alchemy; an empty space, some time, a will to create, and at least one living body, are the basic and essential ingredients. Anything and everything else, including trained dancers and music or noise, are not essential to the making of dance.

I've experienced attempts at dance with inanimate objects, and I've experienced attempts at dance with light, with water, with fire, with coloured balloons and kites in the sky: all puppetry, not dance.

Dance is lending a living body an intended sense of loaded movement. It can be the blink of an eye, the nuanced twitch of a nostril as a dancer pulls breath during the beat after a leap or a lift. It can be subtle, ephemeral, so fleeting it would require an astrophysical device to measure its impact. And it can be brutish heavy, like a bucket of hot lead falling through the skylight of a maternity ward.

To realise a dance piece is to ride a rising escalator of hope and fear. The hope is that a moment, or, better, a series of moments, will emerge from the fug of physical, mental and emotional activity. This unplanned, emergent moment will transform murky clouds of meandering metaphorical puffery into a clean, clear blue sky of cogent, sincere expression.

The fear is of becoming trapped in a state of emotional inertia; that the body will fail to connect with, and interpret, the impulse for movement.

He worked through these intense moment-seeking periods chomping on fruit and smoking Ducados right to the nail.

'Up, up, up,' he chivvied, cupping a half-orange in one hand, a cigarette in the other. 'Inhale the space! Drink the air! Breathe proud! Stand loud!' And he pushed, pulled and bounced his dancers around, urging them to stretch, bend, rip and mend the air between them.

I knew he was having trouble finding moments because my errands became increasingly erratic; he began to send me to collect not just fruit and props but ideas as well.

'Freud's 150th birthday next year,' he announced one morning as he took his regular eleven o'clock cortado at the café-bar next door to the studio. 'I have a feeling I may want to incorporate, make physical, some of his ideas in a piece. What do you think?'

I shrugged. I knew from experience it didn't matter what I thought. I sensed an errand in the making.

'I don't have time to read.' He pulled a long drag on his cigarette. 'Bring me a ten-minute presentation for tomorrow morning, to share with our cast. Something bright, something sharp. An encapsulation of his core thesis.'

'No,' I said. I've no idea where it came from, it erupted, unbidden, like a belch.

He cast me a look; soft, quizzical, slightly pitying, as if questioning my sanity.

'No?' He focussed his eyes on mine; cigarette smoke curling a wispy veil across his features. 'Why no?'

'Freud doesn't deserve your attention.'

He dropped his gaze to the counter as if consulting his coffee. 'And who' he asked, 'is worthy, or deserving enough, of my attention?'

And I still don't know why I said it, it slipped out, unbeckoned, like a silent fart. 'Einstein.'

He nodded, stubbed his cigarette in an ashtray, raised his eyes to gaze along the mirrored shelf of spirits, pursed his lips, and nodded again.

'OK. There it is. Bring me Einstein.'

I expected him to rail, to rant, face down my temerity. Instead, I landed myself with an impossible task and another hastily scrawled shopping-list.

The following morning, as I prepared to give my presentation to his less-than-wholly attentive young dancers, he ceremoniously sliced a large melon into thick wedges and set them on a platter on a stool.

His dancers arranged themselves in a tangle on the floor at my feet; they smelled like primary school kids.

I cleared my throat and opened up a flipchart pad to reveal a hurriedly squiggled bright yellow sun, and they smiled like primary school kids.

He sat there, high on a stool behind his dancers, nodding along with my stumbling explication, chomping on nectarines.

'And so, T1 is the point from which our imaginary observer notes the movement of Earth through space.' My hands quivered as I made marks on the flipchart. 'But all points in this space are moving. And the velocity of light is the same regardless of whether the source of light is moving or still.' I felt as if skating with a bellyful of brandy.

He knew I was struggling, but I knew I had animated his interest. As I drew circles supposedly moving through space along an axis, he plotted an arrangement of fruits on the studio floor.

He placed a line of five lemons, intersecting a cluster of oranges arranged in a crescent. He scattered individual grapes, cherries and tomatoes.

Having created a three-metre-diameter circle with bright green limes, he summoned his dancers' attention.

His dancers looked relieved.

I folded the flipchart easel and retreated to a corner of the studio.

He marched them through a strenuous ten-minute warm-up before clapping them away, like birds, into a flurry of improvised movement.

His six young dancers played a spindizzy game of catch with fruit, dashing about the space, effortlessly scooping pieces of fruit from the floor and tossing them through the air.

Haroun, a lithe Moroccan, leapt into a pirouette, arms outstretched, and released two tangerines. Sílvia dived backwards through the air, caught both tangerines, hit the floor, rolled a perfect reverse somersault and tossed them back into the air. David plucked the fruit from the air, as if catching raindrops, and rolled into a clenched fisted cartwheel, releasing the fruit at the apex of his tumbling arc, allowing Montsy – palms held in front of her like a supplicant – to gather them, drop to her knees as if before an altar, and roll the fruit across the space to Núria.

This furious display of energy lasted one minute, then, in perfect unison, five of the dancers seated themselves in a line on the floor to watch Ruth juggle with four grapes. Responding to an unseen and unheard prompt, Ruth pulled her arms into her sides, stood to attention, and allowed the grapes to fall to the floor.

I scanned the space and noted that apart from the four grapes, all the fruit had been replaced in precisely the same configuration as he had set them out.

Agog, I realised I had witnessed an intuitive, athletic rendering of Brownian motion. A stunning collection of moments.

This brief, virtuouso display lifted morale, unlocking myriad possibilities; and from that point rehearsals rushed by as a blur.

After fifteen days of search and reflect, trial, test and experiment he stitched together a stand-alone four minute thirty-three second piece, what he termed a divertissement; a thirty-second duet; a muscular one-minute solo for Haroun, and a thirty-six minute piece comprised of eight sections.

When I reconciled the pre-production budget I calculated we'd gone through seventy-five kilos of fruit.

I never did find out what he did with the pips, seeds, stalks, and inedible bits.

His attitude to music surprised me. I expected him to be much more discerning and more demanding.

I considered having a composer a luxury – even though, unbelievably, cheaper than the performance rights for his first-choice recorded music.

He listened to snatches of the composer's best efforts with cold indifference, all the while eating bananas, refusing to give notes or express approval.

It amused him to watch me second-guess his thinking and persuade Roger, the composer, to not flounce off the job.

He was much more engaged with the lighting design.

'This is not cinema,' was his overriding injunction. 'Give me cool. Give me warm. Give me hot. Give me light I can feel.'

Sharings – post-dress pre-public peer assessments – are always fraught, if convivial, affairs; juggling apprehension and the joy of meeting up with old friends. There's always booze and food.

The dancers had secretly taken the initiative to lay on a spread of fruit platters, a variety of alcoholic and non-alcoholic sangrías, clëricos and fruit punches and a very able coctelero to mash mojitos, caipirinhas, caipiroskas and whisky fruit sours.

They also conspired with twenty or more of their peers to attend all garbed à la Carmen Miranda.

He got the joke. When he entered the showing space, dressed wholly in black, and saw the tables of fruit arranged like market-stalls, he smiled, and all assembled cheered and clapped.

After ten blurred, nervous minutes of gladhanding, the audience settled to their places, and I removed myself to the wings.

Audience lights to black. Go time. And Ruth stood there, visibly trembling. I nudged her gently and she uncoiled like a spring, diving into centre stage.

Not one missed cue, not a stumble, not a breath out of place.

The pieces fascinated even the most cynical eye and, like gravity, possessed an irresistible pull. I could tell by the profundity of intrigued silence between sections that his audience had become acutely, electrically, aware of their immediate individual exterior space, the proximity of the person next to them and the space between.

He had opened up possibility. All we had to do was connect.

The overall effect of experiencing his work was of being in time, wefted into its flow, passing through life; deep-seam soul mining.

The show closed to three seconds' silence followed by the most enraptured applause I've ever experienced.

After that I don't know precisely what happened. I was preoccupied with tidying things backstage, fiddling around, delaying my joining the throng, when I heard someone call above the din, 'Give him room! Give him space! Give him air!'

I ran onto the stage and looked into the makeshift auditorium to see him laid flat on his back, a cigarette still burning in his left hand, his right hand clutched around his throat.

His lips were blue.

'He was laughing,' someone said. 'Laughing, drinking, smoking. Then he took a bite of pineapple, and then he started dancing.'

A Fraction of the Whole

A snap interview with Steve Toltz

Legend has it that this Australian novelist wrote his debut novel, the Booker prize short-listed A Fraction of the Whole, *under a palm tree in Parc Ciutadella...*

Back in Barcelona...

Yes, I came here in 1992 and then came back in 1999 for about six months. Then I came back, again, in 2002. Barcelona was where I wrote most of my novel and my overriding memory is that of writing a novel in a circus-like atmosphere because at the time I was living with street performers.

Is it true that you wrote the book in Parc Ciutadella?

Yeah, well, I think writers can get stuck in habits. I started writing before laptops, so I often wrote outside, in two hour blocks. I also have a habit of writing in two hour blocks and moving: two hours in the park, two hours in a cafe, two hours on the beach.

Why keep moving?

Well, if you are in a cafe, that's as long as you can sit there on one *cortado.* Plus two hours, like I said, is as much as I can manage in one go and it's good to wander off and see something different, Barcelona is good for that, lots of terraces and parks.

So is it a good city for writers?

It's a great city because you can walk everywhere. I actually ended up walking more in this city than I have in any other city.

And you spent five years on that first novel?

Yes.

Surprising because the novel seems very fluid – almost a stream of consciousness.

That's very gratifying because I don't write in a fluid way at all. It's a painstaking method of writing I have developed – there is hardly a page of that book that was written from beginning to end. I work in blocks of paragraphs because that is as much as I can deal with, then I put the paragraphs together.

With regards to Australia, the books are very damning and sarcastic. How did they take it?

They took it with good humour. They are great at laughing at themselves. When I was writing it I didn't even want to think about publishing it because I had threaded the book with insults to my fellow countrymen. But they took it on the chin.

You have mentioned that you try to write with humour about the human condition. Who have been your influences in this aspect?

I guess, Thomas Bernhardt whose books I love. But until I wrote the first novel I had not read any of my peers. I guess I felt I was playing catch up so I read classics. I figure that if something has been around since the 19th century and is still in print then that's a guarantee. If you are reading contemporary fiction you take more of a chance. But going back to your question, I very much like the Spanish language writers Robert Bolano, Javier Marías and Enrique Vila Matas.

Finally, I wonder if on your latest visit to Barcelona you picked up on the 15M movement that has sprung up on those streets you spent so much time walking around?

Well, not really. I have seen the images from Madrid and Barcelona but I can't help being Australian, and being amused. This would never happen in Australia. You just couldn't get them camping on the street without a barbecue.

Farce

Màrius Serra

In 2004, Barcelona organized a much derided event 'The Forum of Cultures'. At the time described as a kind of cultural Olympics, the event gave rise to much criticism and humour. Here Catalan writer and broadcaster Màrius Serra provides a satirical take on the time...

At the end of the Diagonal, a group of illegal immigrants has launched a full-scale assault on the Barça Museum. This blitz of an attack leaves thousands of tourists bereft of the opportunity to see the treasures of the most-visited museum in this multi-cultural, internationally supportive and ecologically balanced city.

Fed up with being evicted from just about everywhere, the Cathedral included, a by now radical group that forms part of the vast collective of illegal immigrants has decided to attack the most powerful symbol in the country. Having ruled out the Catalan Government, the City Council and the Episcopal Palace, a Ronaldinho strip worn by one of the kids running around during the assembly showed them the way forward. With the efficiency of a battalion of Dutch sappers, the immigrants are slipping into the museum in small groups. At the agreed time, just five minutes before the place is due to close, they unfold their slogan-laden paraphernalia and set up their base camp inside the sanctuary of Barcelona Football Club.

The president of Barça refuses to give the green light to an intervention by the security forces, as proposed by the Catalan Government, and sends two of his men to parley with the immigrants. The meeting lasts two days and two nights. Long enough to ensure that, even though the negotiations are taking place in Barcelona Football Club, famed for its drawn-out deal-making, those observing the situation begin to show concern. When rumours start to circulate that the meeting has turned into a kidnapping, the two Barça negotiators appear with two-day beards and a long preamble to an agreement which contains more clauses than a star player's contract.

A group of Japanese, who have invested six hours of their precious time at the door of the museum, provide a guard of honour to the thirty-six members of the multicoloured, ID-bereft collective, who leave the Barça Museum peacefully. The Barça negotiators have decided on a completely unexpected solution to the crisis.

'One of the club's coaches will pick them up today, with all the honour due a Premier League team, and will take them straight to the esplanade of the Forum,' the club's spokesman keeps on repeating, occasionally in Spanish, occasionally in Catalan, 'where they will be welcomed by a delegation of intellectuals and legal experts carefully selected from the Forum Dialogue on Multiculturalism And Coexistence In the Neoliberal World of Convenience, that is currently taking place.'

The Barça spokesperson is a smart, refined and somewhat thin man, whose clothes fit him perfectly. As he repeats his press statements, he cannot help but be aware of his two-day beard, which gives a dramatic touch to his appearance when he is seen on TV. It is obvious that he doesn't usually go about badly shaven.

At the other end of the Diagonal, a crowd of hacks are unable to comprehend that the Forum, normally so strict about who it allows in, is going to play host to a group of citizens who have no residence permits at all.

'Couldn't there be trouble when the police ask for ID at the gates?'

'The Forum feels it should be directly involved in all conflicts which imply differences between two parties,' the Forum spokesperson responds, not in the least worried by the implications inherent in this reply.

This spokesperson has long hair, and a beard that he's been growing for months; he has been squeezed into an Armani suit he clearly isn't used to wearing.

A wasp's nest of reporters and TV crews are waiting for the Premier League team's bus in the Forum plaza. None of the thirty-six illegal immigrants on that bus has ever set foot within this modern enclosure. Most don't even know it exists. The cameras waiting for them, as if they were star football players, frighten them, but the reception committee frightens them even more. This consists of two Catalan policemen in full gala uniform, whose only function is to offer as formal a reception as possible. That *really* scares them. Ever since they set foot in Europe, people in uniform have meant nothing but bad news.

'Allow me to welcome you to the Universal Forum of Cultures,' says a bearded representative of the management, 'in the name of the minister-delegate, who asks you to forgive his absence but who has promised to squeeze you into his timetable in order to attend to you as you deserve.'

The immigrants look nonplussed but obey their host's indications and go through the VIP entrance without being subjected to any visible form of control; they then get onto the mini-train which will take them around the premises.

In one of the rooms at the nearby Convention Centre, Hausson the Magician and the Great Morelli are debating tradition and modernity in the world of magic. Hausson used to work closely with the poet Joan Brossa and then went on to do conjuring shows in which poetry played a central role. The Great Morelli is quite well-known thanks to his important collection of objects that once belonged to the first great conjurer in history, the Frenchman Robert-Houdin, on whom he has become an expert.

Both have contributed important exhibits to the exhibition on illusionism which has just been opened, coinciding with the start of the Dialogue.

Hausson has loaned several visual poems inspired by magic, dedicated to him by Joan Brossa; the Great Morelli has provided three of the original devices Robert-Houdin used for his tricks, among which is the famous Protean cupboard.

Hausson admits that conjurers today have a low social profile, but believes that this has always been the case.

'Our profession has never been held in any great social esteem,' he declares.

'I must agree to differ,' the Great Morelli breaks in, 'because my much-admired Robert-Houdin ended up travelling around colonial Algeria paid by the French government to use his tricks to discredit the superstitions held by the Republic's North African subjects.'

He has a considerable knowledge of the life and work of the founder of modern conjuring. Indeed, he has translated Houdin's memoirs into Catalan.

'His task was highly specific,' he explains. 'It was to attempt to demonstrate, through the scientific practice of sleight of hand, the superiority of the rational Republic over ancestral local beliefs.'

Before an audience of mainly practising magicians who are disappointed by the absence of David Copperfield, the Great Morelli goes into the details of the journey which the French government underwrote for the father of modern magic.

'Any art which wishes to have a certain transcendence, must have social influence,' agrees Hausson, who is having trouble getting in his pennyworth, given the torrential flow of the other's conversation.

When it comes to the Q&A session, a member of the public who claims not to be a magician praises Hausson's work with Joan Brossa; then a magician who calls himself Jordiet (little George) tells a racy anecdote involving Sofia Loren and the classic bra trick. A third commentary from the audience is more critical.

'All this business about social influence is all very well,' says a woman half-hidden under a chador, speaking in Catalan with a French accent, 'but where would you now find a magician who would do what Robert-Houdin did, or they say he did, in colonial Africa?'

Silence.

'Or, to put it another way, how can a magician today intervene decisively in the social sphere?'

The two speakers look at each other, each inviting the other to respond. There is some doubt as to whether the woman's question has religious implications. Finally, the Great Morelli makes the first move.

'The fact is that magic today has lost its way,' he begins. 'It's as if the special effects of the digital era had hidden it away in a history museum.'

He feels comfortable with this line of reasoning.

'We live immersed in a virtual world, used to all kinds of technological gimmickry which make us distrust our own senses, to the extent that today, perhaps, the French government would send Robert-Houdin to combat the influence of television or the internet, instead of Algerian shamans.'

The woman smiles. She appears to be untouched by the tension normally provoked by religious debates.

'That is why I am convinced that the only way to recover magic from the depths to which it has sunk in these difficult, Harry Potter times, is to ensure it has content.'

'But how?'

The Dialogue audience, consisting mainly of fellow conjurers, echoes the Muslim woman's question to a man. The voices of all the more or less frustrated magicians in the country converge to voice those two words: *but* and *how*.

'But how?'

'Well...'

The Great Morelli looks down and hesitates for a moment, as if thinking things over on the spot, then places his hands on his head, histrionically, and exclaims:

'I've got it!'

He stands up with the solemnity he uses for his performances. He isn't wearing a top hat and isn't exactly dressed up to the nines, as he is on stage, but his whole bearing is of the type reserved for important occasions.

'Are you aware that a group of immigrants without residence permits have entered the Forum, after having barricaded themselves indoors somewhere else, by way of protest?'

Most of the audience affirms that it is indeed aware of this. The better informed people describe the affair to the others.

'Then I shall apply my skills to this group,' says the Great Morelli, at some distance from the microphone.

The general murmuring drowns out his words, but the Great Morelli is an obstinate man, so he picks the microphone from off the table and repeats himself until sure that everyone has heard what he has to say.

'I aim to put the power of conjuring at the service of these unfortunate citizens,' he declares, 'in order to demonstrate the true social force of magic in the world today.'

The intentions of the Great Morelli cause such a ruckus in the room that the round table comes to an end there and then. The moderator suggests that he will forward the proposal to the top-level organisers of the Forum and everyone gets up to discuss this new turn of events.

In the Forum mini-train, the woman moderator of the Speakers' Corner, now acting as a guide, is trying to follow her printed instructions for dealing with VIPs when her walkie-talkie starts to make screeching noises.

Hi, kkkkxxxx, this is management calling,' says a voice drenched in static, 'You've got to take the group of Sub-Saharans to the Haima stage right now, kkkkxxxx, over.'

The girl interrupts her explanation regarding waste disposal plants in mid-sentence. Without switching off the mini-train's microphone she grabs the walkie-talkie dangling between her breasts and answers.

'They aren't all Sub-Saharans. There are also North Africans, Filipinos, Latin Americans, Eastern Europeans, Asians...'

Before she can finish her list with the obligatory 'over', the static-soaked voice on the walkie-talkie hurriedly breaks in.

'Relax, kkkkxxxx, all that matters is that this group of downtrodden citizens of the world that's accompanying you appears on the Haima stage in five fucking minutes, kkkkxxxx, over and out.'

The exchange of words with the static-saturated voice has been amplified by the mini-train's PA and followed with growing interest by the journalists travelling in the other vehicles.

'Head for the Haima!', shouts the man at the head of the first of the two trains.

Both pursuing vehicles immediately change course.

When, ten minutes later, the thirty-six illegal immigrants arrive, dizzy from the journey, at the Haima stage, the hacks are already there, sitting in the front rows.

'Everybody onto the stage,' shouts a short, nervous stage manager who is walking in circles and talking incessantly into his headphone mike, 'right now!'

The girl doesn't know what to do. She feels as if everybody's yelling orders at her today.

'We haven't got all day!' the stage manager urges. 'On this stage in front of you lots of things take place every day, so we need to get this over and done within fifteen minutes flat! We've got a Forum to run here!!'

The girl, flurried, hurries the immigrants off the mini-train and they climb the steps leading to the stage, on which every day, at eight in the evening, 141 questions are asked by the audience to a well-known celebrity.

The stage manager raises his hand and utters a key word into his headset microphone. The people at the sound desk put on the Blues Brothers number which is usually used to welcome guests. At the other end of the stage a small crane slowly raises a piece of furniture covered in blankets. This is the Protean cupboard, the most valuable of all the exhibits loaned to the Forum by the Great Morelli. Its owner is already on the podium, directing operations. The stage manager, infuriated by this interruption, shouts at him.

'And just who are you?' he yells from a distance, 'What do you think you're doing on my stage?'

The Great Morelli doesn't bat an eyelid. He removes a loudspeaker and a set of lecterns that are preventing him from guiding the crane towards the dead centre of the stage, in order to place the cupboard there.

'What on earth are you doing? What are you doing?! Don't touch anything!' roars the stage manager.

When he feels the little man's breath on the nape of his neck, the Great Morelli turns round, touches the back of his ear with his right hand and produces a toy cell phone.

'Any problems, just call up management right now and they'll tell you who I am, you wretched little man!'

Then he turns to the disconcerted immigrants, who have just got onto the stage and are standing upright like a regiment of sepoys waiting for their first uniform.

'But look...' the stage manager stutters, the cell phone in his hand.

The magician doesn't even deign to look at him. He is already greeting the foreigners one by one with a slight bow of the head, shaking thirty-six hands in turn. Before the stage, the audience sits expectantly in front of what looks, so far, like a military inspection.

By the time the Great Morelli has finished his hand-shaking, the frantic stage manager has already received orders on his headgear to give Morelli free reign, the press photographers have had their fill of taking snapshots, and the people who have signed up to take part in the Dialogue Concerning The Social Transcendence of Magic in the Times of Harry Potter have had time to ensconce themselves in the empty chairs before the Haima stage, spread out amongst a crowd of Nunca Máis ecology protesters who are waiting for the writer Suso de Toro, a fellow Galician, to appear for the session of 141 questions, the first of which will no doubt allude to the delay in the start of the session itself.

'Good evening, ladies and gentlemen,' the magician says, using the microphone which needs to be at the disposal of the Galician writer in ten minutes' time, 'What you will see now is completely improvised.'

The deafening feedback from the microphone would seem to confirm this statement. The stage manager shrugs. It's their funeral. If they want to try changing the world without consulting him first, they can take the consequences.

The Great Morelli distances himself from the microphone a little, until the feedback fades.

'As those of you who have attended the Dialogue on magic in the times of Harry Potter know full well, the idea which I am about to put into practice emerged barely an hour ago in the course of a discussion with my colleague, the master magician Hausson, concerning the possibility that magic might play a significant social role in the world today.'

Another burst of whistling comes from the PA. Now it's the walkie-talkie of the guide of the illegal immigrants, that has a feedback problem. The girl goes down the steps at the side of the stage, blushing, while trying to pay attention to the static-saturated voice that had spoken to her earlier.

'Hi kkkkxxxx. The Minister-delegate will be here in three minutes, on the Haima stage, with a group of people in authority, kkkkxxxx, you have got to welcome them and find seating for them, kkkkxxxx, make sure there are at least ten seats free in the front rows, kkkkxxxx, over.'

Silence. The girl's eyes open wide.

'Err…' she tries to speak, her mouth open, but the words 'people in authority' don't make it all the way out of her throat.

'Got that? Kkkkkxxxxx, over.'

'Err…, affirmative,' she answers, her lips pressed close to the walkie-talkie.

The Great Morelli happily expands on his initial theme. He adores the pleasant tickling sensation that comes from being the centre of attention. He has never had so many cameras focussed on him, but he doesn't feel intimidated. He feels as if he's been waiting all his life for this moment.

The directors of the Forum arrive at the Haima stage with a few people in authority who are visiting the area, and the Galician writer Suso de Toro. There are plenty of free seats in the front row, but the guide, flustered, seats them wherever she can.

The magician recognises the authorities sitting down in front of him, and takes advantage of the fact to repeat his thesis on the current state of magic. He then goes on to spend a full ten minutes explaining word by word what it is he is going to do on the Haima stage. The same ten minutes which, in theory, had been granted him so that he could not upset the timetable of events over-much.

'In a few moments, an event will take place on this stage which will move the world,' he declares, 'just as this magnificent Universal Forum of Cultures is doing, this Forum which is destined to become a cultural milestone in the century we have just entered.'

In the stalls, various heads start to move in different directions. The movements of those in authority are longitudinal and those of the journalists transversal. Heads nod and shake. Vertical and horizontal movements,as if in a crossword puzzle to which only the Great Morelli has the solutions.

'Everything will take place in this nineteenth-century cupboard,' he asserts grandiosely. 'We will move from the nineteenth to the twenty-first century without passing through the twentieth, which has seen some of the worst tragedies that have ever befallen mankind.'

The magician opens the doors of the Protean cupboard. Its wheels allow him to slide it around so that the entire audience can see it, both those standing on the stage and those sitting in the auditorium. Its most remarkable feature is its simplicity. It is a cupboard with two swing doors, set on four legs with wheels, so that it can be moved easily over any smooth surface, or even spun around like a top.

'This valuable antique has magical powers,' he roars, his eyes wide open as he caresses the austere form of the cupboard, which, indeed, is so austere it wouldn't look out of place in an orphanage. 'Ladies and gentlemen, I present the Protean cupboard, an antique which, in its heyday, was the property of the great Robert-Houdin, the father of modern magic.'

Once again, he moves it over the stage, with the swing doors open so that everyone can see there isn't a corpse hidden inside.

'Proteus was an ancient sea god who had the power to transform himself into anything he wished. The creator of this cupboard named it after Proteus because it is able to transform those people who enter it.'

The interior is smooth, without so much as a single shelf. The Great Morelli passes his hands over the surfaces, looking for nothing, very slowly, and then spreads out his arms, frenetically. The audience is expectant.

'Today this cupboard will recover its transforming capacity once more in order to demonstrate the power of magic, and it will do so with one of these poor immigrants without residence permits whom the Forum management have so kindly invited in, to see if their contact with this haven of freedom might improve their difficult personal situations.'

The Great Morelli turns to the thirty-six immigrants with his hands raised, opening and closing the palms as if he were in a car, warning them that his sidelight is switched on. Then he goes back to the microphone.

'These men, as you know, have reached their limit in their attempt to integrate themselves into our prosperous society. All come from the so-called Third World and aspire to form part of the First World without passing through the Second one.'

In the stalls, the directors of the Forum give each other knowing looks. They are in full agreement with the magician's words. More than one feels as if they are on the brink of a historical moment.

'Now I will try to discover who is best predisposed as regards undergoing the Protean transformation which will allow him to be successful in our society.'

The Great Morelli pauses theatrically. The photographers mark his movements with a plethora of flashes.

'The chosen one will be subjected to the transforming energy of this old cupboard of Robert-Houdin, the properties of which I am proud to say I have adapted to the needs of contemporary life.'

He goes back to the immigrants and practices a kind of laying on of hands, which puts a few of them off. As the ceremony appears to be taking its time, the little stage manager decides to take control of the situation. An order of his given on the internal PA system activates the soundtrack of 'Mission Impossible'. Three seconds later, the magician interrupts his laying on of hands, turns to the sound cabin and with an energetic gesture demands silence. The stage manager shakes his head in desperation.

'Just who the fuck does he think he is?'

The Great Morelli goes up to the microphone, removes a pack of cards from his pocket, cuts it skilfully and shows the bottom card, first to the stalls and then to the immigrants. It's the queen of hearts. There are no women among the thirty-six immigrants without residence permits.

'The gentleman who selects the queen of hearts will enter the cupboard of Proteus.'

After shuffling the two halves of the pack with the slickness of a croupier, he announces:

'This is the Protean moment.'

He walks ceremoniously towards the men standing on the stage with the cards fanned out. He offers them upside down. Each immigrant takes one and shows it. the first to do so is a Chinese man who has the jack of clubs, then an African, two more Chinese, three men from Santo Domingo, a Pakistani, a Peruvian, a Moroccan...

'The queen of hearts!' shouts the magician, at some distance from the microphone.

The Great Morelli raises the arm of the Moroccan lad in triumph. A very young man indeed, he looks absolutely stupefied. The audience claps, the magician leads him to the centre of the stage and speaks into the mike:

'Congratulations, lad!'

The Moroccan boy looks at him, clearly not understanding a word. the magician points to the black man who came before him and urges him to join them.

'Come here, you shall be my assistant.'

The black man smiles, but doesn't appear to understand much either. When he has both of them close to the microphone, he tries to get a few words out of them. The Moroccan boy speaks very bad Castilian, but the audience manages to understand that he's from Morocco and that he hasn't been in Europe for very long. The black man seems to be a bit older and more on the ball. He also talks better. He is Senegalese. When the magician asks if he will act as an assistant, he nods, smiling.

'This citizen, marginalised by our prosperous society,' sermonises the Great Morelli, as he puts an arm around the Moroccan boy, 'will be the subject of a Protean transformation of tremendous symbolic value.'

The other people without residence permits are invited to leave the stage. The poor girl who has been acting as their guide has trouble finding a seat for all of them, with the result that some of them end up standing to one side.

Taking advantage of the confusion caused by the mass eviction from the stage, the stage manager tries to put the Blues Brothers back on again. Again, the magician demands silence with an emphatic gesture.

'Now, when I ask him to do so, our young friend shall enter the cupboard,' says the Great Morelli.

He makes a few obvious gestures to the boy, bidding him enter. At first, it seems as if the lad is reluctant to do so, but he finally goes ahead, not looking too happy about it. Spurred on by the magician, the audience claps enthusiastically. A single, brief ovation. A deafening one.

'In no time at all you will start to feel that the world can move in mysterious ways,' Morelli snaps at him before shutting the cupboard door in his face.

The black man watches all this with mistrust. The magician, with yet more overt gestures, indicates that he wishes the man to dance a waltz with the Protean cupboard. Once he has made this clear, the magician goes up to the microphone and explains it to the audience, using the four official languages of the Forum. Vals, vals, valse and waltz. The Great Morelli feels like an elder statesman.

When the cupboard doors are well and truly closed, the black man embraces the cupboard unselfconsciously. The stage manager, eager to make himself useful, adds a little detail. He puts 'The Blue Danube' on the sound system and the African tries to waltz about with the bulky cupboard in his arms, without losing his composure. Time goes by, but the music moves in one direction and the rotating man and cupboard in another, as if trying to make it clear they belong to two different realities.

After two long minutes of The Blue Danube, the Great Morelli repeats his gestured request for silence, then waits until the black man places the cupboard so that it faces the audience in the stalls; the magician then does a little act. He utters strange spells in a string of unknown languages, knocks on the door three times in a row and finally, with a flourish, opens the cupboard wide.

A general oooooooh! precedes the ovation. The Moroccan lad is no longer wearing the jeans and T-shirt he had on before. Now he looks like an up-and-coming banker. Navy blue jacket and trousers, a white shirt and a tie in the colours of Barcelona Football Club. The clothes suit him. Of course, he could easily have changed inside the cupboard, but even his hairstyle seems different, and at all events the Great Morelli doesn't give the audience time to reach any conclusions.

'Welcome to Catalonia, lad.'

The transformed Moroccan steps out of the cupboard.

'Thanks, boss,' he says.

The Great Morelli takes him by the shoulders and accompanies him slowly to the centre of the stage, under a huge spotlight. Then he removes the microphone from its stand.

'Now I'm going to ask you a few questions, OK?'

'I'm all ears!', the Moroccan says with an accent from the central Catalan canton of Osona.

'Do you know any traditional Catalan songs?'

'I don't know. Try me.'

The magician gestures to the black man to leave centre stage and place himself next to the open cupboard. Then he addresses the audience.

'This is going to be a bit like a request programme on the radio. Does anyone want to ask him for a song?'

'Do you know *Els Segadors*?' asks a journalist seated next to the authorities.

The lad closes his eyes, takes a deep breath, and begins:

'Cataluuunya triomfant, tornarà a ser rica i plena…'

The lad's passion takes everyone by surprise. Most of the audience rises to its feet to take part in this emotional version of the Catalan national anthem, sung by this immigrant without a residence permit in the Universal Forum of Cultures.

'…endarrera aquesta gent, tan ufana i tan superba…'

The authorities present cannot help themselves. Some place their hands over their hearts. Others raise four fingers in the air to symbolise the four stripes on the Catalan flag. One of the Galicians raises his fist.

'Bon cop de faaaalç, defensors de la terra!'

The entire Haima is bellowing out the song.

'Bon...cop...de...faaaalç!'

But the Great Morelli doesn't seem altogether satisfied. While the tremendous finale of the song is still echoing around the Haima, the magician cuts into the first round of applause with an unexpected demand.

'Ladies and gentlemen, we shall now take a look at the wallet of this lad who has just become a Catalan speaker. Can I have a look at it, please, lad?'

The Moroccan digs into his pockets until he finds a wallet in the inside pocket of the jacket. He seems genuinely surprised. He turns it over in his hand before stretching out his arm so the Great Morelli can describe its contents to the audience.

'Here is a driving licence and an official ID card which, to judge by the photo, belongs to this person,' the magician says with a smile, 'who, by the way, is now called Víctor and also possesses two credit cards, a Visa and a Mastercard, along with all sorts of other cards.'

He plucks membership and credit cards belonging to the Catalan Automobile Association, the Caprabo supermarket chain, Barcelona Football Club (with a life-long season ticket), the *Vanguardia* newspaper subscribers' club, the Friends of the Barcelona Zoo, as well as a bunch of calling cards which the Moroccan doesn't recall having ordered, on which there is an address he doesn't recognise.

'When you get back home tonight, you will remember everything, Víctor,' says the Great Morelli, enigmatically.

The lad looks at him, and smiles. These shining teeth are the only visible link with the timid Moroccan who went into the cupboard a moment ago. The rest of him is completely new. His hairstyle, the navy blue suit, the Barça tie, the watch, the belt, the black lace-up shoes. Everything is new, especially the words he says and the contents of his wallet. His language and his ID.

'Some might think that this is an evangelist preacher's trick,' exclaims the Great Morelli, in a self-satisfied tone, 'like those cases in which the power of suggestion has people talking in languages they have never learnt.'

The Moroccan looks at him, still smiling.

'But that isn't all,' the magician says, more self-congratulatory than ever.

'As the documents in his wallet show, our man here has made a new life for himself. When he leaves here and goes to the address shown on his ID card, he will find he has a comfortable home, a car, a job...'

There is commotion in the stalls. The journalists have started to talk to their editors-in-chief over their cell phones. Many are convinced they've struck oil.

'Headline: "Changing the World and a Name",' a staff writer whispers, "and underneath put 'those who lose their original culture, gain a new identity". No, it's not a hoax. It's for real.'

Three members of a TV crew are barred from approaching the stage by the diminutive stage manager. The photographers aim their most powerful lenses at him.

'If you please, new European citizen,' enunciates the Great Morelli with pompous solemnity, while pointing to the door of the cupboard, 'this is your path to the future.'

The new European citizen walks in determined fashion over to the cupboard. He is glowing with optimism... Before entering, he waves, as if saying goodbye to someone at the airport. The magician closes the swing doors, asks his black assistant to dance a few more steps of The Blue Danube with the cupboard before dragging it to centre stage. Then he signals to the flustered stage manager to allow the cameras up onto the stage, then places the three cameramen right in front of the cupboard, two metres away from the doors; then he starts a countdown, stretching out the numbers as if at Cape Canaveral, and when he gets to zero he opens the swing doors.

The 'ooooh' is even more widespread and louder than before, but this time comes in different stages. First it comes from the cameramen and the other people who happen to be on the stage, and then spreads like a Mexican wave through the audience. Everybody, including the authorities, rises to their feet as if a goal had just been scored. Their 'ooooh' is full of admiration, but also of disappointment, because now the cupboard is empty. The Great Morelli beckons to the cameramen to examine it at close quarters.

'All I ask is that you don't touch it, because it is an old antique that damages easily.'

The camera flashes make the scene look like the moment Barça score a goal.

'As you can see, our new European citizen has begun a new life,' the magician declares, knowing that his voice will attract the attention of all the cameras.

Indeed, in all the viewfinders, the empty cupboard is replaced by a close-up of Morelli's smiling face, lit up sporadically by bursts of flashes. He enjoys making public statements. He feels that there should be plenty of cameras at all his performances.

Some radio journalists have described this prodigious event live. The print journalists are still glued to their cell phones.

'What do you mean, we haven't got anything if the boy isn't there anymore?!' screams a blonde staff writer who is apparently on the point of tears. 'We've seen him come out of the cupboard transformed, we've recorded him speaking in Catalan and there are images available, taken at some distance, I have to admit, of his new ID cards.'

There is a general bewilderment. The directors of the Forum, who have watched the process of transformation with passionate attention, are heading for the stage with a view to asking the magician for an explanation of the Moroccan's whereabouts.

'As if it wasn't enough that three prisoners took advantage of their visit to the Forum to make their escape,' a journalist for a private radio station reports into his mike, 'we have just now been witness to the live disappearance of an illegal immigrant. If we bear in mind that the Forum has the shape of a triangle, this is beginning to look like a Bermuda Forum.'

The stage is taken over by journalists, conjurers who had earlier taken part in the Dialogue about magic and the members of Nunca Máis who are protesting because the act featuring Suso de Toro hasn't started yet. A few journalists have cornered the black immigrant who has acted as assistant to the Great Morelli, eager to get a statement from a Sub-Saharan.

'Yo no sé nada,' (I know nothing) is all the Senegalese can say, again and again.

The other thirty-four immigrants without residence permits, who have gathered at the far right end of the stage, are shouting slogans in favour of their legalisation and against the Forum, taking advantage of the huge media presence.

Some of the Forum directors try to calm them down by offering them the chance to enter into a dialogue.

'We'll sort this out Forum-style,' the minister-delegate with beard and glasses keeps on repeating, in front of a black man who looks like a basketball player. 'There's nothing like a dialogue when it comes to helping people reach an agreement.'

But the anti-Forum slogans don't let up. Those yelled by the immigrants are now overlapping with those of the Nunca Máis people, who also feel they've been tricked by the magician's show.

To the far left of the Haima stage, the same crane which brought the cupboard is now taking it away, wrapped up in the same grey blankets. When the operator raises it into the air, the photographers who were focussing on the demonstrators riddle the bottom end of the cupboard with flashes, but cannot spot any kind of trap door.

'Does anyone know where the hell the Moroccan went?' the stage manager asks on the inside line, 'Have you seen him backstage or anything?'

The back of the stage is full of long black curtains, so that if anyone had slipped behind the cupboard he might well have been able to hide himself among the curtains without being immediately seen by the audience. On the other hand, the stage-hands who work there would probably have spotted him.

'Did you see him get away?'

All the answers he gets on his headgear are negative. Not a single member of the crew which works backstage at the Haima has seen a thing.

'You ought to keep an eye out for the gear,' the sound technician warns him, 'some of it might get damaged.'

The illegal immigrants have taken over the stage. An Indian with a turban, probably a Sikh, takes hold of the main microphone, removes it from its stand, and starts to lead a chorus of protests from the rest of the group. Next to him, a heavily-built Peruvian grabs the microphone stand and starts to bang it against the floor, like an Easter palm frond, harder and harder.

'The vital thing is to know how to listen,' the minister-delegate insists, just a step away from the metal palm frond, 'because only if we listen will we then be able to...'

He is interrupted by a bump. Nobody has pushed him on purpose. He has simply bumped his back against a cameraman who is moving backwards fast to get an image of the Protean cupboard swaying against the background of a huge banner which an anti-Forum group has just unfurled. The fact that, instead of the usual Forum Out, it says Forum Arse No has excited the cameraman.

The minister-delegate keeps his balance as best he can, but his spectacles have fallen off and the Peruvian's metallic palm frond smashes them to pieces in time to the rhythm of the slogans...

There are too many people on the stage. The authorities' bodyguards are starting to get jumpy. Through their headsets, they talk about beating a retreat before a disaster happens. Some of them can't understand why the Forum management hasn't already sounded the alarm.

Without his glasses, the champion of dialogue doesn't have such a clear view of things. He steps backwards and searches for a recognisable face among the blurred images that surround him, so that he can give the order to alert security. He gets it wrong three times. First he gives the order to a sound technician who doesn't answer him, he's so scared. Then the minister-delegate goes up to one of the magicians who has taken part in the Dialogue. The third false subordinate turns out to be a sports journalist who has followed the immigrants from the Barça Museum.

'Aren't you the director of the Forum?' he asks him.

The minister-delegate hesitates. In theory, if he identifies himself that will help him to identify the person he is looking for. But he's afraid of the consequences. The last thing he wants is to appear in the newspapers with popping eyes, having lost himself on the Haima stage in the middle of the immigrants' protest.

'What director? I'm here to listen to Suso de Toro,' he answers, putting on a slight Galician accent, morally convinced that no one could accuse him of telling a lie.

When, finally, the alarm is sounded, a large number of policemen cordon off the Haima area in a matter of seconds. their first victim is a young man in rastas and a Nunca Máis T-shirt. Standing in the middle of the auditorium aisle, he tries to stop the security forces from coming through, while yelling at them. The second policeman from the front doesn't think twice. He whacks him so hard with his baton he leaves him stretched out over the plastic chairs.

'You can stuff your Nunca Máis up your arse, sonny.'

There is chaos on the stage. The immigrants have been the first to notice the presence of uniforms. They have stampeded back to the black curtains at the back of the stage and now they are struggling to get through to the backstage area, pursued by the short stage manager. The Peruvian has used his metallic frond to thwack an obese technician who was trying to block their path and now no one else dares to stand in their way. Until they reach the police cordon. There they stop in their tracks.

'Back up!' shout the cops.

When the officers manning the cordon see the immigrants turn tail, they start chasing them.

The chase ends up in an open battle on the Haima stage. The cops force their way through by hitting out with their batons. Some of the immigrants manage to flee through the stalls, but most remain trapped in the same space where, just a few moments ago, they were being offered the most dazzling of futures.

The fight coincides with one of the itinerant shows that is circulating under the canvas ceilings of the Haima. A huge musical machine made of iron in the form of a white dove called CooCooPeace moves forward on caterpillar wheels while making all sorts of percussion type sounds. A group of musicians perched on the wings of this monstrous dove provide traditional pacifist melodies.

This artefact wends slowly forward until somebody fiddles with the controls and sends it hurtling at top speed towards the Haima stage. On its devastating route CooCooPeace crushes dozens of auditorium chairs, knocks over a loudspeaker tower and crashes into one end of the Haima stage, ending up tilted forward with its beak plunged into the shattered podium. As a result of the impact, the slates supporting the stage floor come loose, shifting the floor vertically so it looks like the deck of a wrecked ship. The sudden change in angle sends cops, immigrants, magicians and everyone else who hasn't yet got off the stage sliding off, and also manages to knock over half a dozen of the poles holding up the huge canvas ceiling of the Haima. A strong breeze does the rest.

The canvas coverings of the Haima, half loosened, flap in the wind around the huge white iron dove, tilted into what is left of the stage, as if drinking from it. From an aeroplane which is beginning its landing manoeuvres over El Prat airport, this image turns out to be of startling beauty. It has the desolation of a shipwreck. A great sailing ship appears to have been attacked by an apparently harmless bird. If the passenger looking out through the plane's window had a pair of binoculars, he might just be able to see that the little black dot which appears to crown the mess of white canvas sheets is a small crane. A black crane which, watched attentively by a man also in black, is hauling away a black cupboard, austere in form and whose contents are unknown, to a safe place.

Tom Chandler

Barcelona: Dreams and Ghosts in the City

Fourmiillante cité, cité pleine de rêves (Baudelaire)

Teeming city, city full of dreams where ghosts,
In broad daylight, accost the passers-by.

Yes, the very air above your heads is filled with dreams
And drunken ghosts laughing and shouting.

Like the crowds below swarming the pavements
Spilling across the red and green of thrumming roads.

Dreams are strumming guitars on wrought-iron balconies
And mingle with the sawdust in the bar beneath.

Ghosts dance sardanas in the Plaza Real
To the echoing notes of a fatal clarinet.

Like scales played endlessly, ghosts ascend
And descend the stone steps of spiral staircases.

Dreams and ghosts, pushing and shoving
For space to cross the sills of open windows.

Teeming city, dreams sit of the jibs
Of your cranes, swinging their legs in the empty air.

Yes, dreams from the delicate jibs of cranes
That guard the spaces round your tender towers.

Gaberdined ghosts drag their shopping trollies
Filled with memories and recriminations.

Dreams discarded overflow from public bins
Ghosts rifling discard dreams, oblivious.

Ghosts picking and sorting the best boxes
For the night behind the bus station.

Dreams fringed by arc lights at the stadium
Buoyed up on the sighs of a hundred thousand.

Dreams sweat shoulder to shoulder in the metro
Swaying into the dark to a busker's accordion.

Ghosts are smoking cigars in the lifts
And tipping waiters in last year's coin.

Dreams flutter from the trees pale yellow
And lie flat on the wet pavement, dreaming.

Ghosts tread wet leaves underfoot in the evening mist
That hangs like dirty laundry from the plane trees.

Fallen leaves in Parc Güell are swept in heaps
And last year bonfires as we walk on.

Aromatic scent of dreams
Smokes past the city's open windows.

Tuesday's Gifts

James Beddington

Her hair tied back, Carla leans over the spare prep sink. This end of the kitchen is quiet. It's usually only busy at peak times. She scrubs the scentless soap up her arms. It's her ritual. It's also the best she can do, short of a shower, to get the smell off of her.

'I smell like Granny's kitchen,' she'd complained when she first started. Her mother laughed. Then Carla went back, visiting Napoli, and sat outside smoking if the women were cooking. Carla had loved the smells as a child.

Pulling on her woolly hat, she slips out of the door without saying good-bye. No point when she's back in four hours. Carla starts down the street for home and the shower that will finally get the oregano, pasata and basil out of her hair. She has thought about cutting it short, but she likes it long. Snapping the end of a cigarette off she lights the stub as she turns the corner. There is plenty of time to smoke but kitchen habits die hard.

She will take the longer way today. Little of the winter sun reaches street level in the Barri Gòtic. She pulls her hat down. She will stop in the narrow street and look up at the windows of the first floor flat. She will take the time to roll a cigarette by hand, and think about ringing the bell, maybe, if the lights are on.

Of course, she doesn't see lights or ring the bell. She looks up. Spending a moment, she wonders what went wrong then heads home to shower.

Dear Stephen,

Just a short one this week.

I hope you're well and that life is treating you better. We're all fine here. Paul's doing well at Leeds.

You remember your cousin Mary? She's finally marrying that boyfriend of hers. It's the first weekend in June. We're all going, I've accepted for you, since they sent the invitation here. You will come won't you?

I think I know why you had to get away for a bit. We'll always be here for you.

Hope to hear from you SOON.

Dad

P.S. Your mom's birthday's next Thursday. Please try and phone her. It would mean a lot.

Stephen flags the e-mail, answer later. The number flagged is now 21.

Darsh stands in the street. Wrapped in his sheepskin coat he sways one foot to the other – hands in his pockets. Another five minutes then back to the electric fire in the back of the shop. But it's important, he smiles at tourists and greets regulars as they pass. Sometimes they stop, for directions, to chat, or buy something.

At this time of day, he doesn't really need to be here except that his cousin always jams the till and invents prices normally short-changing Darsh. Still family is family. This reminds him of the thick letter from his aunt, the de-facto family matchmaker. Darsh opened it yesterday. She's found him another girl, who sounds nice, but very young. Such a gap would never have bothered him thirteen years ago when he came here. He's worked hard to get a shop, and then harder to buy a flat. He has a mortgage and prays his uncle never finds out. It has taken longer than his planned five years. His aunt keeps reminding him that he should be a father by now.

Sometimes he wonders who he is. He's not Spanish but he's not sure he's still Kashmiri either. His hair is frosted with blond tips, which hides the grey remarkably well.

Smiling and shaking the hand of a regular, he follows her into the shop, finished for now with the winter damp.

He will have to write back. Should he say yes this time? Could he leave his cousin to run the shop while he went home to marry? Could a girl from home manage life here? At least this one speaks some English, learnt from a mission school. The last girl his aunt proposed was impossible. She probably would have demanded servants. He was only being practical. He still wants a family and marriage. Perhaps not exactly the family his Aunt wants for him.

He settles behind the till, opening his coat to let the space heater work its charms. He turns to watch a girl. She often passes by, sometimes like now, looking up at the building across the street. Sometimes she buys something but not often. He compares his image of life with his aunt's new find, to a life with this girl. It's unsettling. The Swedes from down the street come in and he turns back to chat to the man while his wife collects their shopping.

'Hi amigo, how are you?'

'Good. Pretty girl,' the Swede gestures out the window.

'You think so? She's thin, that's not so healthy.' The Swede grins at him. Unsettled, Darsh continues, 'a woman who smokes needs a man who smokes.'

'Pretty,' the Swede mouths as his wife deposits the usual yogurts, and fruit. Darsh weighs the fruit.

Dearest Stephen,

I know Dad wrote earlier. Please write back to him he's awfully worried. I know you just "need some space" at the moment. I'm sure It's perfectly healthy. We're all trying to understand. I only ask don't shut us out.

Love, Mum

18th January

In the flat. Everyone's out. It's quiet, been quiet the last couple of weeks but you know that don't you? I should do the dishes, made curry last night but I'll leave them a bit. I've got a class for a new academy today. Academy is what they call private language colleges here. Sounds posh, isn't. I'll have to try not to mess this one up. I never expected to be teaching again. I know you used to love it, but for me it was always just a way to stay in Thailand, to put off England and a real job. That's all gone now isn't it. Writing a diary is supposed to help me sort out how I feel. I don't know if I should be writing it to someone who's dead. I'm still the same coward about emotions that I always was. I know you said it was ok but thank you for putting up with me.

I need a shave. I think, might go one more day, but there's that class. I'll wear the blue shirt. The collar and cuffs are getting a bit tatty, but it's ironed. I've lost weight. Half my clothes don't hang right. Still better than getting fat, you'd never tolerate that.

I got the weekly email from dad. I haven't replied yet but I will, I would even if mom didn't pester me. Mary's getting married and they think this is a good time to reintegrate me. I can see dad sitting in the pub with Uncle Tom. Saying things like 'once we get him home he'll see sense'. Then Tom will say 'We should buy him a girl, someone to make him forget.' Naturally, Tom means dad should hire the girl. Tom only spends money on Tom. If Paul's there, he'll go bright red. Course Tom probably still thinks Paul is gay just because he doesn't talk about girls all the time. I bet Paul's quite the charmer up north.

Stop dodging. The question I should be trying to answer is: Should I be writing my diary to my dead wife? The 50-mil question. I can't figure it out. I doubt that you can google your way out of that one. Do you know? I know you're not online much these days but if you can, send me a mail.

Stupid pathetic bastard. See I can't change. Still joking, hiding my feelings, even here. I write this to you but you're gone. It'll never be read. Probably best that way.

I'm not sure I'll ever be ready. You told me to move on. But I don't know how. You made me promise. I tried. She's Italian. I couldn't do it.

I've got a few hours before that class. I'll go across the street to that Indian's shop and get some wine. I should see if there's anything else I need while I'm going. I always forget to shop if I go out for a long time. It's one thing about living here that I can't get my head round. No 24/7 shopping. No proper shops on Sunday, well only six times a year. They also close for three hours in the afternoon. The problem is that I'm never in the mood to shop by the time they open again. I could always go to the Carrefour but places like that are so depressing. Ok. I'll be back soon, a bottle of wine and some fruit, and a baguette that'll be stale by tomorrow.

Hi Dad,

Thanks for your messages. Yes, I remember Mary. She was bridesmaid at my wedding.

1st weekend July = June 30 & July 1 or 7th & 8th?

I'll try to make it.

Love, Stephen

After showering the stink of the kitchens out of her hair Carla wraps her head in a towel, takes her green-jasmine-tea, the last of his gift, and sits in the patch of sun from her postage stamp window. It might still be too cold to sit outside but it's good to feel the sun on her skin. Soon Pinchu, her kitten, comes to investigate, sniffing the box under the bed in passing.

'We should get rid of that stuff, shouldn't we?' Pinchu settles in her lap to have his jaw stroked.

She follows the sun to the wall with Pinchu making small protests every time they need to move. When the sun leaves, Carla puts Pinchu on the bed and makes lunch. While making the salad she tries to decide what to do this evening. Some friends are meeting but that will involve Italian food, rarely appealing and never after a double shift. Of course, if she's late then she could join them afterwards. They'll probably be going to a bar. Trying to meet boys never seems to turn out well when there's a big group of women. It's better than sitting in the restaurant after closing, drinking with waiters. She decides she's in a funny mood today because nothing seems appealing, maybe she didn't sleep well.

Carla goes into the bathroom and blow-dries the last of the damp from her hair, and straightens it. Looking in the mirror, she draws a heavy black line underneath each eye, but leaves other makeup until she decides what she's doing tonight. Pulling on clean whites and inhaling the crisp pine scent of the detergent, Carla tosses the morning's smelly ones in the machine. She grabs something sexy to stick in her bag, just in case. She promised herself never to go out in whites.

On the way back to work she decides to walk past his flat, again. It's foolish but she'll do it anyway. It barely makes the walk any longer, but she'll have to be quick or she'll be late back to the kitchen.

Hurrying she only notices the van navigating the narrow street at the last minute. She jumps into a recessed doorway as the van edges past. A second look, she realises it's his doorway. Fate or not? She rings his bell then steps into the street so he'll see it's her. If he's in and if he looks.

Dearest Auntie,

Thank you for your kind letter. This type of girl seems much more suitable to be a shopkeeper's wife. Even the beggars are educated here. I have a few questions that ...

'Hola amigo, how are you.' Darsh greets a regular, laying aside the letter. It's the quiet English man who lives close by and drinks too much, but all the English do, here in Barcelona.

'Fine thanks, you?' He replies, opening the refrigerator.

'Oh good, very good. It's cold today yeah?' The customer's in the back of the shop, Darsh turns to face his heater again.

'Everyone's just waiting for spring now.'

'I have some nice oranges just in. Shall I get you a kilo?' Darsh stays by the heater, if he wants oranges, he'll get them himself.

'Any bananas?'

'Later, they're coming but they don't get here yet.' Darsh gazes out the window leaving the man to shop in peace. You can overdo it. His father must have told him a hundred times. A customer is like a wife, if they want to talk they will, especially the wife. Remember you want them to spend money, well, not the wife. The girl from the restaurant is back. Darsh takes the money thoughts elsewhere, as he makes change. His aunt would complain that she is far too thin but maybe his aunt wouldn't need to know. The Swede was right – she's pretty. Absentmindedly he makes change for the wine and oranges as he watches her cross the street to a door and buzz someone. That's why he thinks she knows someone in the street. 'See you later, amigo.' He calls as his customer leaves. Darsh watches them collide as the girl steps back from the door.

'Carla – hi – I'

'Hola, Stephen, how are you?' Don't you dare try to kiss me. Not here, she thinks.

'I'm ok. I glad I ran into you. How have you been?' Do I know her well enough to kiss her cheeks? I'll never get this right.

'Me? Oh, I'm good, thanks.' Carla wants to add nice of you to ask but doesn't. She can smell chillies and cardamom, like his cooking.

'Listen, Carla about the other night...' I should have called her sooner, he wants to say so but isn't sure if she's angry at him.

'What other night? Oh you mean two weeks ago?' Yes – she's angry he thinks, while wondering how to explain, before blurting it out.

'Carla I'm sorry. I couldn't go through with – things. I was married.'

'Oh you were married?' Carla wishes she were taller, so she didn't have to look up to meet his eyes. 'And suddenly now you are not?'

'No – well, yes. But not like that. She died.' Stephen looks down not wanting to risk her seeing a tear in his eye, then away realising where he's now looking.

'Oh, I'm sorry that's – awful.' Why does it have to be something like that? Carla wants to ask. 'You must think I'm a real bitch.'

'No, I – I thought I was ready. I wanted to – really – but when we kissed. I – just couldn't.'

'It's ok.'

'No, it's not OK. I should have said something. I wanted to explain but – I was embarrassed. Can you forgive me?'

'Maybe. I must go now to work. – But I invite you for coffee. Tomorrow is ok for you?'

'Really – great.' Don't grin you idiot, he thinks, 'How about four?'

'Fine. No five is better, or I'll stink of oregano and sweat.' She starts turning to get to work.

'Carla, I think I need to go slow...'

'Tell me tomorrow, I'm going to be late for work.' He watches her hurry away, before turning for home. He misses her glance backwards as she turns the corner, looking up to see her gone.

Picking up the letter, Darsh tells himself you're invisible to western girls. He'll say yes to Auntie. But he doesn't have to make it easy for her.

Catalan Interiors

P.J. Kavanagh

An extract from Kavanagh's acclaimed autobiography A Perfect Stranger *which, in this chapter, sees the poet in 1950s Barcelona and teaching English...*

After the usual initial period of dismay – what am I doing here? – I found myself a room slightly less horrible than the others I'd looked at. One black bombazined widow had offered me the bed her husband had died in four days previously, it was still laid out like a bier beneath a livid crucifix, bleeding after the Spanish fashion. She haggled resolutely through her tears.

I found Spanish, or perhaps I should say Catalan, interiors to be in the Victorian presbytery waiting room style. They always looked as though the inhabitants lived elsewhere. Huge chandeliers that came to rest a few inches above the antimacassared dining-table, heavy black oaken chairs like instruments of torture, and on the walls dark religious pictures, sentimental and blood-soaked at the same time. The shutters were always drawn, and although everything was over-clean it was all coated with an unhealthy clinging silence, worse than dust. You instinctively lowered your voice; I found myself conducting the negotiations in whispers, my heart in my boots.

These were the apartments of the embattled middle class, and perhaps one of the necessary expressions of a regime the chief supporters of which seem to be the old women and priests.

The flats are huge because they're designed to a celibate clergy's ideal of family life – three generations under one roof – a horrible thought. The men either clear out all together or take their pleasures elsewhere, leaving the women to preside balefully over echoing caverns of mahogany, as though keeping them in readiness for the laying out of a corpse.

Spaniards seldom entertain at home, but the few times I was invited home by pupils, some of them middle-aged men still living with their mothers, there was usually this heaviness, this suffocating ugliness, the absence of light and air, the dreadful, empty ceremoniousness without grace or style. And my host out of respect and, for all I knew, love, for his mother, paid lip-service to her narrow, cruel views: a woman of no experience, no reading, whose only point of contact was the clergy whom he affected to despise.

My room was very dark, and made darker by wallpaper patterned in intricate shades of dung. However it had a bed, a chair and a narrow table from which each day I moved the lace doily and put my notebook there instead. Each night I found the notebook put away, the doily replaced. The ornaments I removed and returned to my landlady saying that I was afraid I might break them. This she understood and clutched them to her accusingly, as though in fact I had. She was a woman of curious habits. The flat divided into two, with the lavatory on the landing in between. Every time I used it, whatever time of day or night, there would be a pause, and then a furtive shuffle of slippers and she'd go in there; a few minutes later I'd hear the plug being pulled again. This filled me with a peculiar kind of horror. Once, in the early hours, I looked up from my book and saw her shadow outlined on the wall – she was somewhere out in the hall, watching me. The shadow stayed there for perhaps quarter of an hour, quite still, and then it went away. I can only add that these lodgings were the least sinister I'd been able to afford.

I wasn't paid very much, but the work was pleasant and gave me time to do my own. I settled down in earnest to learn my trade – in a way I now think mistaken, if not absurd. I took Yeats' words as my text but tried so hard to make my verses 'well made' that I jammed up whatever lyricism I might have had left. I was so terrified of being dilettante that the end-result was often professional in the worst sense, although the original impulse was perhaps simple, and strong. I became obsessed with the idea of getting into print; this would give me professional status in my own eyes. I sent a long poem, very Audenesque and called *St Thomas More*, to John Lehmann. I had misgivings about this, I didn't want to be published because I knew his niece, but he was the best literary editor at the time and hadn't struck me as the sort of man who would publish anything he didn't like. I was quite right and he didn't. I plugged on, turning out reams of stuff, trying to get Auden out of my system.

Some years later I was talking to a famous editor about the exciting experimental work in American magazines. 'Ah yes', he cried, thumping the table, 'but they haven't got anyone to call them to order!' I wish I hadn't called myself to order so much.

But I knew that poetry was a way of life as well as an acquired skill. Maybe the age didn't want you, but nevertheless your temperament, however poor a thing, was needed, whether others knew this or not. The job was to find a means of existence (a job) that kept this temperament functioning. Let the poems come or not come as destiny decided, but your ear had to be cocked to inside noises, and therefore to outside ones as well. I didn't like theorising, however, it made me uneasy. I just burrowed away and three days a week taught English.

Heaven knows if I taught it. I didn't know the answers to most of the questions myself, if indeed there are any, and the lessons filled me with commiseration for those who wanted to hear this impossible language. It was very tiring work, more like a performance. When I was stumped for comedy material I made them do quizzes, like the difference between 'washing down' and 'washing up' (poor sods!) and what they enjoyed most were each other's mistakes. The pupils were mostly girls, and I suppose I showed off, but it seemed better to have the full attention of the class, even if you were talking rubbish, than to be feeding them the real stuff (whatever that might be) and nobody listening. I also took classes outside, old ladies in their drawing-rooms, barmen in the bars; I was saving to get back to spend Christmas in England.

Clifford King, a writer who was also teaching at the Institute, introduced me to the Glorieta, the cheapest restaurant in Barcelona – in the world maybe. If you bought a kind of season ticket your three-course dinner worked out about eightpence; the trouble was you had to be very strong to eat it. Afterwards I filled up a bottle with heavy black wine in the fish-smelling cave of the bar next-door, and went home to work on my poem for Sally's birthday – the wine helping me to forget the dinner.

For lunch I went to the same restaurant every day, near where I worked, had the same meal, and read through the complete back numbers of Horizon and Penguin New Writing. I'd found them in the Institute library. There I wrote the first poem in what sounded like my own voice. It was my declaration of impatience with a fuzziness I thought I detected in the work of my near-predecessors. I wanted something more specific, colder, tougher, and I felt that I was hoisting a standard of revolt. In fact it was only a bit of Kleenex pinned to a stick, but it was a beginning. I don't think I changed it, but left it as I'd scribbled it down, between the Cuban rice and the inevitable flan.

Love Poem

Can you forgive the fastidious cannibal
His unusual pleasures? Does your charity
Embrace the noisy whore, forgetting her manners

In front of your daughter? The cocky-walker
Who teaches your wife to care about clothes again
And look in the mirror? And yet defend
Your wife from your enemy and your daughter,
From the convincing whore, your life from the cannibal?
When you can do this, and this, and lose
Your wife, your life and always your curious daughter,
Then we may talk of love and what we mean.

I showed it to Clifford and he was very angry about the reference to whores, which he considered disrespectful. Some of the nicest people he'd ever met, and what about Mary Magdalene?

Don't tell him Jesus never slept with her, and a good thing too! I had nothing against whores and meant them no harm in my poem.

I've no idea whether Clifford was a good novelist or not because he always told me his plots, in detail, so I didn't need to read the book. I riposted by talking about my feeling for Sally, whom I missed to the point of obsession and, bless him, he listened to it all. A gentle, independent, courageous man, he showed me Barcelona, for which he had a passion. He wrote a good book about it later, called *To Barcelona, with love.*

First, he introduced me to his friends, the whores. In those days there were certain quarters of Barcelona where you could push almost every other door and go upstairs to a room filled with bored girls in transparent shifts, some of them asleep, and a few men reading the evening paper. Every now and then one of these would finish his newspaper with a sigh, fold it carefully longways, put it in his pocket, glare at one of the girls (often a woman of motherly proportions and advanced years) and jerk his head towards the door. She'd yawn, stretch, and carry on the conversation with her colleagues until she was almost in the corridor – then she'd remember her role, dig the customer in the ribs and switch on a lecherous grimace of such cosmic phoniness it was a wonder it didn't freeze him in his tracks. But usually he'd stopped looking at her by this time – thinking of something else probably. It was interesting to see the hot-blooded Latins at play.

This was a fairly high class one, about ten bob a time. You could pay anything from five quid to ninepence, and there was a separate establishment for every pocket. The walls of the poorest ones were glazed like public lavatories with yellowing cracked tiles. Exhausted, ill-looking women in Mother Hubbards, their hair hanging down in damp strings, circulated among the crowd, absently rubbing a crutch here and there, eyes empty, trying to raise a spark that would lead a man to spend the pennies he couldn't afford, her share of which would be farthings. One night I saw one of them amusing the other women by pulling out her child-distended nipples as far as they would go, and letting them snap back, like pieces of brown elastic.

In the quieter ones, the seven and six or ten bob ones (God knows these had few enough customers in that poor rich city), Clifford sat and talked with the girls and I admired some of the bodies, wondering at the variety of shapes. Sometimes I got interested, in a pin-up book sort of way, and if only the girls could have acted a little better, or a little less, I mightn't have felt so much like laughing. I felt lust all right, to a burdensome extent, but these girls couldn't have dispelled it – I'd have to regard either them, or myself, as less than human. I didn't have the sort of ideal gaiety that cuts through such things, makes contact. In the first place their attitude was that of a contemptuous nurse-maid – His Lordship wants his dinner does he?.. come along then you... And in the second place these were female human beings who were trapped – we could walk out of the door into the world of possibility, these girls stayed here in this one, as limited as a zoo. Sometimes there'd be a new girl and she'd sit there looking frightened, and that was horrible.

Clifford got their stories from them, and these were suspiciously often of the 'don't darken my doors again' variety; and he'd inveigh against the corrupt society that could bring about such things, and the Church that encouraged it, then he'd disappear for twenty minutes and emerge stroking his beard and looking pleased with life; after that we'd go and pretend to eat the dinner in the Glorieta. I couldn't make up my mind whether he was exploiting the results of a corrupt society, or sending money back into the system that would help alleviate it. Both, I supposed.

Many of the girls were, in fact, unmarried mothers; and as there is hardly any work for women in Spain, in order to feed their children they probably had had no choice. In the mornings they turned the Cosmos bar into a kind of crèche, and then they'd all sit and say the Rosary together before the day's work, praying always for a rich husband. These they sometimes found when the American Navy put into port. There was a paid scribe in the Cosmos who translated the sailors' love-letters – passionate avowals from eighteen-year-olds to 'my pure angel'; and for a fee the scribe composed suitable replies. They were not deceiving these boys, or no more than other women often do; they obviously adored them and the future that they made possible. I don't know what happened when the sailors found out, but I'm sure some of those girls made marvellous wives, though probably fiercely respectable.

But always this terrible, crushing poverty. There was an old woman with ulcerated legs outside the Cosmos bar with three lemons in front of her. She wasn't begging, but I never saw her sell one; how on earth did she eat?

The money seemed to have settled at the top, like scum. The rich were too rich and they knew it, it poisoned them. The air was thick with hate. Stopped by a policeman for jumping a traffic-light, the owner of a car that cost more than most of the pedestrians would earn in their lives shouted at the policeman that he'd make him lose his job, and he stepped back and saluted; this was normal. But it was no use a foreigner being safely indignant when the Spaniards themselves kept so quiet. They were not apathetic, but they knew the cost better than we did.

Robert W. Service

Barcelona

The night before I left Milan
A mob jammed the Cathedral Square,
And high the tide of passion ran
As politics befouled the air.
A seething hell of human strife,
I shrank back from its evil core,
Seeing in this convulsive life
The living seeds of war.

To Barcelona then I came,
And oh the heavenly release!
From conflict and consuming flame
I knew the preciousness of peace.
Such veneration for the law!
How decorous was every one!
And then (significant) I saw
Each copper packed a tommy gun.

Well, maybe it is best that way.
Peace can mean more than liberty:
These people, state-directed, may
Be happier than those more free.
When politics wield evil grip,
And warring factions rise and fall,
Benevolent dictatorship
May be the answer, after all.

The Sleepwalker

Leah Ganse

The neighbor's damp clothing stirred in the breeze, weighing down the laundry line with its solid-colored garments and tablecloths and towels, vibrant against the sandy stucco and brick. Her eyes drifted towards her own laundry, hanging unprettily in stark contrast to the postcard-like image across the street. From her seat on the terrace she had a privileged view of both Barcelona's mountains. It had been the main selling point of the apartment and she spent most of her time at home there, watching the children play in the plaza below her while their grandparents chatted on the benches, or studying for the translation program that had initially brought her to Barcelona.

The phone rang, and she turned back toward the apartment, counted three rings, and waited while she listened to Joel answer the phone in Spanish and after a pause, switch to English.

'It's your mother,' he said, crossing the terrace towards her. He handed her the phone, lifted her bare feet and then redeposited them in his lap as he settled into the teak chair opposite her.

'Are you planning on leaving soon to pick him up from the airport?' her mother asked after they exchanged hellos.

'Fifteen minutes,' she answered. 'Joel's driving me there, but he's just dropping me off. We'll take the train back. How was getting him on the plane?'

'Good, I think,' her mother said. 'But you know Michael, who knows what he'll be like when he gets to you, so just be understanding.'

'Yeah, I know.' She thought back to the endless conversations she had had with her parents trying to convince them to let her 25-year-old younger brother stay with her for a week. Medications had been discussed, the issue of her living with Joel and how Michael might react, how to deal with him in a crisis, and the last and most personal, if he even wanted to come. She had argued that seeing her living on her own and in a relationship would make him realize he could have that for himself, that the exoticism of the Mediterranean, Gaudí's fairy tale buildings, and filling him up on local food would have a restorative effect, like when the infirm were sent to Europe to calm their nerves and cleanse their bodies with sea air and a warm climate. Finally, he was on his way.

After agreeing to call her mother after Michael arrived, they hung up and she set the phone down on the table between herself and the man she had been living with for the past eight months.

'Are you ready for this?' Joel asked, and she drew her feet away from him and slipped them into the tan high-heeled sandals on the ground in front of her.

'We'll be fine,' she smiled and stood up from her seat, bending over to kiss him. 'And in a few days, you'll finally get to meet my brother.'

'I wish I could come with you and meet him today.'

'I know you do, but you know it's best if you let him get comfortable with his surroundings with just me for a few days before I introduce you two. I don't want to freak him out.'

'But just a few days. Otherwise my mother will get used to me living with the family again and won't let me come back to live with you.' He winked at her.

'The scary part is I know it's true.' She jumped out of the way as he playfully tried to pinch her, and after gathering their things, they left the apartment for the airport.

In the car, they were mostly quiet as she watched the late summer landscape roll by, the suburbs of Barcelona where she had worked at an English academy after first moving to the city, the mountains on one side and flat fields stretching out on the other. After five years there, it had become home.

At the airport, Joel held her for a few moments before saying goodbye, but anxiousness made her pull away first, and she looked back at him and waved before going into the terminal to wait.

She tried to picture what her brother would look like after nearly two years of not seeing him, and wondered if he'd had his hair cut recently, or if he was still having their father do it because he was afraid to leave the house. She watched a few bus loads of people pass through the revolving doors of El Prat, and then finally he appeared. His face registered recognition, and rather than smiling, his eyes brightened a little.

'Hi, buddy,' she said hugging him and taking a deep breath to get the air back into her lungs that had escaped in a rush when she saw him. 'How was your trip?'

'Hi, Carla.' He sighed, and she remembered the long breaths or pauses that always perforated his conversations. 'Uh, it was long. I'm kind of tired.'

Carla gave his shoulder a squeeze and gently took his bag out of his hand. As they walked, she tried not to stare too hard at him. Would it be less scary here because everything was new and strange and unknown? Or was he simply trying to get his bearings so he could figure out how to react?

'Hungry?' she asked, as she slipped a ten-Euro bill into the red and white ticket machine to buy his pass.

'A little, I guess.'

They climbed onto the waiting train and found seats across from each other towards the back. Michael rested his suitcase on the seat next to him. An officer was checking tickets, and Michael's eyes flitted towards him as he went from person to person.

'He's just checking our tickets,' Carla touched his arm. 'They do that sometimes.'

Michael relaxed a little and looked out the window.

'It's just three stops to my apartment,' Carla said.

'Is there anybody there right now?'

'No,' she nodded. 'Joel's family invited him to visit like I told you, so he's there for a few days.' She quickly went through the catalogue in her head of the people who had been a part of Michael's life in the last few years. Their parents, his counselor and psychiatrist, an occasional brief visit from an aunt or uncle. After the breakdown, his network of people had shrunk dramatically and quickly, and his suspicion even extended to the few people who did form part of his life.

'So, this is my building!' Carla turned and looked over her shoulder, smiling at him as she began unlocking the first in the series of doors. In the small, carpeted metal elevator he studied the signs in Spanish for the maximum capacity of the elevator and a notice of when the meter reader would be coming.

'Have you been keeping up with your Spanish?' Carla asked.

'A little.'

With a 'ta-da,' she opened the door, pushing it with her shoulder since it sometimes stuck in the heat. Michael looked slowly to the left and then to the right, and stayed still while Carla orbited around the apartment rattling off the list of rooms that required no explanation. Like everyone she showed the apartment to eventually did, he gravitated towards the terrace.

'That's the best part of the whole place,' she said. 'Look.' She slid the glass door open and let him pass through first.

'Wow, you have a lot of plants,' he said, a small spark of interest slightly heightening the pitch of his voice. One of his few sources of pride at home was their father's garden that he had become increasingly interested in. For the year when they lived in separate houses, he with their father and Carla with their mother, Michael would bring her and her mother things like tomatoes, hot peppers, or basil and rosemary. He was holding one of the little basil leaves on the terrace between his thumb and forefinger when he asked, 'Did you grow these?'

Carla nodded. 'Pick some if you want.'

'It's okay,' he said. He asked a few more questions about what Carla was growing (lavender, thyme, a few mystery plants that she had thought looked or smelled nice) until the wind picked up, the laundry snapping loudly.

'Over there to the right is Montjuïc,' she said, turning him slightly to face it. 'Where all that green is. That's where the Olympic Stadium is. We could go see a movie outside there if you're up for it.' When he didn't react, she turned him the other way. 'That's the other famous mountain in Barcelona, Tibidabo,' she said. 'We'll go up there one day. You should see the view of it from the terrace at night though when the cathedral on the mountain is lit up. It's really cool.'

He shook the hair out of his eyes that the wind had rearranged. 'Maybe I will take a nap now,' he said.

'Yeah, of course. I'll tell you more about the city when we're walking around later.'

She showed him to the guest room, where she explained that there were fresh sheets on the bed and that she'd wake him up in two hours so he could start adjusting to the time change. The photo board on the wall caught his eye. Among them were pictures of Carla's college girlfriends, her first trip to Barcelona, a few recent ones of her with her mother and father at college graduation, and one of all of them when Michael and Carla were just three and six.

'Recognize that one?' she asked. He smiled slightly and then turned away to unzip his suitcase.

'Have a good nap,' Carla said, beginning to pull the door shut, then stopped.

'Do you need a glass of water for your medication?' Her muscles tensed as those tentative words escaped her lips. She waited for his reply.

'I don't take it until later.'

'Okay.' She closed the door behind her with a click.

She snaked all ten fingers through her hair and got herself a glass of water before sitting down to make the two phone calls to her parents. After the initial moment of relief that he had arrived safely, they both had advice to dispel. 'Just don't push him,' her mother said. And later with her father, 'Make sure you see him take his medication.' She filed them away in the same place but closer to the surface than the things they had told her over the years that she truly couldn't get out of her head. 'Every day, I wonder if my son will be alive when I come home,' from her father, and her mother's, 'You have no idea what it's like to have a son who wants to die.'

She had detached herself from those surreal anecdotes over the years and the mystery of her brother's mental illness had become a part of her normalcy. Escaping most of the ugliness by fleeing to Barcelona where she had spent the best summer of her life, she was eager to recapture the bliss she had first experienced there. Contact with her family and reality was now about a once a week occurrence, and mainly surface level. When one of her parents would pass the phone to her brother, the conversations were limited, punctuated with his question-accusations, 'Is there somebody else on the line? Did you hear that click? Is someone listening?'

Now with him sleeping in the next room, there was nothing to hide behind but a smile and hours upon hours of exploring Parc Güell, la Boquería market, the beach, her favorite cafes in the corners of Raval, and the pretty plazas in the bohemian Gràcia neighborhood to distract from everything she wanted to say but couldn't.

With half an hour left before the time they had agreed she would wake him, Carla decided to start on the lunch she had planned for him. She chopped potatoes and onions for tortilla and took Spanish ham and olives out of the refrigerator to let them become room temperature. As she was slicing up some soft, red tomatoes, and the oil in the pan started to spit for the croquettes, Michael appeared in the door frame with a yawn.

'Can I help?' he asked.

'You're up!' She smiled, his multi-directional hair reminding her of when they were children. 'Why don't you grab a couple of basil leaves from the terrace and then you can help me finish the tortilla?'

He complemented the smells as he helped her in the kitchen. 'Onion makes anything smell good,' she said dismissively. When they had finished, he helped her bring plates out to the terrace and they sat down to eat, he working through his food more slowly than Carla had remembered. After warming up for a while talking about the plans she had made for their week and how their parents were doing back home, she took a breath, 'Joel would like to meet you,' she said, looking up from her food and stealing a glance at him to see if those few words had garnered a reaction, but he was using his bread to soak up the bit of olive oil he had left on his plate.

She began again, 'I've told him so much about you and since we don't get to see each other that often, I thought it would be a really good chance for the two of you to meet. I mean, things are really serious between us. I wouldn't introduce you if they weren't.'

He looked at nothing in particular blankly for a moment and said, 'Yeah. Maybe.'

They spent the rest of the day having tea in the Born where he took pictures of the street lamps and Santa María del Mar, the cathedral she dreamed about marrying in one day, looking around the Parc de la Ciutadella where he took pictures of the giant fountains and the mammoth replica that hinted of the zoo the park contained, and walking up and down the beach in Barceloneta, where they stopped to buy a cheap paddle set and played for a bit. He smiled broadly as Carla missed shot after shot and then when they were through, said, 'It's okay, you actually did pretty well.'

A natural athlete, her brother was tall and broad-shouldered with uncooperative dark hair. The medication had put more weight on him and dulled his eye color to a grayer shade of blue. But he was undebatably handsome although he had never considered himself so. It was rare to see him smile since he was self-conscious about the slight gap between his front teeth, but their parents' homes in the states were full of photos of him smiling as a little boy. Those were my baby teeth, he would always point out when their parents would ask why he didn't smile like that in pictures anymore.

They went home much earlier than Carla ever would have before on a Saturday night, foregoing the metro to take the longer city bus route, and he was even more uncommunicative than usual. Carla was a little relieved that he was ready to sleep.

While he showered, Carla went into her room to change into her pajamas and as she passed the guest room, her brother's open suitcase caught her eye. His clothes were sort of sloppily folded like he had been rummaging through them, and his socks were loose and strewn about. On top of the organized-looking mess was his pill box with prescriptions taped to the top. The water in the shower shut off, and Carla made her exit.

'Well, I'm going to bed,' he said padding into the living room in the bathrobe and slippers she had given him as a gift earlier that day.

'Your meds?'

'I took them,' he said. 'See you in the morning.'

'Night, kiddo,' she said to his back and wondered if she should insist in the future that he swallow the pills in front of her.

She waited ten minutes after she heard him click the light off before picking up the phone to call Joel. When he answered, she felt the day's tension drain from the top of her head down her spine and out of her body. She sent a quick thank you to the universe for giving her someone she could unburden herself to.

'You had me worried since I didn't hear from you all day,' he said.

'But you knew I'd call eventually.'

'I knew you would. Are things going how you expected?'

How she expected. What exactly had she expected out of it all? A miraculous overhaul of the synapses firing or misfiring in his brain? For him to see her living on her own in a relationship and suddenly want to emulate that? Or for a grand-scale, total meltdown, and the knowledge that she had pushed too hard for the trip?

'Everything's about what I expected. I think it's going well.'

After I-love-yous and I-miss-yous, she pulled a blanket over herself on the couch and shut her eyes for a minute, thinking about how quickly things with Joel had progressed while the TV droned softly in the background. Being with Joel made Michael's problems seem far away, the happiness she'd been feeling for the past eight months since they had moved in together nearly eclipsing the worries that normally hung over her head. Am I really that self-involved, she wondered, or so obsessed with happiness that I could forget about Michael?

When she had driven the three hours home from college to see her brother before he was checked into the psychiatric ward of the hospital because he had taken a bottleful of pills, she had been fairly certain that he had fully expected to die that night. But now more than six years had passed since then, and while he hadn't attempted suicide since then, something had died inside of him, condemning him to a sort of purgatory that he seemed unwilling to leave. She had read the books, though, and knew that until he was ready to begin living, no one could force him to do anything differently.

She flipped off the TV and set her alarm for the next morning. She had become unaccustomed to sleeping alone, and when she eventually slept, it was restless and the night seemed long.

'Not a lot of tourists seem to know about this place,' Carla said, mounting the steps to the labyrinth park the next afternoon.

'Hm,' he said. He was wearing a new dark brown leather jacket even though it was too warm for it. They passed through the gates.

'Over there's the labyrinth,' she said. 'Maybe we can explore around the park a little bit first and then leave that for last.'

'Okay,' he said, pulling the new black camera their father had ordered for him exclusively for the trip out of his pocket.

'Stand over there,' he pointed to a patch of coral-orange flowers. 'I think Dad would like that picture.' Carla smiled and he counted to three, snapped, and checked the image on the screen before he nodded and said, 'Good,' handing it to her for approval.

'Let me get someone to take one of both of us,' she said, taking a few steps in the direction of a couple of girls with dreadlocks and sketchbooks.

'No, it doesn't matter,' he said.

'But it'll just take a – '

'I don't. Want you. To.'

I handed his camera back to him after his clipped words and he jerked it away, shoving it into his pocket and almost breaking it when the still open lens caught on his pocket.

'Let's just go over here then,' she forced herself to say. They climbed a graying set of stairs and Michael stopped to take a picture of the Grecian looking statue of a woman under a gazebo.

'What's that?' he asked, looking at the pavilion at the top of the steps.

She sighed and cocked her head, sweeping a fistful of hair away from her eyes. 'I actually don't know.'

She started to climb. After a moment, he followed her and said, 'It kind of looks like the Parthenon.' She glanced back over her shoulder at him but his eyes were still on his feet as he navigated the stairs just behind her and to the right.

The columns gave the peachy building a self-important air and after Michael tried unsuccessfully to open the door, they walked around to the back where a long black rectangular pond ended in a statue of a woman reclining under a stone canopy. He took a few pictures of the goldfish in the pond and watched the girls with dreadlocks out of the corner of his eye as they climbed onto the statue.

'Wanna do the labyrinth now?' he asked.

'Sure!' she said and began trotting down the steps, slowing her pace when she realized Michael was content to take them at his normal pace.

'So this is it,' Carla said as they looked at the inscription at the entrance under a depiction of Ariadne and Theseus. 'Right or left?'

'This way I guess,' he said. For the first few minutes their instincts seemed to match up as they wound through the hedges, stopping once to turn around at a dead end. The sounds of the other walkers drifted over the walls of shrubbery and occasionally they caught glimpses of them through the parts of the wall where the hedge had been cut away and the exposed wire showed through. They rounded another corner and hit another dead end, Michael running into her as he turned sharply around.

'Watch out!' he barked and took off at a faster pace. 'You tried to make me go this way, didn't you.'

'Michael, I don't know which is the right way either,' Carla said, still fully capable of astonishment even after knowing that side of her brother for years.

'But you've done this before.'

'That was a year ago – I can't remember which way I went.'

'Let's just go,' he said, and right on cue, they turned into another dead end. 'Why did you bring me here?' His eyes were wide.

'I thought you'd like it. Please just slow down,' she said to his back. They spent a few tense, long minutes while she followed him through the labyrinth, Michael letting out a strained, deep curse every time a dead end came up or they went in a circle. She was so focused on the shifting leather on Michael's back as he tried not to swing his arms while he walked that she almost ran into him when they finally reached the center.

'Oh,'she said. 'You found it.'

It was just a small circle in the center with a statue of Eros in the middle. She watched as Michael's arms then hands relaxed by his body, and instead of looking up at the statue, the labyrinth's hidden treasure, he fixed his eyes on his feet. Carla took a few steps closer to him and took his shoulder in her hand, extending the other one out in front of him with her palm open.

'Here, give me your camera. Mom and Dad would want a picture of this.'

As soon as Michael had gone to bed after their quiet dinner, Carla ran a bath for herself and lay in the tub whispering on the phone to Joel.

'It sounds like you're handling it the best way you can,' he said, after she had recounted the day's events.

'I just can't tell if he's better or worse than the last time I saw him.'

'Is there a better or worse with him?'

She sighed, dragging her fingernails lightly up and down the leg she had hung over the tub's edge. 'Not for a long time. But I still keep looking for any signs of better.'

'I want to make you feel better.'

'You do.'

'No, I want to be with you right now.'

'I want that, too.'

'There's a lot more that I want right now, too.' Joel's voice relaxed her body, giving her the release she so desperately needed as she imagined her own hands were his, magnified under the water as they left trails of heat on her skin. She went to bed trying to fall into a dream that he was making love to her, but when she woke up later in the middle of the night it was with no memories of dreaming.

She thought she had heard the door to the guest room open, and then told herself that it was only part of her nonexistent dream or the neighbors upstairs. A few quiet footsteps sounded in the hallway, and she lay tense for a few more moments, waiting for the sound of the bathroom door opening and closing that never came. A few more sleepless moments passed while she futilely tried convincing herself to go back to sleep. She snapped on the light switch by the bed and called out to her brother after she opened her door. The only light in the apartment was coming from the dim table lamp she and Joel had inherited from the apartment's previous tenants, dimly filtered through a navy canvas lampshade.

'Are you awake, kiddo?' She flipped on both the light switches to the bathroom and spare bedroom, knowing that he wasn't in there either.

'Michael?' Kitchen light, flip. Hall light. Something impelled her to look in the hall closet before flipping the last light on in the living room.

'Seriously, where are you?' She tried to control her voice, thinking about how her mother would have behaved in situations like these. Michael used to sleepwalk as a child, and it had always frightened Carla. Once their mother found him in the laundry room holding a bottle of bleach, another time she found him in the garage right before he knocked over a bin of deflated basketballs and sports equipment. One night when Carla was fourteen, she had awoken to the slow sound of her doorknob turning beneath a sleepy hand and her brother's silhouette in the doorway. He had turned the hall light on but instead of allowing her see him better, it blinded her dilated pupils.

'Go back to bed, Michael,' she had told him, and he did without shutting the door behind him. That was the night she had started locking her door. She had never been afraid that her brother would hurt her, but rather she was afraid of him in that state when he wasn't himself, but something alien and unrecognizable.

Remembering being blinded by the light of the hallway that night, not seeing something that was right in front of her, she turned toward the glass door that led to the terrace. It was obscured by the glare from the light she had just turned on.

As soon as she slid it open, she saw him standing on a chair looking down into the plaza. The noise of the door opening surprised him and he spun around, offsetting his balance and causing him to fall towards the railing.

'Mikey!' The sound that came out of her mouth sounded distorted and wrong, like it had come from another person. He slipped backwards, knocking his elbows on the railing and bringing the terracotta planters crashing to the ground as his hands flailed out in search of anything to grab hold of. Something like a scream had come rumbling up from his insides, too. He lifted his bleeding hand and held it in front of his face, waiting to feel the pain.

'You almost made me fall off!' he shouted.

'I thought you wanted to jump,' She crumpled onto her knees next to him and bunched his hand in her shirt.

'I wasn't trying to jump. I was trying to see that thing on the mountain better.'

Carla began to cry, still holding his hand through the fabric that showed spots of blood where it had soaked through.

'Don't you ever, ever try anything like that,' she choked out. With his good hand, he awkwardly patted her shoulder.

'I'm sorry,' he said.

'I'm sorry I almost made you fall.' She wiped her face on her shoulder and surveyed the damage. They were sitting in potting soil and herbs. 'I'm worried about you. You don't seem any better, and I just want you to be happy. Or I want you to believe that you can be happy. Do you?' She brushed dirt from her knees while she waited for him to form a response.

'Yeah, I guess so. But it's not that easy.'

'I know. But that's why you have to keep up with seeing your counselor and taking your meds and trying to push harder.'

'Carla, I'm tired,' he sighed.

She looked up at Tibidabo in the distance and told herself to pull it together. 'Okay,' she said, and kissed the top of his head. 'Come on, let's wash your hand and put something on it.'

They had spent one day exploring modernist architecture on Passeig de Gràcia, another in Montserrat hiking in the mountains and exploring the church, another in the MNAC and the Fundació Joan Miró, one in Sitges at the beach, and one shopping for souvenirs and eating too many tapas. She had tried to fill the days as much as she could so he would be tired enough to sleep through the night, and so that he would tell his parents he had had a good time with his sister. And as she had predicted, the week came to a close much more quickly than either of them had expected.

'I'm sorry I didn't get to meet Joel.' They were at the airport again, Michael wearing his new leather jacket with his arms stiffly by his sides.

'That's okay. Another time you will,' Carla said, touching his arm and pulling on it a little, seeing if he might let it swing and relax a little.

'Well, I had a really good time,' he said.

'Me too.' She pulled him into her arms, noticing how strange it felt that he could make her feel small. 'Call me when you're home. I love you.'

'Love you, too.'

She waited with him at security until he reached the belt where he took off his shoes and jacket and walked his stiff, meek walk through the security gate. Then she watched until he was gone.

Outside, Joel waited for her in his car. She hadn't seen him the whole week. The sun was full out and his car was sauna-like when she climbed in.

'I can't wait to show you how much I missed you,' he told her, squeezing her thigh and hiding a few fingers under the hem of her shorts. Carla smiled at him and said she'd like to sit and have a beer first while she told him more details about the week. Maybe sit on the terrace, where she still hadn't cleaned up the soil and spilled plants. They hadn't gone out on it for the rest of the week. There would be broken terracotta too that she would have to be careful with, and she hoped that the blood hadn't stained any of the chairs. It wasn't important, though, she thought. It was just a mess. Not better, not worse than before. But this one she could clean up.

Groves of Wrath

An interview with Elena Moya

Moving between the shadows of the Spanish Civil War, the business battles of a global economy and a young girl's sexual awakening, Elena Moya Pereira's potboiler The Olive Groves of Belchite *has been released in the UK and will be published in Spain next year. Here she talks about her work and writing 'away from home'.*

Most of the writers we feature come from outside Spain to settle in Barcelona or Catalonia. You are the opposite case. How did this come about?

I went to the US with a Fulbright scholarship to do a Masters in Financial Journalism. Back in Barcelona, I soon discovered Spain's very young democracy translated in a far-from-independent press, not suitable for a young and hungry journalist like me, willing to call things by their name. I went to London, where I joined Bloomberg News, and stayed for 9 years. I am now at *The Guardian*, as a business reporter, after 2 years at Reuters as well.

As a novel author, I also thought that I had more chances of being published in Britain, a bigger market, and more open to new authors, than Spain. It worked.

Would you consider yourself 'in exile'? Do you ever consider coming back?

Yes – as a Republican, I still reject the backwards, macho society that still controls Spain. There are freer countries, and I feel privileged to have lived in both: the US and Britain (less so than America).

But I dream of coming back every other day, opening my windows and seeing the Mediterranean sea, not paying a fortune to eat fresh vegetables and good fish, meet up more spontaneously, all a bit less rational.

What was your motivation for writing the novel?

The need to say, out and loud, that Spain is still a very young democracy and that has some very bad, tough and unfair implications that still affect every single Spaniard – regardless of whether they're in Spain or abroad: a society that's far from meritocratic or democratic, where effort is not rewarded, where authority isn't legitimised, all for good reasons – those in power seldom deserve it. A lot of talent and lives wasted. And those at the biggest disadvantage include women and minorities – two groups where I belong, as a woman and as a lesbian.

Not to mention the state of gays in Spain. I know we have one of the most forward-looking pieces of legislation with the approval of gay marriage: but how many prominent lesbians are out there? I can't think of any. Sad. Sad. Sad.

'Leave the dead alone. Still to this day they won't shut up.' How much do you think the Spanish are still in need of 'closure'? And how do you feel about the current campaign to criminalize Garzón for trying to investigate the crimes of Franco?

Yes, still, many older – and not so old – Spanish people feel like shutting up as they were brought up during the very repressive Franco years, and that lasted until the 1970s. So plenty of middle-aged people are still willing to keep things quiet. Not to mention those who feared for their lives or that of their family or relatives.

And absolutely, Garzón's case is the ultimate example of all the above: let's not dig in the past. There are many people who were main characters in those years who are still alive, or people who are in their powerful positions now because they were named by people from that regime – or they're their sons or daughters. All still too tender.

The boycott of Catalan products also features in the novel. How far do you think that anti-Catalan sentiment in Spain is a reality or is it part of that famous Catalan *victimisme*?

No *victimisme* at all. The anti-Catalan campaign is well and alive, one just needs to travel throughout Spain to feel it. Parties like the PP do quite a lot to stir it. If you listen to 'Cope'..! That's not Catalan victimism, but a very real anti-Catalan campaign.

You draw heavily on the Opus Dei and the University of Pamplona. Just how much of this is from your own personal experience? Were you the teenager spirited away by 'colònies' described in the book? As an Opus Dei university it seems a strange choice for someone like yourself...

I went to Pamplona because it was the No. 1 journalism school. And yes, I've drawn some experiences from my time there, and the Opus people

I met there. And yes, I went to one of those 'experiences' – it was just before starting uni, a weekend to get to know the university, and I stayed at one of those colleges. Wow – an experience I will never forget. But I never went, by any means, for religious reasons; only that time, to get to know the university. But once there, I declined all my invites.

You wrote the book in English. How do you feel writing in a second language?

Yes, I wrote *The Olive Groves of Belchite* in English, not because I ever thought I could write a novel in a foreign language, but just because I'd finished the Creative Writing Diploma at Birkbeck College, and I joined a group of alumni who met once a month to workshop each other – we brought our writing to every meeting, and we would criticise and help each other. Since they were all English, I had to write in English.

Do you feel it limiting/liberating?

True, writing in a foreign language is limiting, but also true, English gives me a distance and a rationality that I don't have in my mother tongue.

My novel spells some truths that are very close to my heart, and to that of many Spaniards, about the War, Franco, and all the trauma behind them, that perhaps would have been difficult to spell out that clearly in Spanish. Maybe I am too close – like every Spaniard.

The Nature of Love

Anna Chieppa

Once I was wandering behind the cathedral in Milan, and saw a fortune teller sitting in a corner, at a small desk, with a sign: ASK JUANA.

I dropped five euros into the palm of her hand and asked when I would find True Love. The woman told me that True Love would come soon.

How soon, I wanted to know.

The woman traced a circle with her right hand.

Soon is soon, she said. I can see the face of a nice man, waiting for you.

Is he waiting for me now?

Perhaps. I can see you love him very much.

Is he good-looking?

She sighed. Not really. But they say that beauty is in the eye of the beholder.

Can you be more specific? How am I going to recognise him when I meet him?

That, she said, is the difficult thing. You've been waiting a long time for nothing, yes? You must have help now.

Yes, I need help. Can you help me?

She opened her hand towards me. She had a dark face, and black shimmering eyes, sinking into her wrinkled skin.

Five euros, she said, I can help.

I did not have any more money, and there were still three days to pay day.

I'm broke, I said. Can you just give me a clue about how to recognise him?

She opened her mouth wide in a smile. She had two teeth only, at the front, one on top of each other as if they were about to quarrel.

No money, no clue, she said.

I went back home under a round, yellow moon. It was only the beginning of Autumn and I was surprised to find my bed so cold, when I finally went to sleep, long past midnight.

Eight years later I was living in Barcelona and had a best friend whose name was Milo.

Milo was from Buenos Aires. He was a bass player, although he made his living as a bingo caller. I did not know a lot about music, but Pablo the Mexican did, because he was a bass player too, in a band that got a record deal with Sony Music. And when he listened to Milo playing, he went straight to him and asked for bass lessons. That was the kind of player that Milo must have been, but he never gave Pablo the lessons, because after twenty years studying music, day and night, Milo decided he wanted to be a poet.

I met Milo by chance, on my second day in Barcelona. He was the most intelligent person I have ever known. In the evenings when he was free, he would bring a book by Alejandra Pizarnik to the bar and start reading aloud, while I would get distracted ogling men, biting my nails, hunting drunken thoughts. At the end he would ask what I had understood, which I would have found a bit pretentious if he wasn't my best friend.

The fact is, he usually said when I confessed not having listened to a word, you will never be a real writer if you are so easily distracted.

I'm a woman, I always replied. I can multitask.

Now I had been in the city for two years. I still worked on the tourist bus, a temporary job I could not get rid of, and carried around stacks of Moleskines where I wrote down my notes for the Greatest Novel of the Century, which I was about to start, hopefully.

It was decided years ago that the subject of my novel would be the nature of love.

Milo was in love with Pola, the wife of Diego, his best friend, and she was, according to him, the most intelligent person he had ever known.

From the pictures, Pola looked short and muscular, an average-looking woman. She was a painter in Buenos Aires, decorating her works with her own menstrual blood, animal excrement, tissue from aborted fetuses. Diego was also a painter and beat her when drunk.

Milo spent his nights on Skype, trying to convince Pola to leave Diego and move to Europe, but she feared that Diego would commit suicide.

On Saturdays, Milo and I drank Guinness and ate fried shrimps on a terrace near the beach. I think the day I told him about my plan, it was November. I watched the sea, white and foaming, breaking up in long waves. The morning was dropping its shimmering light onto our table, and it was a good day, a day when all that mattered was to have a friend and a beer, and you knew you were lucky because you had both.

You see, I said to him, to make love possible, such a constellation of coincidences is needed – not only being there, not only liking and being liked, but also being there at the right time, and having the will and the skills, and so on – that I can't understand how there are so many couples around. You've got more chances of being killed by a tiger escaped from the zoo.

They settle for what they've got, Milo replied. They are shit people in shit relationships.

All I am going to say is that Milo was an uncompromising person. Not flexible.

They deserve to be shot, he carried on. The human race should be extinguished.

He sat cross-legged, leaning to one side, his right arm up in a languid pose. He was not good-looking but did have beautiful, long hands. From behind he could be mistaken for a woman, with his short ponytail and the round curve of his back, but his voice was like the sound of a sax, deep and modular.

Fact is, honey, we don't want to compromise. We want the great fuck and the great conversation.

I thought of something that I could do, I said, to increase my chances of finding perfection in a non-perfect world.

What have you thought, honey.

An ad on Loquo. An ad for the perfect lover.

We drafted the ad together, and signed it Anaïs, in memoriam of Anaïs Nin.

On the first day I got 447 replies and one pornographic picture.

Jeez, Milo said, staring at that number, 447, appearing in bold in my Inbox. People are really insane out there.

I went to meet the first one, an NLP practitioner from Germany.

I don't think he's the one, I said to Milo over the phone that night.

Why not?

Well, it was weird...there seemed to be no physical feeling whatsoever.

You mean he's ugly.

Well, I wouldn't know, it was like meeting a stranger.

Honey, he is a stranger.

I kept looking for the one. I met a Finnish DJ who was addicted to ketamine, a French photographer obsessed with his ex wife, a Catalan journalist who was scared of being gay, tons of married men. I was due to meet a sculptor but he emailed the day before to say that 'due to personal reasons, he had to withdraw from the competition.'

I spent long evenings at the computer, scrutinising the messages and the smiling pictures attached. On the seventh day I came across Jay from San Francisco.

I immediately forwarded it to Milo.

Well, he said, at least this one doesn't make spelling mistakes.

And he signs as Henry M. He's the only one who got the hint. And he's a photographer. It's him!

I went to meet him on a Saturday night, in a bar next to Plaça del Pi. He was good-looking, in an up front, perfect Californian kind of way, with flashing teeth and suntanned skin, denim and black trainers. He took my coat and ordered Mojitos for two.

We slowly came to life thanks to the drinks. I talked about the other guys from the ad, he talked about his work, which involved, he said, talent, travelling, more travelling, and beautiful women. He laughed.

Why did you reply to the advertisement, I managed to ask after another drink.

Because, he said slowly, I was curious.

Curious of what.

Curious of meeting the person behind it. I liked your ad. He sipped more drink. And now, I quite like you.

I flushed. He looked straight at me, making me flush more.

Anaïs, he whispered.

A message from Milo flashed on my mobile.

Honey, has he hit your G spot yet???

I turned the mobile off. At two in the morning we went to his loft, where he gave me a toothbrush still wrapped in plastic and a towel, before vanishing into the bathroom. Sitting on the edge of a leather sofa, I stared at the toothbrush in drunken disbelief, and lit up a cigarette, while a psychedelic reproduction of Venus by Andy Warhol stared at me from the opposite wall. Next time, I thought, I must remember to drink less.

Jay came back, showered and smelling of mint, twitching his nose.

Too smoky in here, he said. Let's open the window.

Don't, I said. I could throw myself out.

He did not laugh, nor did he go to the window. He came closer instead and lifted up my dress, breathing heavily in the silence of the flat, his cold fingers moving up my leg. His body fell onto mine and before I knew it, my head was banging against the bolster. Too late to do anything, and after two minutes he flipped me over on all fours.

I raised my head and noticed with horror that a mirror was covering the ceiling, reflecting our image, a huge pornographic picture above us: my ass like a shaking pudding, still wrapped in a black g-string, my calves tight in fishnet stockings, and his body in and out of mine, a piston triggering embarrassing gurglings from my insides.

Until he came.

Sometimes I tried to remember why I moved to this city. How come I need to change my postcode each time I split up with someone.

Sometimes I wondered how I found the courage to sift through stacks of belongings again, sorting out what needed to be taken and what could go in the garbage, what was essential to life, and what was not. How I managed to look for cardboard boxes, choose flight schedules, write my work notice, plan another life from scratch, like the draft of a new novel.

How I managed to speak to him, resist his surprise, the fear widening his eyes, act.

You don't love me anymore, he said.

His name was Rob, and I had waited too long for him to leave his wife. When he was finally ready, love had transformed into indifference.

He still sent postcards from his travels. He wrote the same four words each time, with his quick, stretched handwriting, the same four words from the streets of Tokyo, Bali, Hong Kong.

From Rob, with love.

Jay emailed three days later. Thanks for the evening, etc, and would I go to his place on Thursday as he had something for me.

Three days of waiting to hear from him had transformed our encounter in my mind into a romantic date with an American celebrity. It was not realistic to set too high standards, but Jay was gorgeous, liked Fellini's movies, and cooked waffles in the morning.

Milo was arguing with Pola via email and was not in a good mood.

If this Jay is so cool, he asked, why was he on Loquo?

I was on Loquo too, does that mean I'm not cool?

You know what I mean.

He says it's difficult in his job. Too much travelling, people always busy and nobody has time for these things.

At his place on Thursday, I discovered that he had developed some pictures that he'd taken on the first night.

I'll show you, he said, unplugging his laptop and carrying it to the bed, how sexy you are, Anaïs.

I'm not sexy, I said.

You're not supposed to say that. You're supposed to say thank you.

In the pictures my body looked smooth and soft, flooded with amber light, something fragile and alive, unseen before. I was confused.

You used Photoshop.

Don't be daft.

He opened a bottle of wine.

Do you like the pictures, Anaïs?

I love them.

He held a glass and stared at me.

Now tell me, who is Anaïs?

I quickly drank my glass and started a fire in my empty stomach. I looked at his eyes liquid with ink, his bony face, and sensed that his beauty made him distant, a remote star. Beautiful people, I thought, sipping more wine to drown the pain I was feeling, are different. They can be themselves. They don't need to please you.

I drafted a bio for him. Studied literature, lived in London, Paris, Barcelona. The wine made me passionate. Books, I said with too much emphasis, are my life. Some people want to live, I prefer to read. I prefer art to life.

At that point I was drunk and nearly shouting. Sweating. My swollen words seemed to bounce against the hard surface of Jay's body, leaving him untouched. I was afraid of boring him and tried not to think about the beautiful people he was used to having around. What kind of conversation do beautiful people have? I only knew conversations with Milo.

I told him about the novel.

Have you started writing yet? he asked.

I'm still... researching.

What is it about?

I didn't know how to explain it, which proved how far away I was from starting the damn project.

Love, I mumbled, and sex.

Sex?

That caught his attention. Tell me, have you ever slept with a woman?

I beg your pardon?

Are you interested in sleeping with a woman? I'd like to watch.

Perhaps he was joking. In doubt, I burst out laughing.

I'm serious, he said.

He was taking me for some kind of sexual goddess. I wasn't sure I liked that. Must ask Milo, I thought, if a guy who wants a threesome with you can become boyfriend material eventually.

After more wine he started giving advice. His first undergraduate job was as a typist for Paramount.

I hated it, he said. But each morning I caught glimpses of the big guys, the ones who made the films, and I knew that one day I would be sitting with them. Day by day, I knew. And that's how I started, sexy. Day by day, I was there for it.

That's so American, I said.

He shrugged. Well, I'm American. You're wasting time on that bus. Go and find a publisher to work for. Do something you love, and you won't have to work one single day in your life. I never work, I have fun.

The lounge backed onto the terrace and we listened together to the sound of the city coming up into the night, a mixture of glasses tinkling, jazz music, life happening in the bars, and I felt lucky to be with him. I felt that his words could be a door opening, that next to him I could invent a new me.

You know, one day baby, I'm going to make a fucking huge amount of money.

Last night I couldn't sleep and began rereading your emails. I wanted to go back to my fantasy of you, that fantasy where I sleep next to you, and your breath is rocking me, like the waves of the sea. Then I went to my studio and made this, an assembly of paint and wood and gum, my gift for you. Under the threads, there is this string of words: the essential the nurture the eternal, EVERYTHING.

One thread is white and one is red. The white one, appearing and disappearing under the gum, is me, because I appear and disappear, and the red one, dying the wood around with its blood colour, is you, because you help me not to disappear, because you protect me, because you are everything.

It was the last email from Pola, printed on a piece of paper. Milo put the paper down and gave me a triumphant look.

How can you not be in love with a woman like that? he said. This is an artist, not a business fucker.

I frowned. Don't you think it's all a bit too poetic?

Pola is poetry. You wouldn't understand.

If she's so intelligent why is she with a drunk?

She has...personal problems.

Tell her, I shouted, to read *Women Who Love Too Much*.

We argued because, he said, I became a bulldog when he mentioned her name. For a little while we met less often, and I kept myself busy getting ready for Jay, waiting with the mobile in my hand, in case he called. Sometimes he did. Once when I was walking back from my shift at the bus.

I was wondering, he said, if you could come round now.

Now? Did you say now?

Are you deaf?

I could not come round now. My legs needed shaving (oh remember, to carry a razor with you at all times!), I had no make-up with me, and my hair was frizzy.

At eight in the evening, hairdressers were shutting.

I'll see what I can do, I said.

I bought a hair straightener and rushed home. It was midnight by the time I was ready and when I texted him, I got no answer. I had two drinks and texted again. I had three drinks and rang. His mobile was off. It was three in the morning and I rang Milo, who had just finished with Pola on Skype.

Diego and Pola are practically over, he said. This time she'll come over here.

I was crying on the phone.

What's wrong, honey?

Do you think he's with someone else now?

Who's with someone else, honey?

Jay!

Jeez, he said. If one day I behave like this for a woman, please shoot me.

Thank you Milo. Thank you.

No matter how hard I tried to get closer to Jay, he kept his glazing of coldness. He asked to see me from time to time, we drank some wine, discussed his work, and had sex.

Anaïs, I don't understand how you can work on that bus. You live like a slave.

I kept saying that he worked too much and needed a holiday. He kept saying he did not need a holiday, and that he never worked, he had fun.

He would move away if I tried to touch his face, and breaking the glass wall around him became my new mission.

Each night with him left me bulimic, wanting him more and more. I spent hours on the PC, searching for information about him. After interviewing him, one female journalist wrote that 'his beauty and talent made you scared.' I had an attack of jealousy. I imagined him at parties, surrounded by celebrities, and when I saw his work on the web or read about his awards, I could hardly believe I had been in his bed, under his skin, even if only for a few hours.

One day I managed to text asking to see him. It was mid December and I was on the bus around Montjuïc. The sight of the National Palace, emerging in the glowing mist of the morning, gave me courage. His reply came straight after.

I'm off to Japan, Iceland afterwards. Then Canada. I'll see you on the day I'm back, the 22nd of February.

I sat and waited but the 22nd of February came without his call.

Most of the time I waited. I got used to tuning myself into this hanging mode, where I was doing nothing, except taking tourists to Sagrada Família, and checking my phone.

Normal people have a life, and have a love life, I said to Milo one afternoon. With me, my love life is my only life. I'm so boring. I'm pathetic.

Milo was unhappy too, waiting for Pola to do what she had promised. We met in bars and drank cheap house wine, got back home hugging each other. When Milo was drunk he became nostalgic for Argentina, something he would not normally allow himself while sober, and talked for ages, sitting next to the gas heater in my room, listening to Joy Division. We could hardly see each other as my room had no window, and Milo had shredded the electricity wire when drunk. We lit candles and drank.

Why do we love one person and not another, I asked Milo one night, walking back from the bar. What is it that you most like about Pola?

The streets were deserted, wrapped in a film of silver light, like sparkling tinfoil.

That she understands me. That we share a language, a perspective.

And us, don't we share a language too? Don't we understand each other?

It's different, he said. He walked fast and his lips were cracked from the cold. He wore rumpled trousers, a sweater stained with yellow paint. She understands where I come from. Why I'm this way and not another. It's like with your mother, with your brother. It's the blood.

And why do you think I like Jay? I finally asked.

Because he's what you'd like to be. But you don't see that he's just a businessman. I mean, he does commercials, he's not exactly Ingmar Bergman, right?

He's talented and beautiful.

Alice.

His voice made me stop. He stopped too and brushed my cheek with his frozen knuckles, forcing me to turn to face him. He blew smoke in my face.

You are too.

We got home in a thick silence, and he fumbled at his street door, searching for the keys.

Sometimes I wonder, I said, holding the door for him, why you and I aren't together, do you ever wonder that?

The fact is, he immediately said, as if he had thought about this before, that we don't fancy each other.

He shut the door and his figure blended with the darkness of the hall. Good night honey.

He was right, we didn't fancy each other. Still, I thought later in bed, I quite liked the hard cut of his cheekbones, those shadows settled like dust at the bottom of his eyes.

I was eight years old when my father left.

We lived in a one-bedroom flat in the suburbs of Milan, cement and more cement and one little park, a grid of syringes and dog shit where old people went for their daily walk. I remember the sun streaming down the balcony grating, at dusk, like a pool of dirty blood, and the winter Sunday afternoons, watching television till bedtime, my mother and I, each of us locked inside our private cellar, waiting for my father to return from somewhere.

That night we set the table for dinner, and waited. There were breaded veal cutlets on the table, and a jug of tap water. At ten o'clock my father was not there.

Perhaps, my mother said, he got held back at work.

At eleven my mother told me to go to bed.

I'm sure, she said, that he got held back at work.

I don't remember how many days we waited, setting the table for three at night, eating in silence. My ears ached from the cold that winter, while skidding on the frozen grass of the garden, and everything was white, muffled by a gelatinous mist. I remember the sky like iron and everything silent, and dead.

After a few months they found him in the South. My mother spoke to him on the phone and when she hung up she had watering eyes. She kept his shirts, pressed and folded with a bunch of dry lavender, in the top drawers of the wardrobe, and a suit of his on a padded hanger, and the picture of their wedding in the closet.

On Sundays she scraped the bathroom tiles and sang old songs from her youth, songs about the loss of love and the impossibility of hope. All morning she sang, until she had no voice.

We hardly spoke to each other. She was too sad, she was a really sad woman.

At 2 am my mobile woke me from a sleep as thick as an ethyl coma. It was a text from Jay.

Still awake?

I had not heard from him in the last two months. In the meantime, I had tried to date someone else from the ad, someone who turned out to be Married Man Number Eleven.

I jumped out of bed, and 47 minutes later I was ringing his bell. He opened the door in a white bathrobe, smiling sleepily.

Nice to see you, he said, kissing my face.

We sat on the terrace with a bottle of wine. Barcelona lay in front of us, with spires of gleaming light, and the night, blue velvet and the smell of seawater. I was so excited I wanted to cry.

He politely asked after my nonexistent novel.

Really, Anaïs, how can you still work on that bus?

Long time without seeing you, I remarked casually.

He was back from New York, he said. He was making a short film there, and then, he said, there was this girl he fell in love with.

My heart skipped a beat. A girl?

Yes, a girl.

Love? Did you say love?

Wait a minute. He went to the living room for a bottle of scotch. I need...this, before I can talk, right?

He sat with his head back and shut his eyes, drink in his hand. A Russian model, he met her in Milan. His shoulders sagged. He never, ever, had fallen for someone like that.

All of a sudden I realised that before meeting her I was dead. Do you understand what it means?

I think I do, yes.

I wanted to marry her, you know.

It hurt. A bit. Like a crack of ice, melting under my bones. The coldness. Then numbness.

One huge star vibrated in the sky. White and more white, trembling.

I rented a car and drove from Milan carrying her belongings, he said. I made another trip the following weekend. And on the following one, until everything was here, including her.

I inhaled and exhaled. I concentrated on my chest, compressed with smoke, going up and down.

What happened, I asked.

He washed his mouth with the last of the whisky, and sighed.

She told me she had second thoughts. She flew back to the ex-boyfriend, three days after moving here. I'm sure they never stopped seeing each other, behind my back.

I'm sorry.

Oh, I cried so much but it's over now.

You were crying?

I spent whole days walking along the beach, just crying. But I had time to think a lot about myself. I believe it was good, after all.

Half of his face was in darkness, and half was cast in the reddish glow of a glass lantern on the table. The leaves of the trees behind him were red too, glossy and luminescent, and everything was still.

You know what I found out, he said. I have no friends. Not one. I've never, ever had a friend in my life.

I was holding my breath. I became cold from the damp, seeping into my bones.

He leant forward and grabbed my hand. How do you make friends? Please teach me.

I can't...teach you that.

Now I was embarrassed, about this unexpected display of emotion, more repellent than the nakedness of the body.

Ah.

The dawn was breaking, with a yolky light softening the darkness, gradually revealing his eyelids drooping with tiredness. Orange and apple trees were lined up on the terrace, and lilac bushes, and an Indian hammock swayed, tied to the house wall.

You know, I loved her so much, yet everything was a fantasy.

Perhaps, I said, slowly chewing the words inside my dry mouth, perhaps love is always a fantasy. Perhaps you needed the fantasy.

He swept the ash off the table with his hand and regained his usual voice, stripped of any emotion.

Each time you came to me we had sex, he said. That did not mean anything to us, so why don't we agree to something different today?

It was like a needle, perforating the tissues of my being, scraping under my skin. How long, I thought, before I forget this?

Sure, I said, and I saw him handing me my jacket, taking me to the door, because our chat was over.

I cleared my throat.

This is the first time you've spoken like that, Jay. I appreciate it a lot.

He grinned. Thank you.

Tell me, I asked, because I wanted to know, what was her name?

Misha.

His expression became softer and a shadow clouded his eyes. I could not stop looking at him and it dawned on me that I would spend the rest of my life searching in men's eyes for that same shadow.

You know, he added, now that I know what love is, I'll miss it forever.

Of course.

He waved at me. You take care, Anaïs.

While going down the stairs, I turned to say that my name was Alice, but his door was already shut.

I stepped out into the morning, now rainy, soaked with humidity. The clean-up crews were washing the streets and a few lamps that were still on cast globes of spectral light onto the wet asphalt. I took a cab to the bingo, where Milo was finishing his night shift. He came out wearing his uniform, a black jacket with golden cuffs, and we drank gin and tonic in a bar.

Honey, you must be the clone of Bridget Jones.

I love that you're so nice to me all the time.

He raised his glass. Let's raise a toast to Jay, the American asshole.

We watched out of the window, the city flowing under curtains of rain. I wanted to ask him if there was a way we could try something better, something better than the bingo, and the drinking, and the ads in Loquo. Something better than Jay and Skype with Pola all night, but he spoke first.

Pola went to hospital last night, he said. Diego broke her arm.

Oh.

I'm going over there. I need to see, speak to her.

Going where?

Buenos Aires. Home.

Hi lit a cigarette with a match, and watched the flame leap before dying. I realised that I knew too little about his family in Buenos Aires, that nobody rang him, or wrote.

There's a nice quote by Einstein, he said. If you're after a different outcome, don't do the same old thing.

I wanted to ask if he would be back, but I didn't. We sat listening to our hearts beating, feeling the dampness inside us, and I wanted to ask questions for which I had no courage, describe things for which I had no words.

Two months before he left us, my father and I were sitting in the car, in an outdoor car park, while a fine rain washed the windscreen.

Staring at some place ahead, across the wet patch of grass beyond the car park, my father said:

Ali, I've got something to tell you.

Each time I recall the pitch of his voice, full of solemnity, like a storm approaching, I shiver.

I was a good kid. My parents' education was strict, and I was not allowed to shout, or protest, or ask inappropriate questions. Therefore I kept quiet in my seat, patiently waiting to hear the story he had to tell, my gaze locked onto his profile, sensing that something important was coming.

Your mother and I, he began, don't get on very well. There are things...

Suddenly the rain grew stronger, and we listened to the cascade of water falling down the windows. My father's body twisted in his seat.

Listen, he finally said, let's forget this and go home now, yes?

He brushed my shoulder, put the car into reverse, and drove off.

My mother kept repeating that we did not know my father. He was someone whose silence was hard to decode, someone who could easily lead a secret life, somewhere else. We did not know whether he believed in God, what we wanted from life, we could not even decide whether he was good or bad. We did not really know why he left, what waited for him outside our house.

Despite being with us for a few more weeks, my last mental picture of him was shot that afternoon. I always remember him as he was at the wheel. I remember his greyish eyes, a shade paler than his pullover, his lips tightened, and his face flushing, as if suddenly becoming hot in the car, or as if something was bottling up under his skin, something to feel excited, or ashamed about.

I replayed this sequence thousands of times, in the years following that afternoon, each time trying to guess what was so important that could not be said, which string of words, out of all the possible combinations, could have spared what happened afterwards. I have collected hundreds of lucid dreams, hundreds of drafts for an event that will never be rehearsed again.

There are a few fixed features though. In my dreams, I am always someone else. I am a real person with a real personality, not a shadow clinging to broken hopes, unspoken desires. There are things I want to do and be, in my dreams, and I believe I will do them and be them.

In my dreams I am not afraid to speak to my father, that afternoon. My voice comes out clear and strong. I never shake.

I turn to my father and say:

Please don't go.

In my dreams, there are at least twenty different ways I say this, but regardless of how I say it, I always manage to make him stay.

In the end, Milo flew to Buenos Aires, but Pola never left Diego.

All this happened three years ago. Milo stopped sending emails, but I know from Facebook that he is still there, with a girl called Sonia. His pictures show him fatter, less pale, with short hair and a new contentment about him. Sonia is always close to him, their heads touching, their faces smiling, and each morning he writes sweet, sticky love messages on her Facebook wall. I wonder how easy it was for him, the apparently impossible task of wearing a new life like a new jacket.

I have googled Jay's name today, and seen that he is getting divorced from another Russian model.

I am still here, recovering from Married Man Number Seventeen.

I have never told anyone that I once published an ad for a lover. People would think that you must be really desperate, really lonely, to publish an ad like that. I have never told anyone about Milo, how I miss travelling across the lunar landscapes of his brain.

I do not have his number. If I did, on nights like this, I could pick up the phone and call him. Lock myself in the toilet like now, half drunk, half desperate. I could forget how scared I am, and three years too late I could say that I understood nothing, that perhaps that was love, perhaps it could have been true love.

Tom Edge

Hebe and Heracles on the Metro

(Pentecost Monday 2010)

All men have need of the gods – Homer

Gleaming with dentistry
they ascended at Drassanes.
A head and a half above
the rest, they stood.

Contrary to legend
he was close cropped,
golden. She with dark ringlets
gently. They glistened among us.

Brilliant in their aerial whites
they suggested ambrosia
and the asset-rich credibility
of a fully flossed future.

Then, I noticed his eyes –
a shade too close
for Deity. And she was
chewing, gum. Open mouthed.

Immense at first sight
I now believe them,
sadly, to have been
only Americans.

The Green Bikini Top

Tony Tysoe

From where we live at one end of a winding flat-bottomed valley tucked in amongst the thickly wooded slopes of Les Gavarres, which at this time of the year emerge from out of the early morning mists like floating clumps of giant calabrese, it takes me half an hour to drive into the university: ten minutes to get to the other end of the valley, fifteen minutes cruising the highway that runs the length of this central part of the Costa Brava, and five minutes more edging through traffic-choked suburbs before I can finally cut the engine and sit for a moment in silence with the car stationary beneath the towering walls of Girona's old quarter.

The best part of the journey is crossing the valley. There are orchards on both sides of the single-track road, and vineyards, and wheat fields. *Masies* with low roofs and thick stone walls shelter behind copses of eucalyptus and pine. In spring I drive past meadows bursting with the most vivid colours, as if it is the colours themselves that have seeded in the red fertile earth. There is all manner of wildlife, too: foxes, red squirrels, wild boar; at the beginning of autumn a pair of buzzards took up residence. They wheel and turn now on the warm up-currents from dawn to dusk, their familiar silhouettes visible for miles around.

Few outsiders come to our valley, save for the Africans who ride in on patched-up bicycles looking for work. We don't stop to consider how they get here or the stricken villages they might have come from because we've largely lost that way of thinking about things. And that is not all that has changed in us since we arrived in this place, and slowed down, and started wondering how the course of our lives might look in years to come under the unblinking gaze of eternity.

The first puta appeared at the side of the highway one Monday morning about two months ago. She was standing at a well-chosen spot just before the airport turn-off, on the edge of a bamboo grove near a track leading to an abandoned farmhouse where her clients could turn off the road and park unseen. As I drove past I was thinking about the lecture I was due to give that morning and almost missed her. (The title of the lecture, in case it is felt to be of significance, was: 'The Spanish Civil War and its Aftermath: the Death of Reason on the Battlefield of Ideas'.)

The next day she was joined by a friend. They wore the same clothes: short yellow skirts, white boots, and high-necked fluffy jumpers with shiny satin jackets.

The following morning the first puta, undeniably the prettier of the two, caught my eye as I drew level with her, and waved, not a cheerful wave but a commanding gesture she must have brought with her from wherever she came from. I was considering this when I had to swerve to avoid knocking off his bicycle an African pedalling slowly along at the side of the road going in the same direction as me. I saw him wobble in my slipstream. The reproach in his eyes lingered in my rear mirror as I drew away from him and continued on my journey.

From then on, the putas were at their posts every day unless the weather was particularly bad. They brought white plastic chairs from somewhere and then replaced them with more comfortable ones upholstered in fake red leather. Usually they sat apart but once when I drove by, the second one was perched on the pretty one's lap. They had their heads close together and were bent over what I guessed was a mobile phone. They were laughing and looked very happy.

Hoopoes are a regular sight on grass verges in this part of Catalonia. They are elegant-looking birds with a striking plumage, but the Book of Leviticus tells us to shun them because they are unclean and foul their nests. I was reminded of this when it became obvious the putas were fouling their nest too. They hung carrier bags from the bamboo canes behind the chairs, left plastic water bottles lying on the ground and carelessly discarded scraps of toilet paper that became snagged in the grass.

I got used to the sight of them on my daily journey and grew to look forward to their appearance as the spot where they stood drew near. Sometimes I only saw one of them and was anxious for the rest of the day about the other, though I felt slightly embarrassed about this and told myself not to be ridiculous. Then, about a week ago now (though it seems longer) the weather became freakishly warm and the putas changed with it. The pretty one suddenly took to wearing her thick chestnut hair lifted up of the nape of her neck, instead of over her shoulders. And the next day, she had shed her satin jacket and fluffy jumper in favour of a bikini top which, I was astonished to see, was exactly the same shade of dark green as a swimming costume my wife had picked from a rail outside a boutique on the Corniche of Beirut back in '82 or '83, and had bought with my enthusiastic approval.

This association of places and objects was very strong, as well as disorienting, because my wife and I haven't talked about those days in Beirut for ten years or more (it goes without saying the swimming costume from the boutique on the Corniche is long gone). But the fact is that for the rest of that day the puta and her dark green bikini top filled my thoughts and destroyed my concentration. Work was all but impossible. At one point during the morning, I even imagined asking her if she had chosen the colour herself, or if she had had it chosen for her, and my lips moved as I framed the question.

That same evening I set off back home later than usual. As I drove, my head felt heavy and I heard myself repeating the harsh words I had directed at one of my younger faculty colleagues before leaving the university building. It had started as a trivial argument over the basis on which the fictionalisation of real events might ever be justified. We had been discussing a young man, a former drug addict, who had written a best-seller purporting to be the true story of his life. He now stood accused of making most of it up. His publishers were under attack. The media were making hay with the spat. The young man, who was American, had even made an appearance on the Oprah Winfrey show.

My argument with my colleague followed predictable lines. Her position was that in such cases truth per se (her expression) was not the important consideration. The only criterion by which a writer's integrity should be judged was what she called the 'truthiness' of their work.

'The concept of truthiness encompasses the essential latitude every writer must be allowed when portraying real events,' she proclaimed with evident satisfaction at her choice of words.

At first I did not reveal my true feelings but merely remarked that as far as I was concerned there was no halfway house when truth, or what we were pleased to describe as 'real events', were under discussion. It was only later, when my young adversary (who, like the author she was defending, was American) implied that I had an authoritarian nature, comparing me with those academics of the thirties who abandoned their independence and clambered aboard the Soviet Realism bandwagon, that my language became intemperate.

'Do you have any idea at all what awaits us in this profession if we abandon true and accurate detail as our ethical yard-stick?' I asked her, in a raised voice, I regret to say.

At that, she levelled Jean Genet's notorious quotation from *The Thief's Journal* at me: *Here are the loves with which I have been preoccupied... Having noted them, I now make use of them. May they serve the purposes of this book.*

'Surely you would agree that Genet is speaking for all writers there?' she said.

She was completely ignorant, of course. Sartre called *The Thief's Journal* Genet's most beautiful book, the 'Dichtung und Wahreit of homosexuality'. It has a wider timbre than any other confessional autobiography I know of. To continue arguing with this young lady would, I was certain, be completely pointless. Even so, I persisted.

'Novelists, perhaps. And probably Governments. But not us, I hope.'

'Ah, I see,' she said, with a truly infuriating smile.

I should have known better, of course, but I was angry, and I couldn't stop myself. 'You don't see anything,' I said. By now I fear I may have been shouting. 'Poetry and truth in a book by Genet is one thing. Truthiness and your fucking country's foreign policy for the last forty years is quite another.'

'Let's leave it at that, shall we?' she had answered, reasonably enough.

The sun was already low in the sky and there was no sign of the putas when I passed the spot where they always stood. Without planning to, I slowed down and then found to my surprise that I had stopped completely. As I sat with my hands on the steering wheel wondering what to do in this unexpected situation (I can now see that by then my judgement was almost certainly clouded by my approaching bout of illness), the reflection of a container lorry began to fill my rear mirror alarmingly quickly before the real thing passed in a rush of wind with its horn blaring, leaving my car rocking violently. I hurriedly pulled onto the side of the road, turned off the engine, and set out to walk the fifty yards back along the road in the direction I had come.

It was a curious thing but as I walked I heard no noise from the passing traffic. All was silence until I reached the track that led to the abandoned farmhouse and stopped before the two chairs in fake red leather, still set at what was no doubt the correct angle to the road. The only sound now was the rustling of the bamboo canes, stirring in the evening breeze.

I noticed the patched-up bicycle, thrown down carelessly behind a bush a few yards from the chairs, before I heard them. A woman was singing softly in a language I did not recognise, a man was making low animal noises. I took a few steps forward, and parted the bamboo screen. The pretty one was lying on her back and gazing at me from over a man's broad rippling shoulders, smiling, as if she had been expecting me. She said something that I did not understand but knew was not directed at me, though all the time her eyes were fastened on mine. The other puta raised her head then. It occurred to me I was looking at three people adrift on an old mattress in a sea of trampled bamboo, holding on to each other for survival. It was a big mattress, and would have been awkward to carry. I wondered what help the putas had needed to get it there.

These were the things that I saw, and these were the thoughts that came to me at the time. It was only later that I thought of Freud's visit to the Acropolis as a young man and began to consider anew the effects of the condition of disassociation on a character like mine. It is true that I did have a momentary feeling I might finally be on the edge of a breakthrough of understanding but it did not last. And, I am quite certain, on reflection, that this was for the best and that it was something I somehow half-realised even while I was standing there. It would, after all, have been irresponsible in the extreme, and selfish, not to have recognised that at our stage of life such a breakthrough could only have come at a very heavy price.

I may have cried out, I'm not sure, as I stood on the edge of that bamboo grove. But I do clearly remember stumbling backwards and the man rolling onto his side and turning his face towards mine, and I do remember seeing the familiar reproach in his eyes as he did so.

That night I slept badly and dreamt of birds with dark green feathers, and a silver plane falling towards me from out of a blue sky. By the morning, a fever had taken hold and I asked my wife to phone the Faculty secretary to say I would need a week off work. Later, she sat on the edge of the bed and we talked. She said I had been working too hard and I did not disagree with her. Perhaps, in the weeks ahead, we will talk some more, and I will be able to explain to her something of how I really feel and she will understand.

Yesterday I returned to work. When I drove past the spot where the putas had stood, by the side of the bamboo grove just before the airport turnoff, they had gone. They were not there today either. But I did see a group of Africans riding into our valley on their patched-up bicycles this morning, and this evening the buzzards were wheeling and turning in the open skies above me, visible for miles around. I shall look out for them tomorrow, too.

Genre-bender

An interview with Rupert Thomson

Once described as 'a twisted British fabulist', the writer Rupert Thomson has written eight highly acclaimed novels including Divided Kingdom *and his latest* Death of a Murderer *which was short-listed for the Costa Novel Award. Following stints in Athens, Rome, Sydney and Berlin, he has been in Barcelona for five years where he now lives with his wife and daughter in Sarrià.*

Our conversation takes place in Plaça de Sarrià and is occasionally punctuated by the chimes of the nearby clock tower.

In a lot of your books there seems to be a theme of escape. Is that why you are here?

Well, my first novel was called *Dreams of Leaving* and that just relates so much to where I come from; I come from Eastbourne and I couldn't wait to get out of it.

As for the reason as to why I am in Barcelona – it's a long story. It's not escape so much as liking the feeling of being in exile. You might say that's a form of escape, you are escaping your own identity but I like being a foreigner, I like not being able to understand the things I can hear around me. I like the isolation that can give you, I also like the process of discovery, so…erm, I've never really thought about my books being about escape. I see them as being about trauma.

As to Barcelona, we'd lived through a very difficult four years [He refers to a period in Cheshire in the Northwest of England] and we needed to go somewhere with light and air and a place that had that kind of atmosphere – the opposite of what we'd been doing.

You mention a lot of cities. We recently asked Colm Tóibín if he thought Barcelona was a good city for writers and he replied that it was probably a better city for poets. Is there such thing as a good city for writing?

That's interesting because your first image of Barcelona is as a city of distractions. I have to be very careful not to get drawn into that.

I mean even on a disciplined night you don't get home until past three in the morning and I get the impression that it's almost normal to have breakfast before you go to bed, in which case I would do very little work.

That said, I find Barcelona a great place to write, but then, for me, most cities are. I find it much more difficult to write in the country because there are no distractions. That sounds paradoxical. I love the idea of the distractions being there because I can resist them. Because normally the world that I'm in when I'm writing is equally if not more attractive and magnetic. I like the tension between the world I'm writing about and the world outside waiting.

Given the distractions, do you set yourself a timetable for writing?

Well, people are always astonished by my discipline. You look at most novelists, as opposed to poets or short story writers, I think most of them have a fairly strict routine.

I work from about 9.30 in the morning until 2.30 in the afternoon and then again between four and seven; I do that six days a week and I get up on Sundays. I never go out on Saturday night because I have to get up earlier on Sundays than any other day. I get up at 7 and work for four hours. So I work about six and a half days a week, that's my compromise. I had to make a compromise when I got a family – my wife doesn't see it as such a great compromise but I used to work seven days a week! But I need to be in touch with the material everyday. I find that if I stop for a day or two it takes me another two or three days to get back to where I was. I think it was Rilke who said 'the ultimate intuitions and insights will only approach a writer who remains in his work'. That idea of remaining there is crucial to me.

It's hard to pigeonhole your work. Mystery novel, fantasy, satire, allegory. Where do you see yourself?

I simply write what I find interesting. I've been compared to everybody from Gárcia Márquez to Elmore Leonard. Mervin Peake has been mentioned too.

At this point I mention Jonathan Swift and George Orwell. He laughs when I say he is in good company.

I find it difficult to make any sense of it because of course I'm inside that process. I'm simply writing and don't see myself as a jackdaw picking bits of different genres unless I'm forced to by a critic and then maybe I can see that I do use genres. I have even been described as genre-defying. But when I'm writing I'm not aware of using genre. I don't think of it that way. I simply write and I never know what it is going to be at the beginning, I only find out when I've reached the end and I look back and think…ahh, so that's what it was.

It's only now with eight books behind me that I can begin to see certain patterns and themes in my agenda.

In your books *Dreams of Leaving, Divided Kingdom, Death of a Murderer*... they all seem to have an incredibly bleak view of England...

Really?

Yes. And I quote from *Divided Kingdom*: 'It had become a troubled place, obsessed with acquisition and celebrity, a place defined by envy, misery and greed…for decades, if not centuries, the country had employed a complicated web of manners and convention to draw a veil over its true nature, but now, finally, it had thrown off all pretence to be anything other than it was – northern, inward-looking, fundamentally barbaric.'

There is an aspect of England that's like that, isn't there?

But it's more than that. Many of your characters are continuously portrayed as mean, petty lowlifes and the general impression is one of somewhere you wouldn't want to live.

But Billy Tyler in *Death of a Murderer* is written with great sympathy, isn't he? I admit his life is bleak but…

…but he's surrounded by these horrible characters like the Fletchers (a particularly nasty portrait of council estate trash)

(laughs) Mmm, I'd forgotten about them.

But these characters that come up over and over again and it begs the question: do you hate England?

Mmm, no-one has said that before but I have to say that people often describe me as being very English but I've never felt I fitted in at all. I feel Mediterranean. I feel as if the sense of humour is the same and as if there is a response as a person and a writer that I don't get in England. It's different if you are talking about London. I mean London is not really England but having lived in the provinces… I just don't fit in there at all. They don't know what to make of me and I don't really know what to make of them. I have tried going to the pub…

I don't hate anywhere actually, it's just that I feel more comfortable out of England.

As an exiled writer, do you not fear losing your English – the way local expressions creep in to your language which are actually nonsensical? Typical examples of this here are replacing 'I don't mind' with 'It's the same' or adding *yes* to the end of every sentence.

I know what you mean. I have a friend in Rome who speaks Italian English and I did the same thing the other day. I said 'God I've got a real feeling of crispation today'. But for me that's just adding to language. I do know what you mean though and you do have to keep contact with your own language. I do go back to England often enough not to lose it and I remember reading an American writer who lived in Naples, he said just that, he had to leave because he realized he was losing his American. He couldn't write American characters anymore. But that's never bothered me because my characters, very often, are never from anywhere. And we all know about Beckett or Joyce who wrote about Ireland from Paris. You could say paradoxically it's easier to write about the country you come from when you're not in it.

Would you consider setting a book in Barcelona?

What tends to happen with me is that when I'm in a place, I'm not writing about it, I'm absorbing it. So later, down the line when I'm living somewhere else, I will write about that place. The curious thing is that because of 'The Crisis', I thought earlier this year I was going to have to leave and move back to London. I was panic-stricken and desperate because I love Barcelona and I don't want to leave so I thought…I know what I'll do, I've got three ideas for three short pieces of fiction and I realized they were all set in Barcelona and they were all love stories, so in May and June I wrote them – in seven or eight weeks. It was my love letter to the city thinking 'I might have to leave' but now I don't think I will have to leave so I'm putting it on one side.

Rupert Thomson returned to London shortly after this interview.

Lola

Lesley Galeote

Barcelona, 1937

When Dolores crossed Plaça Rius i Taulet she saw a gypsy boy trying fruitlessly to attract some pigeons with what looked like bread crumbs.

'Pigeons don't trust people anymore,' she thought. 'People are eating up all the animals they can grab.'

She held her basket more tightly and started walking faster, looking away from anyone she came across. The smell of the dead leaves filled her senses and did not leave her until she turned into a narrow side street and entered an old, dark building. The iron and glass door clanged behind her. Dolores felt her way along the poorly lit hallway. She reached a dilapidated staircase and climbed three flights with barely a sound. On entering her flat she heard children's voices. Javier, her firstborn, met her in the hall.

'Have you been to the black market, mamá? What did you bring?'

'Shut up, boy!' She tried to slap him but he dodged her. When she saw the door had closed behind her, she added more calmly, 'Go to Tibidabo and get some wood.'

'Again!' he muttered sulkily.

'Yes, again. How are we going to light a fire if you don't? Make sure nobody sees you. I won't bolt the door so we don't make any noise when you get back. And don't make any noise on the way out. The neighbours are watching everyone. Is your father home?'

'Yes.' Javier opened the front door and he left, angry but silent.

'I'm so sick of worrying that one day they might arrest him for gathering wood in Tibidabo,' Dolores thought. She entered the kitchen, pulled a key from a pocket and opened the larder. She took out some sausages, eggs, fresh vegetables and two big round breads from the basket she was carrying and put them on the shelves. Nuria had told her that her uncle from the countryside had visited her the day before.

She was so busy tidying up the larder that she barely heard her husband's boot steps as he left their bedroom. He spoke and his deep voice remained in the air. It was only after the front door was shut that his words took shape:

'I'm going to get shaved, Lola.'

She ignored them but then she heard the children shouting on the back terrace. She slammed the larder door, and locked it securely. Only then did she rush down the hall to the terrace. Fernando was hitting his little sister and calling her a fascist and the little girl lay curled up on the floor, crying and screaming. Dolores grabbed them both and dragged them inside. She pushed the terrace door shut and she cuffed Fernando.

'I've told you not to lay your hands on your sister!'

'She started it! She scratched my face!'

'I don't care! It's bad enough that everyone in the entire country is killing each other to have you beat each other to death too! I don't want to hear you say those words you hear in the street. Don't let me catch you playing war again!' Lola pushed the little girl, who was drying her tears, 'and Ana, I've told you not to play with this brute anymore.'

Fernando gave her a look of uncontrollable hatred. Dolores froze for a moment. He looked just like his father.

'Go to your rooms,' she ordered. The children obeyed.

Dolores went to her bedroom and she dropped into her rocking chair, shutting her eyes as she leaned her head on the back of the chair. The rocking transported her to the seaside, to that beach from her childhood where she watched the Mediterranean waves turn into foam over and over again until she felt sleepy.

A loud bang in the distance startled her. Shots? She cradled her right arm with a grimace. Could they be shots? She pulled up her sleeve carefully while she kept listening. The bruises on her arm were turning yellow. She didn't hear anything else except for the faraway sound of lorries. She leaned back on the rocking chair again.

Her husband had left the wardrobe open. From the mirror framed by mahogany, a pale woman with black hair and fine hands was staring at her. She never wore jewels anymore and her clothes were simple but well cut. Dolores smiled back at herself.

'Yes, even though I no longer have what I used to have you can tell what kind of family I come from.' She sighed. 'And to think that nowadays I have to apologize for not being from the lower classes.'

Her gaze settled on the wardrobe's top shelf. The embroidered linen and lace tablecloths lay there all folded up. The tablecloths had turned yellow over the years, but sometimes she would still unfold them to remember the dinners she had dreamed she would invite people to. She had dreamed of immaculate white lace cloths, silver cutlery, Bohemian glassware and Sèvres porcelain, and of mixing with the most important and best dressed officers and ladies from some military post. Her mother had taken her to so many balls and had told her she would marry someone important.

She slowly dozed off in her rocking chair.

Loud insistent banging on the door woke her up. She struggled to open her eyes.

'But I didn't bolt it because Javier… Is it because of Javier?'

Dolores got up and went to the door. She feigned composure and she put the safety chain on before opening the door and looking.

'Milicianos! Open the door.'

Through the crack of the door she saw a gun barrel, boots and uniforms.

'What do you want?'

'Open the door. We have orders to search your home.'

She closed the door and took off the chain with an air of offended dignity, although her hands were cold. When she opened again she sensed someone looking through the spy-hole in the door opposite. She stepped aside and a man marched in, followed by three dark, uncouth and scruffy young men.

'Why don't you bolt the door? Aren't you afraid someone might break in?'

'Who's going to break in? There's nothing worth stealing here. And you come in if you want to anyway.'

The leader, a short man with a square face touched her shoulder with his gun.

'Mind your words, lady. Where is your husband?'

'He went out.'

'When?'

'I don't know. A while ago.'

The leader looked at the children, who had come out of their rooms and were hugging each other, squeezing up against the wall.

'We're not going to do you or your children any harm. Is your husband a Guardia Civil?'

'His accent…he's not from around here,' she thought. 'Is he El Murciano, that man who has sent so many people to the checas, to be tortured and then executed?' And she said aloud 'No. He left the Guardia Civil years ago. Now he works for the City Council.'

'Was he a captain?'

'Lieutenant. He left before being promoted.'

'Why?'

The other three milicianos remained still behind him, but their boots squeaked now and then from the young men's barely muted uneasiness.

'He said the military police was not for him.'

The leader was not listening to her. He started walking and looking around.

'We have orders to search and check his loyalty to the Republic.'

'Search whatever you like. My husband is not involved in politics. You won't find anything here.'

'Jaume, Enric, search the rooms…You, search those cupboards over there.'

The leader strode to the dining room and started to open drawers and scatter the contents on the floor. Behind her, Dolores heard doors slamming, rifle butts banging furniture and men pushing beds. The fourth miliciano had opened the built-in cupboards at the end of the hall and he was tossing towels and folded clothes on the floor.

'And the neighbours can hear everything,' Dolores thought, mortified.

She went towards the dining room and saw the leader rummaging among the glassware.

'Be careful! Those are my best glasses!'

'Comrades,' yelled the young man in the hall 'there is a loft in the ceiling.'

The leader took a chair while the young man opened the storage space by hitting it with the butt of his gun. Dolores leaned against the wall. The young man got on the chair, trampling the velvet with his muddy boots, and he felt the area inside the loft. He pulled down a box and gave it to his superior. The slamming around in the bedroom, the nervous movements of the young man searching receded in Dolores's mind as her eyes became fixed on the hands of the man who was opening the box. She was suddenly fascinated.

The dismantled gun and the bullets! The leader of the milicianos took out pieces of the rifle and, with a piece in each hand, he glared at her.

'So there was nothing here? What about this?'

'I had forgotten. It's been years since he left the Guardia Civil.'

'Possession of firearms. Your husband can be executed for this.'

'It's dismantled and rusty. We had forgotten about it.' Dolores heard the indifference in her own words.

'Your husband knew that he had to hand any gun in his possession to the authorities. The Popular Army doesn't have enough weapons to defend the Republic and you are hiding firearms!'

Dolores stared at him in silence. She saw a man with a gun and his look of triumphant hatred and she only felt contempt for him. 'These bullies think they can scare me with their guns and their bullets… me, the daughter of an Army captain, me, who grew up among firearms.'

Pedro had just applied the last brush stroke of shaving foam when the sound of boot steps approaching outside could be heard, then someone kicked the glass door open.

'Where's Ángel Lanzón? We've found weapons in his house!'

Ángel heard the voice booming behind him, but he could barely make out a few dim shapes in the mirror.

'We know he came here.'

He tried to get up, but the firm hands of the barber had jammed him in his seat.

'He left about twenty minutes ago. There weren't many people this afternoon and I shaved him right away.'

'Which way did he go?'

Pedro pointed to the right.

'That way.'

'Did he say where he was going?'

'No. Lanzón never tells anyone anything.'

The milicianos ran down the street and left the door squeaking on its hinges. Ángel's hands were sweating and they stuck to the metal arms of the chair. He stared at the image in the mirror, at the foam and the man who had saved his life.

'Pedro,' he said quietly, 'I don't think I want you to shave me today.'

Dolores was sitting looking at the mess in the dining room. She had told her children to tidy the bedrooms but she felt too weak to start clearing up in here.

A sudden banging on the door made her jump and rush to the hall. She had forgotten about Javier and his pile of wood and had locked and bolted the door. She opened the door without putting on the safety catch.

Leaning on the door frame, unshaven and holding a cigarette in a shaky hand, stood Ángel. Dolores looked at him in silence.

'Lola,' he said with a bitter smile. 'You told them where to find me.'

Shock Therapy

An interview with Lydia Lunch

Musician, performance artist, writer or photographer – whatever the discipline, Lydia Lunch could never be accused of shying away from controversy as she shines a light into the murkier corners of human existence. Somehow, she finds herself residing here in the city ...

Why did you come to Barcelona?

To escape Bush. I knew he was going to steal the second election so I got the fuck out; and anyway I had been coming to BCN since 1984 on and off and I couldn't support myself in the States...

But why specifically Barcelona?

Well, it was thirty years out of fascism as America was going into it. I think it is one of the sanest countries in the world right now. When I'm dealing with heavy subjects I don't need to live in the cancer zone, when I'm speaking about the enemy it doesn't mean I have to be living in their backyard to know what they are doing. Right now, because of its time in history it feels sane.

I'm not sure the locals would agree with you...

Yeah, but that's their issue. I'm an outsider. I don't party every weekend and I live in Grannyville [she lives in an apartment near La Sagrada Família]...my building is mostly 90-year-olds and one floor of students and I like it that way. They don't hear me...

But it seems a little sedate...

Where the fuck am I supposed to live? In the Born? Are you nuts? Look, I lived in ghettos my whole life, I was born in a ghetto. I lived in New York, Pittsburgh, outside of San Francisco, LA... LA is a ghetto. I did my time. I didn't need to live in the ghetto anymore.

Is it a city you work from or a city you work in?

It's easy for me to create here because I'm not distracted by anything. I can get a lot of work done here. I can do a lot of performances here. I can play anywhere from Heliogàbal to the CCCB and it's interesting for me to be in Spain because they have more respect for me as a multi-faceted artist. They are not afraid of me here... The other day I was doing my solo show 'Sick with Desire' and I'd do this piece called 'Ghosts of Spain', which is about the ghosts of the civil war and Spanish amnesia but also brings in Faluja, Islamabad, Darfur and so forth, but it starts with the ghosts here and I just love antagonizing the audience. I'm showing pictures of Belchite behind me and I'm saying "It's in your constitution, amnesia, and I won't forget your fucking dead". I mean I've accused America long enough so now I'm accusing the country I live in and don't even belong in for 'Crimes of Amnesia' and I love it. I mean I called my book *Amnesia* because it is a constitutional right that they decided to forget the Spanish Civil War. To me it's astonishing... but anyway, I still feel that wherever I live I'm an outsider: that's one reason I love living here. I refuse to learn the language – it's arrogant to some degree but I don't do it out of arrogance – I do it so I don't have to hear the mundanity of normal conversation. Especially grannies in the butcher's shop. I feel outside of every community I've ever worked in. I live in an onanistic universe which doesn't exclude other people, I just don't need them. I will do what I do, with you or without you and I think that's ultimately where my strength lies. Ultimately I see myself as a lone figure on the railroad tracks with a polka dot handkerchief tied to a stick, maybe a cat on a leash. That's how I feel no matter where I am.

You say you 'don't want to be understood'...

I don't have a philosophy or a dogma I'm trying to preach. I'm ever a 'mutable'. The problem with most people is that, first, they are pigeon-holed by gender, then they are pigeon-holed by socioeconomics. Then as an artist they pigeon-hole you even more. I mean, fuck you. I'm at the tip of the volcano and it is not necessary for every word to be understood. It's like poetry – I hate that word – some lyrics don't always make sense, it's not sense that is the important thing, it's emotion and passion that's the important thing.

So have you got a message?

There's no fucking message. What's the message? Me against them? If there's a message it's 'I am the voice for whatever dilemma I hope I can voice in you that you can't find a voice for'. That's it. I am the eternal scream into the endless void: trauma, torture and night.

You work in many disciplines. Are you more of a musician, a poet, a visual artist?

I am a confrontationalist in whatever form I choose.

So how would you describe yourself?

I am a faggot truck driver, mainly. I'm a serial killer who decided to knit. My work is like crochet, knitting, architecture. Whatever format it takes it all goes back to the word and the word is basically AGHHHHHH. To make poetry out of the battle cry. That's what I do, because for me, it's like the title of my recent exhibition [a show of photographs in Valladolid], 'The War is Never Over' and I've been speaking about wars since under Ronald Reagan and it's not going away. It's perpetual industrial military complex and you'd better get used to it. It ain't going away. And in some ways I take great delight in this fact because it's man at his worst, which is what I've been complaining about since I was born... man at his worst. Fucking assholes...and the bitches who allow it to go on... Jesus Christ.

You once said you were 'busy being mad at everything'. Are you still mad or are you mellowing with age?

Whoever isn't mad is an idiot... and if you don't want to be slapped awake, don't come here. It's OK... go turn on your MTV... go listen to The Ting Tings... that's cool. I don't care.

Mark Reading

The Rambla (R.I.P.)

Was it here at the Pitta Inn
Those fascist bastards did 'em in?
Firing squad sorts
Tanks full of gin,
Did they park up at Hogan's
And watch Kentucky FC
Loading their guns
For their Bugger King
Before going on
To spill some guts
For patria
And a handful
Of ill-starred bucks?
No. It was at the UGT
Further down
A las cinco de la tarde
They gunned 'em down
Franco's blues
Had come to town:
Calling time
At the union bar.
And now, Che Guevara
Is a human statue
On Miró's star
Wowing the crowds
With his joke cigar.
Jaume, Manuel,
Amadeo and Alba,
Cheers to you.
Wherever you are.

Note: The UGT is a Spanish trade union. There is a plaque on their building on the Rambla in memory of Jaume Compte, Manuel Gonzalez Alba and Amadeu Bardina who died defending the building during the Barcelona revolution.

Acknowledgements

Pauline Stainer's poem appears courtesy of Bloodaxe Books and appears in her collection *The Lady and the Hare.*

P.J Kavanagh's *Catalan Interiors* is an extract from his autobiography *The Perfect Stranger* and appears here courtesy of Carcanet Press.

Farce is a translation of part of Màrius Serra's award-winning novel in Catalan *Farsa,* published by Planeta, translated here by Matthew Tree.

Vanishing Point is a translation from Gloria Montero's Spanish novel *Punto de Fuga,* published by Editorial Meteora, translated by the author herself.

Home to Barcelona is published by PPU, Barcelona.

The photo-montage cover of *Barcelona INK 1* is by Conxita Puigarnau.

The cover of issue *Barcelona INK 2* includes a painting by Gonzalo Goytisolo, *The Lying Sky,* www.goytisolo.com, used with permission of the artist, to accompany the poem by Ryan Chandler, from his work *Night and Day.*

Barcelona INK 3, photo by Tom Chandler.

On the cover of *Barcelona INK 6,* the art work was produced by Lydia Lunch from the photo montage *The Body is a Battlefield* featuring Beatrice Dalle.

 The poem is from *Amnesia* by the same artist.

All other cover artwork and poetry is the work of Ryan Chandler.

Thanks to Hannah Pennell for her tireless proofing of the first seven issues, and her guest editorship of the women's issue, and to Helen Francis for her work on number eight, and Tom C for his careful reading of this anthology.

Thank you to all the hundreds of writers who have so made this project possible.

And of course, thank you Barcelona.

Index

Lightning Source UK Ltd.
Milton Keynes UK
UKOW051138230312

189461UK00001B/23/P

9 781611 500264